Praise for *An Infatuation*
by Joe Cosentino

"Joe Cosentino proves there's more than one way to a happy ending in *An Infatuation*, a story of first love and heartbreak delivered in a fresh and funny voice."
—The Novel Approach

"Don't miss this one, friends, it is a heartfelt story, magical in the telling! Thanks, Joe, for putting your heart on the page for us to savor!"
—Bike Book Reviews

"It's unusual for me to get sucked into a book in the first chapter but it grabbed me early and I read the whole thing in one day".
—Nautical Star Books

"I think you will be left breathless with the reality and emotion behind *An Infatuation*."
—Diverse Reader

"I really loved this book and having an ending that made me laugh and cry at the same time is testament to the brilliant writing."
—Books Laid Bare Boys

"Like an onion, Joe Cosentino's stories have layers. I would really recommend them. This is a Bittersweet novel, but it has laughs-a-plenty despite the sad and ugly lurking beneath the veneer. A truly fabulous read."
—Boy Meets Boy Reviews

"The author executed his storyline with a marvelous precision that would be the envy of many authors.… If you can only afford to buy one more book this year, buy this one."
—Three Books Over the Rainbow Reviews

Praise for *A Shooting Star*
by JOE COSENTINO

"…unbelievably beautiful… a masterpiece"

—Love Bytes

"This is a bittersweet love story, so don't be surprised if you find tears running down your face… But, as Joe Cosentino proves time and time again, with his wonderful writing and storytelling ability, love will prevail…"

—Kathy Mac Reviews

"*A Shooting Star* could easily function as a master class in how to write short fiction… Joe Cosentino has provided a work that will leave you thinking and wanting to savor and re-read it again and again."

—GGR Reviews

"Of all the books I've reviewed, or attempted to review over the past year, this is only the second book that was well written."

—multitaskingmommas Book Reviews

"*A Shooting Star* will deliver the traditional mask of theater—tragedy and comedy—in equal measure."

—Vance Bastian Reviews

"…polished prose at its best. Intelligent writing, a thought-provoking plot and characters befitting the theater genre make *A Shooting Star* one of my favorite reads this year."

—Love's Last Refuge Reviews

By JOE COSENTINO

A Home for the Holidays
An Infatuation • A Shooting Star
In My Heart

Published by DREAMSPINNER PRESS
www.dreamspinnerpress.com

IN MY HEART
ANTHOLOGY

JOE COSENTINO

Published by

DREAMSPINNER PRESS

5032 Capital Circle SW, Suite 2, PMB# 279, Tallahassee, FL 32305-7886 USA
www.dreamspinnerpress.com

ISBN: 978-1-63477-103-0
Library of Congress Control Number: 2015921057
Published March 2016
v. 1.0
An Infatuation previously published by Dreamspinner Press, February 2015.
A Shooting Star previously published by Dreamspinner Press, September 2015.

Printed in the United States of America
∞
This paper meets the requirements of
ANSI/NISO Z39.48-1992 (Permanence of Paper).

An
INFATUATION

Joe Cosentino

To Fred for everything over all these years,
to everyone at Dreamspinner Press,
and to anyone who has ever had an infatuation!

CHAPTER ONE/NOW

PASSION. FLAME. Cherished one. Infatuation. Words don't measure up. How can I tell you how I feel about Mario? *Mario.* It's as if the universe created one perfect person, and put him next to me with a *Keep Off* sign dangling from his neck. The universe can be sadistic like that. As I stand here in front of my great room fireplace, as always, I'm thinking of Mario.

"Hi, babe."

Stuart's home from work. Let's can the Mario talk… for the moment. Stuart (tall, thin, blond) and I (short, stocky, ginger) have been together nineteen years.

"Nineteen and a half years, babe."

"Thanks, Stuey."

Stuart is having his 5:15 p.m. piece of fruit.

We met freshman year in the registration office at college. I was filling out my schedule the day before classes started. Stuart was making his schedule too… for his senior year. He invited me to his off-campus room for a special dinner. He had prepared and frozen it the week before in case he met someone. That night, after we made love (Stuart had ten packs of condoms in his night table, though it was his and my first sexual experience), we fell asleep in a pretzel position in each other's arms. We have been cuddling in blissful and monogamous love ever since. True to the oldest child/youngest child theory, Stuart is a planner, and I'm a procrastinator. We make the perfect couple. He plans, and I put off. We fit together like a fundamentalist and an anti-gay discrimination bill.

My father is just like Stuart. When we'd go to an amusement park, my dad would give each of us a printed schedule with the time limit for each ride, time and location for snacks, and leave time and location. When I told my parents I was gay, my father disappeared into his office and returned with a timetable of when I should come out to the rest of the family, come out at school, have my first date, have my first kiss, marry, and adopt children. Maybe boys really do marry their fathers.

Sticking to Stuart's schedule, like toilet paper to a shoe at a job interview, we rise at 7:00 a.m., do yoga and meditation, eat breakfast (organic), and get to work at 8:30 a.m. Dinner is at 6:30 p.m. and bed at

11:00 p.m. On Saturdays we clean, do laundry, and volunteer at the local LGBTQ Center. Saturday nights from 6:00 p.m. to 10:00 p.m. we go out to dinner (organic) and to a movie with friends, careful to come home and go to bed at 11:00 p.m. Sunday we go to church (open and affirming), have brunch (organic), read the newspaper, watch PBS, call our parents, and go to bed directly at 11:00 p.m.

We live in a three-bedroom house with Hudson River views in upstate New York, complete with a double-story great room with a floor-to-ceiling limestone island fireplace, french doors, and interior balcony. The master bedroom, with a canopied four-poster, marble fireplace, sitting turret, and chaise lounge, is for us, as is the his-and-his spa bathroom. The second bedroom, with the wooden mantel, is currently Stuart's study. The adjacent room is my study. The third bedroom, with a toy chest under the window seat, is decorated for our son. Except we don't have a son. Now don't get all *Who's Afraid of Virginia Woolf* on me. It's Stuart's future planning. For now our nieces and nephews use it when visiting.

Stuart designed and prepared the layout and furniture for our house the day we met. Thanks to Stuart, we have two 401K plans, an IRA, life insurance, death insurance, medical insurance, car insurance, home insurance, health care proxies, living and dying wills. Over the years we were legally married in so many countries and states that I lost count.

After working all day at the office, Stuart has kissed me on the cheek, started dinner—from the menu for the month on the refrigerator—and picked up the mail from the kitchen island, whose shape, size, design, and granite and cherry wood finish Stuart planned when he was in eighth grade. He has gone upstairs to his study to research online and plan the itinerary of our summer vacation to Spain… three summers from now.

Okay, back to Mario. To tell you my story, we need to go back some years.

"Twenty years, babe. You have to be exact, or they won't get all the facts."

"Thanks, Stu," I call upstairs.

Okay, let's start at the beginning and go back twenty years. Isn't time travel fun?

CHAPTER TWO/20 YEARS AGO

MARIO AND I first met when we were in high school. The start of senior year. I had seen him many times before, but on that clear autumn day at 1:32 p.m. in chemistry class, I finally got the nerve to introduce myself. Boy, did we have chemistry. Mario—five-nine with jet black hair, dark brown eyes, Roman nose, full red lips, and very muscular body (but who remembers?)— swaggered into class late wearing a tight aqua-blue T-shirt, jeans with button-down fly, and black work boots. After Ms. Hunsley had the nerve to scold Mario for being late, Ms. Hunsley (my new favorite teacher) assigned Mario a lab partner—*me*. Mario's response was incredibly stimulating.

"Whatever," he said, as he sat behind the counter on the stool next to me.

Not missing the opportunity to rub shoulders (literally) with the captain of the football team, I took in a deep breath and said confidently, "Hm… aghm… my… my… ah… chemistry."

Unfazed, Mario rested his black work boots on the countertop, nearly knocking over a vial of sulfur, and placed his strong elbow on my quivering shoulder. "You do the experiments and write the reports. I trust you." Mario winked at me, then asked Ms. Hunsley for a hall pass to "wring out a kidney."

Isn't he the best? He was handsome, strong, intelligent, witty. Okay, two out of four, but he captured my seventeen-year-old heart. Emily Dickinson, Elizabeth Barrett Browning, and Jane Austen never knew such love. I changed my walking route at school, so instead of avoiding the gym as usual, I passed it as much as possible. I'd dawdle to talk to a teacher about my grades (which were all fine), ask a classmate when homework was due (which didn't matter since I'd do it at 2:00 a.m. the night before anyway), or pretend to read the notices on the bulletin board about… whatever they said. I, who had no school spirit or interest in sports or clubs, joined the school band (tuba—don't ask) and attended all the games, pep rallies, and award assemblies to cheer on my new lab partner.

Each assembly, when our principal, Mr. Ringwood, known to us as Mr. Ringworm, smiled and pontificated about our wonderful football team, I counted the minutes until Mario was introduced. When Mr. R. finally called out Mario's name, the gymnasium erupted like a volcano with screaming and clapping for Mario, none louder than mine.

One Friday afternoon I *accidentally* ran into my hero in the boy's locker room. I'd had enough of the big guys banging me into gym lockers, pushing me into cold showers, and hanging me from the gym ropes. So I was on my way to give Mr. Adoni a note from Dr. Dlorah excusing me from gym class for the remainder of the school year (due to my highly contagious disease being studied by my doctor in Guatemala, where he could not be reached for the next year).

The locker room smelled of an odd combination of soap, cologne, sweat, and desire. Mario was getting ready for football practice, standing at his gym locker, without a combination lock on it. Nobody would dare to break into it. (Except for me that one time I smelled his jock strap. Okay maybe it was a few times, but not more than ten.) Mario slid his T-shirt (red today) up and over his thick, black hair and threw it on the nearby bench. No longer harnessed by cotton, his arm, back, chest, and neck muscles swelled to full size. I was half-hidden behind the adjoining row of lockers, wearing my usual green and blue flannel shirt and brown corduroy pants. Mario, who wasn't looking in my direction, said something really beautiful to me that I will never forget.

"Hi."

"Did you just? Oh. Hi. Hello. Good afternoon. Nice to see you. I mean, change with you." I looked down at the floor (but cheated a bit) as Mario kicked off his boots, slipped off his jeans, and then threw them in the lucky locker. His red underpants (briefs) revealed ample manhood. *This is better than the newspaper's underwear ads.*

"Good gym class today with Mr. Adonis, I mean, Mr. Adoni." *Did I just say that?* "Harold High."

"Hi."

"High." *How can I get my pulse down to 260?*

"Hi." Mario reached into his locker for his sweat clothes.

Shouldn't people be doing that for you? "Oh, my last name is High. Like a kite." *How can I stop my arms from waving like an airport flagger on speed?*

"Mario Ginnetti. Like nothin' else imaginable." Mario smiled, revealing a row of perfectly white teeth, and held the sweat clothes in his hands as if he was a mere mortal.

"I know. I watch your body play." *Why can't I stop talking?* "I mean, I watch you play… football… on the field… in your football outfit." *I feel like Michelangelo with his David.*

As Mario put on his sweats, I continued to sweat.

"I'm voting for your body… I mean I'm voting for *you* for president of your… our… *the* student body." *I need my jaw wired shut.* "I'm your lab partner in chemistry class. Ms. Hungry's class… I mean, Ms. Hunsley's class.

His olive-colored face glistened as he registered recognition—*of me.* "I thought I knew you from somewheres. Hey, thanks for doing the lab reports."

"It's my honor… I mean my pleasure. It's fine. If you need help putting up posters for your campaign, I can…."

Having just tied the laces of his sneakers, Mario stood absolutely still. He looked at me as if he was staring into my heart and somehow knew what I was feeling. "I gotta take a wicked piss."

Can I watch?

"Thanks for helping me out, buddy." He slammed the locker door and left.

He called me buddy. Mario held my heart in the palm of his hand like his soap on a rope.

The next day I was eating lunch, alone, in the cafeteria when Mario, wearing a tight jade T-shirt, put his foot on the empty seat next to mine and leaned toward me. I unobtrusively spit my tuna into my napkin and sat on it to hide it.

"Harold…."

He knows my name.

"…I'm worried about my grade."

"The 97 we got in chemistry, right? I'll try harder next quarter, Mario."

"No, the 97 was great. It's my advanced algebra." Mario sat next to me.

Sweat dripped down my back onto my napkin. "What did you get on the last quiz?"

Mario rubbed a thick thumb on his smooth forehead. "A two."

"How did you get a two?"

"How the hell should I know? Harold, if I fail that class, Coach will throw me off the team, my father will belt me, my old lady will cry, and my grandma will pull out my hair—including my pubes. I'm not doing much better in my other classes either. Will you help me?"

I wasn't sure if it was the nauseating smell from the sweaty tuna fish or Mario's request for *me* to help *him*, but I saw tiny white dots in front of my face, and I started to keel over.

Mario put his arm around me. "I need you, buddy."

He called me buddy again. We are Jonathan and David.

After Mario's friends teased him for sitting with me at lunch, he followed them to the gym, but not before giving me a secret thumbs up. *We are Hercules and Hylas.*

As he requested, I happily came to Mario's academic rescue. Our first tutoring session was in my bedroom after school. I sat at my desk as Mario did pushups on the rug below me. When I first got home, I had tried on five different shirts, but ended up wearing my usual green and blue flannel shirt with jeans. Mario wore his regular attire of a tight T-shirt (baby blue today), jeans with button-up fly, black work boots, and leather jacket—resting comfortably on my bed.

As we began, I sounded like a nervous grade school teacher on his first day of school. "Mario, which subject would you like to tackle first?" *Or can I just tackle you?*

With each push-up, his biceps looked like ripe melons on display.

"I don't got no preference," Mario said, not missing a push or an up.

"Let start with spelling, grammar, and punctuation," I said, opening our grammar textbook.

"I already know about them things."

"It might be good to review." I turned to the first chapter.

"Mr. Tyler don't do grammar no more."

"I have the feeling he will start up again soon."

"I don't need to speak the King's English."

No worry there.

"I just need to pass, Harold."

Then I'll just sit here and watch your biceps bulge with each push-up. "Tell me if this sentence is correct? 'Mario don't go to football practice no more to be with them people.'"

He changed to one-handed push-ups. I dribbled on my grammar book.

"That one's easy. It's wrong," he declared like an expert grammarian.

He knows more than I thought about grammar.

Mario continued. "I'd never stop going to football practice. And I call the other guys on the team my *teammates.*"

Guess again.

"Mario, the sentence that I read to you is grammatically incorrect because the word *don't* should be the word *doesn't*, the word *no* should be the word *any*, and the word *them* should be *those*."

He stopped exercising and sat on the rug with his muscular forearm resting on his massive knee. "Why?"

I explained patiently. "Because when using *he*, *she*, or *it* as the subject in a sentence, you use the word *doesn't* before the verb to make a negative statement."

Mario wasn't so patient. "Hey, I ain't no *it*."

"And you know that 'ain't' is slang, don't you?"

"Are you making fun of the way I talk? Kiss my ass."

Don't tempt me. I stood next to him, thinking that if I got closer he might understand the grammar lesson better. *Sure, that's why I moved closer.* "Mario, in the sentence I gave you, the subject or the noun, *Mario*, is in the third person, so it matches with the word *doesn't* rather than with the word *don't*."

He laughed. "I got you there, Harold. There's only *one* of me. I am one of a kind."

No argument there. I cleared my throat. "If the subject was *I*, *you*, *we*, or *they*, you would use the word *don't* before the verb to make the negative statement."

"Harold, I'm worried about you. *I* am Mario. That's who *I* am."

It's times like this I wish I were a teenage alcoholic. "Let's move on to the rest of the sentence. *Any* is correct instead of the word *no* because *no* answers a yes or no question, precedes a noun that has no article, or can be used before a noun that is preceded by an adjective, but not before *any*, *much*, *many*, or *enough*. In all other instances, you use the word *any*."

"That don't make no sense." Mario stretched out on his back and did sit-ups.

I watched Mario's eight-pack contracting in and out like a stunning white cloud formation dancing in a clear blue sky. *What were we studying again?*

"Shit. My knees keep popping up. Harold, hold them down for me, will you?"

I happily obliged and rested my sweating palms on his perfectly shaped knees. From my vantage point in front of him, I could see the jet black, shiny, perfectly stationed hair on his ankles peeking out from the hem of his lucky jeans. As I lifted my head, I came nose to bulge with his massive crotch, which inspired me with a new teaching tactic. "Mario, let's try something else."

"You're the teacher."

"Every time you sit up, say the words, *I don't*. And every time you lie back down, say the words, *He doesn't*. Can you do that, Mario?"

"Sure." Mario did sit-ups in the manner I prescribed.

I continued on to our next lesson. "Good. Now let's change the words for the sit-up to *They don't*, and the lie back down words to *Mario doesn't*."

Again Mario did as I asked. We went on that way for a while. Eventually I changed the mantra to *no* versus *any*. Mario followed my orders to the letter, or rather to the word.

We moved on to squats with *done* versus *did*, leg lifts with *which* versus *that*, chin-ups with *see* versus *seen*, push-ups with *those* versus *them*, push-offs with *got* and *have*, hamstring stretches for *good* versus *well*, and my favorite, taking a rest with *lay* versus *lie*.

As we lay, backs flat on the rug, mentally and physically exhausted, I felt like Annie Sullivan at the water well. To my surprise, Helen Keller—rather, Mario—rested his arm on my chest.

He touched me. My heart stopped beating.

"I'm bushed, Harold. You're more of a slave driver than the coach, and he don't... *doesn't* give us no... *any* breaks."

His flawless strong arm, pumping with his perfect blood, is resting on my chest. I couldn't speak.

He breathed in and out deeply. "I should get going, but I can't move from *lying* here."

I couldn't breathe.

"You did good... *well*, Harold. You're a well teacher." Mario squeezed my chest with his hand, then stood over me. "Same time and place tomorrow?"

I somehow managed to sit up and focus on my amore. Not able to give in to my carnal desires, I suddenly sounded like Miss Gulch. "Yes, we will move on to learning about singular versus possessive nouns, subordinate conjunctions, and prepositional phrases."

"Whatever you say... or just said." Mario threw his leather jacket over his shoulder. "Later."

Mario was gone, and my bedroom transformed from heaven to a mere room with a bed, a dresser, and a desk.

Mario turned out to be a dedicated student, and I was his devoted teacher. Day by day we covered subjects ranging from chemistry to advanced algebra to government to world history.

One session, in my bedroom of course, we were discussing World War II. Well, I was discussing it. Mario, dressed in his usual attire with a canary T-shirt that day, had brought over hand weights and was deeply engaged in his reverse curls, as was I. It was hard to concentrate on the war to end all wars with Mario's triceps being waved in front of my nose like a steak dinner. Mario kneeled on my bed, and I sat on the rug beside our history textbook, wishing it was bedtime. I had gone over the frivolous facts about the war, like the beginning and end dates (1939-1945) and the number of fatalities (85 million), so I moved on to cover the more pertinent information.

"Mario, who was the president during World War II?"

"Hitler?"

"Hitler was the president of Germany during the war."

"So I got it right. You just said president. You didn't say of which country." Mario stood to do flies. His shoulders looked like the Italian Alps.

I'm ready to go mountain climbing. "Okay, who was the president *of the United States* during World War II?"

"Lincoln?"

"Franklin Delano Roosevelt, the great Democrat with polio from Hyde Park, New York."

"What's polio?" Mario asked between reps.

"A virus that causes paralysis."

"How could he be president if he had polio?"

"He sat down a lot."

"Then you could be president." Mario continued exercising.

Standing up, and moving to my real agenda, I said, "Franklin supposedly had a girlfriend, and his wife, Eleanor, was supposed to have had a girlfriend too."

Mario didn't respond.

"What do you think of that?"

"I think it sounds like everybody was happy." Mario grew lines on his forehead. "Is that in our history book?"

"No, they leave things like that out."

"Too bad. It would make learning this shit more interesting."

"I agree." *On to Plan B.* "Mario, who was the Prime Minister of England during the war?"

"How the hell do I know? I never went to England."

I sat at the edge of the bed. "It was Winston Churchill, who was rumored to be lovers with Ivor Novello, the famous actor."

"Will that be on the test?"

"I doubt it. They left that out of our textbook too."

He put down the weights and sat next to me on the bed. "Harold, let's stick to what will be on the test, okay?"

"Okay, but what do you think about that, Mario?

"I think it sucks."

"Why?"

"'Cause I don't like taking tests."

"No, I mean about Winston Churchill and Ivor Novello?

He thought a moment. "I think history is full of lots of fruits. I mean, I knew that J. Edgar Hoover dressed like his mother, like the guy in that movie, *Psycho*—"

"Anthony Perkins. He was also gay."

"Was he in World War II?"

"No, he played Norman Bates in the movie *Psycho*."

"I thought we were talking about World War II."

"We are." I pretended not to notice that Mario's massive shoulder was pressing against my not massive shoulder. "Okay, Mario, during World War II, who was the top military commander… *for the US*?"

"Alexander the Great. And I know, he was gay too, and it won't be on the test."

"Actually he *was*."

"Harold, if the test was about who people in history slept with, I'd get a hundred."

I smiled. "It was Eisenhower."

Mario looked confused. "Was he gay?"

"I seriously doubt it."

"Good, because I have a few questions about that."

Finally, questions about man-to-man love. "Okay, Mario, let them roll." *Be still my erratically beating heart.*

Mario sat hunched over his knees. "The US fought *against* England for our independence. Then we fought *with* them against the Germans in World War II."

Oh bother, questions about World War II. "Right."

"How come?"

"How come what?"

"How come we changed sides?"

I thought about that one. "I guess because times changed. Our two countries had so many cultural similarities that the US and England formed an alliance."

Mario threw back his head and laughed. "Similarities? I don't think so. You ever see rock stars from England?" He stood up and spread his arms to do flies. I wanted to sing *The hills are alive…*.

"Mario, the US formed many alliances during World War II. For example, we formed an alliance with France too."

"Good thing. I like their fries."

"No, Mario, french fries don't come from France."

He stopped exercising. "Then where do they come from?"

"Right here in the good old US of A."

"Then how come they don't call them US fries?"

My head… and libido are spinning. "I haven't the slightest idea."

He put down the weights and ran a strong hand through his thick, black hair. "And another thing. In World War II we were fighting the Chinese—"

"You mean the Japanese."

"Same thing. We were fighting the Japanese, but now they own half of our country. How'd that happen?"

"The Japanese designed and manufactured technology that we bought. Eventually they became wealthy enough to buy US businesses."

He sat down next to me on the bed again. This time his shapely thigh pressed against my grateful, unshapely thigh. "That don't—"

"Doesn't."

"…*doesn't* make no—"

"Any."

"…*any* sense, Harold. That would be like if you and I had a fight, and I kicked your ass then you bought my house and evicted me."

"It could happen, Mario." *Did I just make a joke… with Mario?*

Mario grinned like a bad baseball player with a blind umpire. "Oh yeah, tough guy? You think you can take me?" He reached for my neck.

I jumped up and ran… as cliché as it sounds… into my closet. I did this partially for cover, but mainly to shield the raging erection growing in my pants.

"Ah, hiding from me, huh? You can run, tutor. But you can't hide."

Mario followed me into the closet. He placed his arm around my neck and pulled me back into the room. As I pretended to resist, my back enjoyed the warmth of his firm pectoral muscles pressing against it. Next, as he placed my arm behind my back, my hand rubbed against his abdominal muscles like laundry on a washboard. Mario forced me down to my knees next to the history textbook on the rug, and said, "Back to work, tutor. I have to ace the next test."

As he stood over me, I looked up at his crotch. *It's doubled in size.* I gasped.

Mario fell to his knees next to me. "Did I hurt you?" He put his powerful hand on my unworthy shoulder.

"No, I just lost my breath for a minute."

He seemed to understand. "Good. I don't want to lose my teacher." He smiled and revealed his pearly white, perfectly straight teeth.

I smiled back and unleashed my school-bus yellow, crooked teeth. "Don't worry, Mario. You won't."

As the weeks went by, Mario became Eliza Doolittle to my Professor Higgins. One night we were studying in my bedroom as usual. I was strategically lying on my bed. Mario, wearing a tight emerald T-shirt, sat on the windowsill, throwing a football at the overhead light.

For the third time that night I asked, "The log (base 10) of 10,000 equals?"

Mario thought long and hard and finally said, "4?"

I think he's got it. "Yes, Mario, yes!"

"That's it? 4?"

"Yes, Mario!"

"Holy shit!" Mario stood, threw the football down onto the rug, and spread out his massive arms. As I joyously ran toward him, anticipating a congratulatory embrace, Mario clasped his hands onto the window molding and did chin-ups. "I did it! I can't believe I finally got it right!" Mario jumped down and grabbed his leather jacket from behind my desk chair. "See you tomorrow, Harold."

Sitting at my desk, I asked, "Where are you going?"

He picked up the football. "Meeting my friends at Cosmo's for pizza."

"What about your *other* classes?"

"I learned enough for one night."

"Mario, we have a literature quiz tomorrow. You should stay and cram with me." *We can be Anne Frank and Peter Van Daan or Tom Sawyer and Huckleberry Finn.*

He turned around to face me. "It's just a quiz. No sweat off my ass."

What a way with words. "Mario, I can't believe you don't like books. I'd read all day if I could." *Next to you.*

Putting his jacket and the football on my desk, he sat on the floor next to my bookcase. "Books don't make sense to me, Harold." He pulled out a book. "Like *Romeo and Juliet*. If I ever dated a girl whose old man hated my guts, I'd kick his ass. And another thing I don't get about that book is if Romeo and Juliet were so head over heels in love, how come they don't end up happily ever after?"

I rested my elbows on the desk. "I guess because sometimes things don't work out the way we planned. That's why if we love someone, we need to stay close to him, and commit ourselves to him, whether our family and friends like him or not. And we should never, *ever* let him go."

"Will that be on the quiz, Harold?"

Yeah, the test of life. I nodded and hid my erection behind my desk. *New tactic.* "Mario, did you know that... originally... during Shakespeare's time, all the roles on stage were played by male actors?"

"So?"

"So a male... a young male... played Juliet... in love with Romeo."

"So how come Shakespeare didn't call it, *Romeo and Julio*?"

With a book covering my lap, I sat next to Mario on the floor. "Let's move on to *Our Town*."

Mario grimaced like a kid facing a bowl of pea soup. "I hate *Our Town*. Who is that Stage Manager character anyway? If any guy came into my kitchen and started making comments and rearranging things, my mother would cut his balls off with a steak knife."

I covered my lap with a second book. "It's an amazing story, Mario. George and Emily were only... our age... but they were totally in *love*.

"I don't get it."

"That's because you won't give it a chance." I looked into his dark, questioning eyes. *Please give it a chance, Mario.*

"Okay. Read it to me." He leaned his back against my bed.

"Now?"

"No, when we're forty years old in an old people's home."

I opened the book. Mario closed his eyes and rested his forearm against mine. Despite my cracking voice, I somehow read the section where George asks Emily if she will write to him if George goes away to agriculture college. After I finished, I asked, "Do you understand?"

Mario looked at me like a Rhodes Scholar. "What do you think I am, stupid?"

How did I not notice that cleft in your chin before this? "What does it mean?"

Mario cleared his throat like an orator. "George wants to keep Emily busy writing letters, so she won't visit him at college and catch him rolling in the hay with the college babes."

His mouth was inches from mine. "No, Mario, George is testing Emily to see if she *loves* him."

"Well, does she?"

"What do you think, Mario?"

"How the hell do I know what's in some crazy broad's head in some stupid book?"

I gave him a hint. "Emily *marries* George, doesn't she?"

"My old lady married my old man, and no way *they're* in love."

"Trust me, Mario. George and Emily, like Romeo and Juliet, were star-crossed lovers. You should remember that for tomorrow's literature quiz." *And make sure we don't share their fate.* I reached over Mario's muscular arms to take another book. "Let's move on to *A Separate Peace*."

"Another book I hate. Why do the two guys want to hurt each other?"

Here's my chance. "Maybe because they don't understand their feelings toward one another." Our lips were so close they were nearly touching. "Maybe because of pressures from society, the two boys can't express their… mutual admiration and… caring for one another, so their frustration turned into violence and tragedy."

"What a bunch of bull. I'd never hurt someone I cared about."

"You wouldn't *intentionally*."

He grabbed my arm. "I wouldn't any way at all."

Somehow, even at my tender young age, I knew that wasn't true.

"Speaking of peace." Mario jumped up and removed papers from his jacket pocket. "To keep peace in the Ginnetti family, can you fill out my football scholarship applications for college? They're due next week. They want an essay about why I want to go there. Write extra good stuff for the Ivy League schools, okay, Harold?"

Somehow recovering, I said, "Sure, but why do you want to go to an Ivy League school?"

"To shut up my old lady." He pointed to the bookcase. "Use something from one of your books, but not *Romeo and Julio*."

"Okay. I have an essay to write too. I'm going to State. My parents don't want to saddle me with big college loans for an education degree." *Is it my imagination or does Mario look disappointed?* "As they say, 'There's nothing wrong with New Jersey. We have clean water, honest politicians, and it's safe for children with a Catholic church on every other corner.'"

Mario laughed. "You're funny, Harold. I like that."

Just call me Funny Boy.

He handed me the applications. As our hands grazed one another's, I asked, "Mario, if you go away to school, will you write to me?"

Mario tossed the football in the air. "I don't write too good... *well.* Nobody knows that better than you, Harold."

I sat up on my knees. "But who will tutor you in college?"

Again seeming to understand, Mario placed a hand on my head. "Harold, stop worrying, you'll always be my buddy."

I suddenly felt sad inside. "But people grow apart, Mario. My parents don't see any of their friends from high school anymore. My sister's away at college and she doesn't either."

Mario looked down at me and smiled. "Okay, stand up and bend over."

It's not what you're thinking.

"Now I'm teaching *you* how to do something, Harold."

Mario handed me the football and told me to pass it through my legs to him standing behind me. I awkwardly followed his orders. Next, he brought me to a standing position and put the football in my hand. With his massive chest resting against my mortal back, and his large hand covering my smaller hand, he moved the ball backward. "Now, Harold, wind back, follow through, and let go."

I'm trying so hard not to let go. "You're the football hero, Mario, not me." Like a model on a game show, I pointed to other books on my bookcase. "Let's move on to Tennessee Williams, Truman Capote, and Virginia Woolf."

Holding the football like a boy without a playmate, Mario said, "You should learn how to play football."

Agenda still firmly intact, I responded, "And you should learn about art and music. Let's start with Michelangelo, Leonardo da Vinci, and Beethoven."

"Them—"

"What?"

"...*those* people don't matter no... I know... *any* more. You taught me enough to pass the quiz."

"But we still have to—"

"You're gonna get hurt." Mario blocked my way back to my desk.

I stopped like a mime hitting an invisible wall. "What?"

Avoiding my eyes, Mario spoke to the carpet. "I hear what some guys say about you. Maybe if you played a sport—"

"But I'm not good at sports. And they bore me."

"Then at least quit the band."

"I can't." Our eyes finally met.

"Why?"

"You know why, Mario."

After a long, awkward pause, Mario recovered his fumble with, "You can't quit the band, because you have to play tuba with Horrible Hannah."

I couldn't help but laugh. "Hannah's a nice girl."

"Who's hot for you."

"No, she isn't, Mario."

"Yes, she is, Harold. I heard her tell one of the cheerleaders that she's hot for *your* bod."

"And *all* the cheerleaders are probably hot for *your* bod."

"Don't change the subject, Harold. You like playing the tuba so you can be near Horrible Hannah with the big zits, small boobs, and braces on her buck teeth." He messed my red frizzy hair.

Without realizing it, I pushed Mario away. "Hannah's a nice girl."

"Who is horny for *you*. Horrible Hannah is horny for Harold!"

"She isn't." I pushed him again.

"Harold and Horrible Hannah!" Mario pushed me back.

I hope I don't split my pants.

"Have you done her yet, Harold? Have you done Horrible Hannah?"

"Screw you."

We laughed our pants off—well, not literally. I pushed Mario again. He pinned my arms and wrestled me to the ground, where our eyes met. Suddenly, Mario leaped off me like I was on fire. "You're right, Harold. We should study some more for the grammar quiz tomorrow."

I sat up on one elbow. "It's a literature quiz."

"Yeah, right. Come on, tutor, tutor me."

Still thrown, literally, from Mario's sudden wrestling move and sudden desire to master American literature, I taught Mario everything I knew, or rather everything that I thought would be on the quiz. As we studied, I wondered about the sudden change in his behavior.

Our tutoring sessions continued each night. Mario didn't tackle me again, but he did tackle everything from geometry to geography. It was clear that when Mario put his mind to it, he could master most any subject, except poetry.

On one especially excruciating evening two months later, we were lying on our stomachs, shoes off, shoulder to shoulder, with an anthology of poems nestled on the rug between us. It was a safe position for me, for obvious reasons, and a comfortable one for Mario. Certain that Tennyson was turning over in his grave, we left his poems and moved on to interpreting the poems of Robert Burns.

"Do you understand the imagery that Burns is using in this poem?" I asked.

Mario raised his eyes like a valley girl. "First of all, there are lots of words spelled wrong in this poem. I thought poets were supposed to know how to spell."

"There aren't any words spelled incorrectly."

"Oh, yeah? How about *luve's*?"

"That's the way they spelled it in Scotland back then."

"And people think *I'm* stupid." Mario read on. "And here's a mistake."

"There are no mistakes in this *classic* poem."

"Sure, there are." Mario pointed like a grade school teacher with a globe. "Look, the word *red* is repeated two times."

"Mario, this poem is about a seaman…."

"That's disgusting."

"…who compares his love to a red, red—meaning very red—rose that is newly sprung in June."

He rested his head on his palms. "How did you know that? This thing isn't even in English."

I recited romantically, "And I will come again my luve, Tho' it were ten thousand miles."

"That makes no sense."

"Why not?"

"If this Scottish guy loves this chick so much, why don't…."

"Doesn't."

"…*doesn't* he stay home instead of leaving her to go so far away?"

"He's a seaman."

"Harold, stop talking dirty. It don't… *doesn't* fit you. It freaks me out."

"Mario, he has to leave the person he loves for his *other* love, the open sea."

"Why?"

"Maybe he's a fisherman, or maybe the whole poem is a metaphor for the love of the sea that he returns to every ten years. Perhaps it's like Shakespeare's sonnets and the poem is a metaphor for a man he loves… maybe another seaman. Like Shakespeare, Burns was rumored to have had male lovers."

He groaned. "That's what I can't stand about poetry. It's never about what you think it's about. If you didn't tell me these things, I'd be totally in the dark."

I wish we were in the dark. I sat up yoga style. "That's what I love about art, music, novels, theater, *and* poetry. Each viewer takes from a piece of art what he gets from it. Haven't these poems awakened anything in you, Mario?"

"Yeah, bile."

Here goes. "I mean, don't they make you think about someone you… *love?*"

He thought about it. "If I was in love with someone, I wouldn't talk about sea and sand."

"What would you talk about, Mario?" *I may need to lie on my stomach again.*

A crease formed between his eyebrows. "I'd talk about how terrific she was, how happy she makes me feel inside, how I want to take care of her for the rest of her life, and how I couldn't live without her." Mario shut the book and sat up next to me. "I wouldn't say any of this shit."

I opened the book. "Let's look at Browning again."

He shut the book. "No more Browning. Neither one of them."

I opened the book. "Okay, then let's read Dickinson?"

He closed the book. "No more Dickinson."

"Then which poet do you want to study next, Mario?" I held the book up to him.

He took it from me. "I'm done reading this crazy shit from crazy dead people."

"Mario, don't you want to pass the poetry test tomorrow?"

"I know enough to pass." He put the book behind his back.

"Mario, give me the book."

"No."

"Mario, we haven't read all of the assigned poems yet. Give me the book."

He held up the book. "You want it, big guy, take it from me."

"Mario, be serious."

"I am serious." His dark eyes dared me. "You want it, take it."

I laughed to fake him out, then lunged for it, and fell next to him with the book under my stomach.

He looked like a precocious child with a new babysitter. "You want to play rough, do you?"

He tickled my sides, garnering fits of laughter from both of us. I let the book go and Mario dove on top of it. We were both surprised at my strength as I grabbed his foot and pulled him backward toward me and away from the book. Laughing even louder, Mario reached for the book in front of him and threw it onto my bed. When I got up to retrieve it, Mario tackled me, and we rolled on top of one another onto the bed. Mario's breath smelled like cinnamon, his skin like coconut, and his hair like almonds. *I'm ready for dessert.* I could see my amorous reflection in his large, dark eyes as we lay on the bed with his firm thighs and thick erection pressed into mine. As if in one of my recurring awake dreams, Mario's lips covered mine, and we shared a long, sensuous kiss. *Did that just happen?* My back arched as his warm tongue caressed my mouth. His large hands pressed inside my underpants, scooped up my bottom, and squeezed. My hands moved under his T-shirt and caressed and massaged the muscles in his perfect V-shaped back. His warm breath tickled my ear, and I let out a satisfied moan. I stroked his pectoral muscles, abdominal muscles, then lower abdomen. As I lowered my hand to his jeans, Mario suddenly jumped up to a standing position. "I gotta go."

I looked up in a daze. "Mario—"

"This never happened! Do you understand?" Mario's eyes were full of fear and panic.

"Why are you—?"

Mario reached down and grabbed me by the shoulders. "Harold, we can't *ever* talk about this, not to each other, not to our families, not to anyone at school or anywhere. Do you understand me?"

I wasn't sure if the tears in my eyes were from the pressure on my shoulders or the pressure in my heart, as I whispered, "I understand."

"Good." Mario picked up his jacket and walked out the door.

It took me a few minutes to catch my breath. *Was Mario really kissing me like in my dreams, or was it a nightmare? And if he was, how did I move from heaven to hell so quickly?*

Bringing me back to Earth, my father appeared in the doorway, and asked, "Did you borrow my good tie?"

Only if I was going to hang myself. "No, Dad."

"I was setting out my clothes for tomorrow and noticed it was missing from its spot."

Third tie to the right. Next to your color-coordinated shirts.

"Maybe your mother sent it to the cleaners." He started to leave, but noticed my hair was messed, a tricky task given it always looked messed. Doing a double take, he asked, "Harold, are you okay?"

"Yeah. I'm fine." *The guy I love just kissed me, then broke my heart.* "Thanks, Dad. How about you?"

He took a sip of his pre-dinner wheatgrass juice. "I'm great." Looking at his watch, he added, "Seven minutes to dinner, and one hour to my favorite television program." He smiled and stood awkwardly in the doorway.

"Is there something you want, Dad?"

Standing with one leg inside my room, his head nearly touching the top of the doorway, he replied, "Harold, I know I'm busy at work, and your mother is at the Buddhist monastery a great deal, but we are always here… to talk… if you need us."

"Thanks, Dad. I'm okay." *I think.*

Dad was on a roll. He moved his other long leg inside the doorway, but his body still leaned out to the hallway. "I know I spend a lot of time making schedules and doing chores, but I'm available, Harold, if you want to talk."

At least for the next seven minutes.

"If you want to talk about school, the band, current events… or *anything*."

"I know, Dad."

He lingered like a cat before a fondue tasting. "It's nice of you to tutor your friend from school. I like him. I know you do too. He's always welcome here. Anybody you like, I like."

"Thanks, Dad."

"Harold, I know we're… different, but I'm really proud of you."

"Thanks, Dad. I'm proud of you too."

"And you deserve the best." His long, thin hand scratched at his scalp. "Don't believe anyone who tells you to take anything less."

I walked to the doorway and gave my dad a big hug. "I love you, Dad."

"Well.…" He looked at his watch, mumbled something, and left my bedroom.

Since Mario wasn't as evolved as my father, in accordance with Mario's wishes, he and I didn't mention *the love that dares not speak its name*. Our tutoring sessions went on as usual until the following week. During one evening session, I knew something was wrong with him, but Mario kept insisting he was fine. We plowed through math and science like whipped horses. After a very tense session on tenses, I had finally tired of Mario's vacant stare and sad expression.

"Mario, I think we've had enough studying for tonight."

That got his attention. "What? Why? We haven't done psychology yet."

"Exactly." I closed the book and put it on my desk.

Mario followed me sheepishly. "Harold, I know I haven't been so smart lately."

Really? "Mario, what's going on?"

He sighed and looked away like a soap opera character. "Nothing."

"Mario, I know there's something wrong. Tell me, please."

I sat on my desk, and Mario sat on top of the adjacent dresser. I felt like a psychiatrist at the start of a session as I asked, "Do you want to tell me about it?"

"No." The dimple in his chin was reborn. "But I know you want me to, so I will."

I was falling deeper and deeper in love.

"Harold, your parents are like the Huxtables."

If the Huxtables were a white efficiency expert and a white Buddhist.

"They love and accept you… whatever you do, or don't do. It's not like that in my house."

I took his hand. He held on so tightly my circulation cut off. I didn't care. It would have been an honor to lose a hand for the man I loved. *Captain Hook did it for Peter Pan.* "What's it like in your house, Mario?"

He looked at me and tilted his head. "You want the *whole* story?"

I pointed to my bookcase, overflowing with books. "You know how much I love a good story."

Mario squeezed my hand, I think. "My parents argue a lot. It's more than arguing. Screaming, pushing, hitting is normal for them."

"That must be hard for you."

"Yeah." He looked so adorably sad and vulnerable. "It's harder for my little brother, especially since my father treats him like shit."

"But your little brother has you, Mario."

"Right."

"Who do *you* have?" Now my cheek dimple made its entrance. *Please say me.*

Mario looked away. "My grandma."

Not the answer I expected, but let's go with it. "Tell me about her." I sat next to him on the bureau. His shoulder rested against mine.

"Nonna came here with her family from Italy when she was just a girl. Their first week living in a tenement in New York, a bum throws a lit cigarette into their window. It hits a curtain and the place goes up in smoke. Only Nonna got out alive, because she was always a light sleeper. After that she lived in boxes under fire escapes while she worked fifteen hours a day sewing hems and buttons in a sweatshop. Eventually she made enough money to get off the streets, marry a tailor, and have six kids. After her husband died from a heart attack, she raised all six kids herself from what she made at the sweatshop. When her kids grew up, she was supposed to live with my parents and get a rest. No such luck. She raised me and my brother, did the housework, cooked our meals, did the laundry, and gave me and my brother… *my brother and me* our allowances."

"She sounds like a very special woman, Mario."

"The best. See, Harold, no matter what I do or say, it's never right with my father. I win football games, become class president, thanks to you pass my classes, but it's never enough. To him I'll always be a dumb loser, like he is. He keeps telling me I should go into the plumbing business with him. No thanks. That's why those college applications are so important."

"All finished and mailed."

"Thanks." He squeezed my shoulder.

"And your mom?"

Mario's expression turned from anger to apathy. "She cares more about what happens to the characters on her soap operas than she cares about what happens to me."

"Is it really that bad?"

"It's really that bad."

I wanted to take away his pain. "I'm sorry, Mario."

"Yeah, me too."

I smiled and rested my head on his shoulder. It felt warm and inviting. "But you have your nonna, right?"

"Nonna always believed in me." He smiled for the first time all evening. "And her cooking! All my favorite things like manicotti, veal francese, chicken parmigiana, Sicilian pizza."

Guess who's coming to dinner.

"Nonna always said I was smart."

Okay, that's a bit of a stretch.

"…handsome…."

She obviously still has good vision.

"…and the most important person in her world. The love of her life."

I can relate.

"Nonna always said I could talk to her about anything, and that no matter what I ever said or did, she would always love me."

It suddenly dawned on me. "Mario, why are you talking about your nonna in the past, pardon the term, tense?"

Mario's eyes filled with tears. He enveloped me in his strong arms and wept into my neck.

"I'm so sorry, Mario."

After what seemed like seconds but was more like five minutes, Mario released me and drew my face into his like a rescued castaway at a buffet. Each kiss grew in intensity until the last kiss was an explosion of heat, passion, and a bit of pain. He looked at me with desire raging in his eyes. I reflected that back at him and more. He unbuttoned his pants and placed my hand over his genitals. They felt smooth, thick, and throbbing.

"Mario, do you want to stay here tonight?"

Mario shook his head, released me, and buttoned his pants. As he reached for his leather jacket and opened my bedroom door, he said, "I want to sleep in Nonna's bed." And he was gone.

CHAPTER THREE/20 YEARS AGO

THANKS TO our tutoring sessions, Mario's grades, and my blood pressure, had risen. Mario spent less time with his football friends and more time with me. I even started going back to gym class, with Mario as my protector. That and the fact that Mr. Adoni figured out the *Dr. Dlorah* on my excuse note was an anagram for *Harold*.

One week in gym class, Mr. Adoni took out the dreaded medicine ball. This is a torture technique, no doubt created by Hitler himself, where the strong boys lob a huge, heavy ball to knock down the weak boys like bowling pins. In the past I would generally be hit pretty quickly and happily retire to the side benches. Once in safety I would read a book, or use the book to shield my head from any foul balls that bounced off the wounded.

As usual, the football players rallied to select their classmate targets, as the rest of us prayed, shook, or made our wills. Tommy, an especially large football player, threw the first grenade, which knocked the breath, and dignity, out of Manuel, who was glad to be relegated to the bench. After Tommy and Mr. Adoni shared a laugh, Keith, Tommy's best pal, threw next. Seymour hit the deck and crawled gratefully to the sidelines. Keith and Mr. Adoni slapped hands, and Mr. Adoni headed for his office to read the latest edition of what we called a *girly magazine*. After Henry, Simon, and each small boy went down for the count, I looked over at Mario getting ready to make the next shot. He wound back and aimed directly at *me*. I closed my eyes and held my breath, but nothing happened. I opened my eyes to a warm wink from Mario, and the sight of Toneless Tony lying on the floor rubbing his bruised shoulder. *My hero.*

Each gym class was the same after that. The other football players started to come after me, but one look from Mario changed the game plan and kept them in line. I was even picked for a relay team once. Mario was truly my gym guardian angel.

Unfortunately, not everyone shared my elation over my new gym status. At one session we each were doing, or in my case *attempting* to do, a maneuver on the pommel horse. Of course Mario and the other football players flew through the routine like professional gymnasts. I chalked up and jumped on the horse to the sound of Tommy saying *Ride 'em, cowboy* in a mockingly high falsetto voice. As every muscle in my body strained in a failed attempt to lift my right leg over the horse, Keith called over Mr. Adoni to ask him a question about practice that afternoon. Taking advantage of the planned diversion, Tommy gave me a wedgie, and I fell back flat on the mat with my undershorts bunched at my back. When I looked up, I noticed Mario arguing with Tommy. To my surprise, Tommy came over, helped me up, and apologized. *Miracles really do happen, especially miracles like Mario.*

After a gym class where Mario had chewed out Tommy and Keith for dribbling a basketball on my head, I was changing next to Mario in the locker room. Mario, having just stripped naked, stood next to me, wrapping a towel around his waist. I was putting my clothes on over my gym shorts.

"Thanks for picking me for your team, Mario."

He produced that winning smile. "You did okay, Harold."

"I know. I only fouled three times."

Mario laughed and slapped my behind.

Now I know why guys play sports.

We made our study plans for later that day and said good-bye. As Mario headed for the showers, I left the locker room. Tommy and Keith followed me. As I walked down the hallway on my way to study hall, I heard it.

"Faggot."

No, please God, no. I kept walking, quickening my pace. Just before I turned the corner toward the principal's office, I felt a strong hand push me, and I landed in an empty history classroom, appropriately under a poster chronicling the Holocaust. I heard the door close behind me, and I turned to see two football players standing over me.

"What do you want?" The pitch of my voice, and my pulse, rose like a rollercoaster.

Tommy, the bigger of the two, kneeled next to my face. I could smell the dirt-soiled knees of his jeans. "We have a question for you, Harold."

Keith was on my other side. "You like to answer questions, right, Harold?

Sitting in a pool of sweat, I tried to steady my quivering body. "What do you mean?"

"You tutor our pal, Mario, right, Harold?" Tommy's garlic breath singed my nostrils.

I thought fast. "Sure. If you guys would like my help too, I can—"

Keith put his thick arm on my back. "See, that's our point, Harold. We don't like our pal Mario being your… *protector*. I mean, if you want to be a fag, that's your business. We don't have a problem with it."

Tommy got even closer, if that was possible. "We think it's unnatural and against God, but hey, who are we to judge? Right, Keith?"

"Sure, Tommy. But, Harold, when you start going after our buddy Mario, forcing your lifestyle on him, we feel we need to step in."

My lips trembled. "I didn't force anything on Mario."

Tommy's voice got louder. "We disagree. See, our boy has changed. And we think *you* changed him."

Tommy and Keith shared a secret look.

I choked out, "Leave me alone. I didn't do anything to you."

"Actually you did, Harold, when you messed with our boy, Mario." Keith smiled menacingly at me. "But hey, Harold, don't sweat it. We aren't here to hurt you. We're here to *help* you."

Tommy chimed in. "As a matter of fact, this is your lucky day, Harold."

"I don't want any trouble." *God, Jesus, please help me!*

Tommy took the lead, as usual. "No trouble from us, Harold. Here's how we see it. You want to be a faggot. We can help you out with that. But you gotta promise to leave our friend Mario alone. Deal?"

"Sure. Whatever you say." I peed my pants.

"Good." Tommy winked at Keith, then punched me in the face as Keith kicked me in the stomach.

It all happened so fast. As I gasped for air, they flipped me over onto my stomach. Tommy pinned my hands as Keith pulled down my pants and held down my legs. Next, I heard Keith's fly unzip and felt his erection on my buttocks. With red covering my eyes, and intense pain in my nose and stomach, I screamed again.

"Stick it in as hard as you can," ordered Tommy. "I'll take over when you get tired. Let's teach the tutor a lesson. He wants to be a fag. Let's make him a fag."

I heard the palms of their hands slap and then I felt my butt cheeks separate. Getting my breath back, I screamed louder.

Suddenly I heard shouting and pushing around me. I pulled up my pants and hunched in the fetal position in a corner of the room. Fists flew and punches connected, while I prayed that Mario had found me. My prayers were answered as I looked up at Mario, standing over me in shock.

"Are you okay?" Mario wiped the blood from my nose with the bottom of his T-shirt, and I wiped the blood from his knuckle with mine.

I'm better now. "How did you find me?"

Mario rested my head on his chest. "Your friend Hannah was stalking you. She found me and told me what was happening in here. I would have killed those guys if she didn't tell me to come help you while she got the assistant principal to take them to his office."

"Hannah's a good friend. So are you."

"I'm a piece of shit." Mario buried his Roman nose in my cheek, and his dark, wavy hair nestled against my forehead.

"I'm sorry, Mario."

"For what?"

"Getting you in trouble with your friends."

Mario lifted me by my shoulders to face him, then rested his hands on either side of my face. "Harold, what those guys did to you. That had nothing to do with you. And they're no longer my friends. I'm talking to the coach and getting them thrown off the team."

"But you lost your friends, Mario."

"Harold, don't you get it? Those guys don't mean anything to me. You mean more to me than…."

After a long, deep, piercing kiss, Mario hugged me like he would never let me go. Unfortunately, all too soon he did.

After a long pause to think, Mario finally said, "Harold, we have to stop this."

I looked into his eyes and wanted to dive into those dark pools of splendor. "I've been thinking the same thing, Mario." I sat up on my knees. "Hannah told me about a Young Democrats Club starting up at school. She said we can join and team up with other kids who are tolerant of people who are different, including kids who are gay. Maybe we can make some new friends."

Mario looked like he had seen a ghost… in drag. "Did you…? Did you tell Hannah about… *us*… in your *bedroom*?"

"No, no way, Mario. I'd never do that."

Mario sat back on his heels and exhaled. "Thank God."

I took his hands. They felt like home. "You're the class president. You're nice to everyone. Hannah assumed that you… and I… would want to join the club."

"Harold, I can't do that."

"Why not?"

"Didn't you see what just happened? What those assholes nearly did to you?"

"You just said that had nothing to do with me."

"Harold, it had to do with *me*. Because guys like *me* can't be gay. And guys like *me* can't be in love with guys like you!"

Mario sucked in his breath as if hoping he could take it back. I wasn't sure if he was more upset over saying the gay part or the in love with me part.

He released my hands, and they fell to my lap. "Something's gotta change, Harold."

"I don't understand."

He exhaled and helped me up to my feet. "You sure you're feeling okay?"

"No." *You're breaking my heart.*

He put his arm around me. "Come on, let's go to the nurse."

"Why? All she can do is give me a cough drop."

"Then let's go get you a cough drop."

After Mario and I left the nurse's office, we ran into Hannah, who told me that Mr. Ringwood wanted to see me.

Mr. Ringwood's ancient secretary, who used so much hairspray it looked like she was wearing a helmet, led me into the principal's large office. I stood on the other side of his enormous oak desk and could barely see the principal sitting behind it. Mr. Ringwood was a short, bald, rail-thin, older, gentle man who wore bowties and smiled a lot.

"Harold, please sit down."

He motioned for me to sit in a chair facing his desk.

"Hannah told me about the *incident* with Tommy and Keith. Are you all right, son?"

I felt my nose and my stomach. "Yes, thank you, Mr. Ringworm—I mean, Mr. Ringwood."

Mr. R. smiled his familiar smile and adjusted his bowtie. "It is a *terrible* thing what those two boys did to you."

I looked down at the cracked wooden floor. "I know."

"We have a zero tolerance policy at this school for any kind of bullying or violence."

I nodded in hopeful anticipation of hearing about Tommy's and Keith's permanent expulsion from school.

"So I have decided…."

Can someone's voice crack at his age?

"…to suspend each of them for one week."

One week? That's it? A week's vacation for attacking me? "Mr. Ringworm, I mean, Mr. Ringwood, Tommy and Keith didn't just hit me, they tried to—"

Mr. Ringwood motioned for me to stop talking. He quickly rose and closed his office door, then hoisted his small body up onto his huge desk. For the first time in my life, I saw him not smiling. "Harold, I am going to ask you not to mention that to anyone, not even to your parents."

"Why not?"

He wiped a glob of sweat off his forehead with his handkerchief. "These matters are hard for someone of your age to understand."

Explain it to me.

Mr. R. sounded like a defense attorney at opening arguments. "Harold, this school has a stellar reputation. I know you want to keep it that way. I work every week to protect that."

That and your retirement pension.

"Unfortunate *occurrences* like this, while—of course—they must be dealt with, we don't want to make them... fuel for fodder. Do you understand?"

"I don't think so."

"The assistant principal will meet with those boys and read them the riot act. Every threat will be leveled against them—from telling their parents, to permanent expulsion, to making sure they never get into college, to suing them, and to arresting them. They will also be evicted from our football team."

Now that the season is almost over.

"You are excused from your physical education class for the rest of the year. Harold, I give you my absolute word that you will be safe in this school. And if you should ever encounter a problem with them, or anyone else again, I want you to go directly to the assistant principal immediately and tell him. Do you understand?"

"Yes." *I think I'm beginning to.*

He sat on the chair next to me and whispered as if the room was bugged. "Harold, boys like you, and to be perfectly frank, like me, we have to be very careful. Because we are... *different*, we can make other boys like Tommy and Keith... *angry*. And that's a dangerous thing to do. So sometimes, we have to... *contain* ourselves. Control our... *feelings*. Keep certain things... *hidden*, so we can remain safe, and so there aren't any... *problems*."

Is that what you do with the school board? "Mr. Ringwood, do you think what happened to me is my fault?"

"No, Harold, absolutely, not! You were the victim. But this whole thing can be a good learning experience for you." The infamous smile was back. "We who are... *atypical*, rather than wearing our idiosyncrasies on our shirtsleeves, we need to learn how to... *fit in*, to conform in society... to help make our lives, and the lives of those around us, safe and productive."

"So what do you think I should do?"

He put his small hand on my shoulder. "Go home, take a shower, eat dinner, go to bed and try to forget this ever happened. And in the future, when faced with boys like Tommy and Keith, keep your distance, walk a different route, and stay in the shadows. Hold on to good friends like Hannah and Mario for protection. Make sure something like this doesn't ever happen to you again."

Mr. R. put his arm around me and walked me to his office door. "You are an excellent student, Harold. You have a successful academic career ahead of you. And a wonderful life ahead after that. Learn how to make everyone like you. Learn how to stay safe in this world... that so often can be unsafe. Protect *yourself*. I have confidence in *you*."

He released his arm, opened the door, unveiled his customary smile, and shut the door.

At the time I thought that I had somehow provoked Tommy's and Keith's wrath against me. I also felt it was my fault that Mario was upset. So as the principal recommended, I kept my distance from Tommy and Keith, and tried to be the friend that Mario wanted me to be.

I also attended the Young Democrats' meetings. When I say the Young Democrats, I mean the YA. Mr. Ringwood approved the establishment of the club, provided that if anyone asked our club name, we were to respond "the YA" or "Youth Association." Every Friday at 3:00 p.m., we met in our advisor's—Ms. Hunsley's—classroom with Hannah as our leader. The club membership consisted of Hannah, me, and four other students who wanted to take advantage of the time to work on their chemistry experiments. Most of the time our topic of conservation was anti-environment, anti-gay, or anti-women legislation proposed by Republican legislators. We also talked about closet gay celebrities whom Hannah had a crush on. We did initiate a buddy system, however, where we each promised to come to the other's rescue if Tommy, Keith, or anyone at school came after us. I will always be grateful to Hannah for that. Since Gay Straight Student Alliances had not yet been invented, the YA club was the best our high school had to offer, and I took advantage of it.

Ms. Hunsley sat and knitted during our meetings and said very little. So I was surprised after one of our meetings when she asked me if I would stay afterward to speak with her.

My chemistry teacher was a soft-spoken, middle-aged woman with long, dark hair tied at the back and a soulful look in her large, hazel eyes. The gray roots of her hair peeked out, surrounding her face with a silver glow. She wore a white smock over a simple light blouse and dark skirt each day. Ms. Hunsley wore no wedding ring, and appeared to be devoted to the field of chemistry.

That afternoon she put down her knitting, moved away from her desk, and motioned for me to sit on one of the stools near the window. I noticed the clear, crisp day outside matched Ms. Hunsley's aura.

"You wanted to speak with me, Ms. Hunsley?"

She nodded and shut the classroom door.

After she sat on the stool next to me, I asked, "Ms. Hunsley, did I do something wrong?"

She stared into space for a few moments, appearing to be lost in her thoughts. "What? No. Of course not. You're one of my best students." Her smile made the sunny day more sunny.

"Is it something about the club? If so, shouldn't we ask Hannah to join us?"

"It's not about the club, Harold. Well, maybe it is… in a way." She leaned forward and our eyes met. "I heard what Tommy and Keith did to you."

My head dropped. "Oh."

Ms. Hunsley pushed up my chin. "Harold, that was a terrible thing. It should not have happened. And those boys should not have been let back into this school."

My mouth grew dry.

"Are you all right?"

I nodded.

"Are you keeping away from those boys?"

I nodded again.

"If those boys even so much as look at you again, I want you to promise that you will come and tell me. Promise?"

"Yes, Ms. Hunsley."

"Good." After a thoughtful pause, Ms. Hunsley asked, "Harold, why doesn't Mario come to these club meetings?"

I squirmed on my stool. "I'm not really sure."

"He should."

"I've invited him."

She put her hand on my shoulder and smiled. "Harold, I put you two together in lab for a reason. I sensed that you each possessed what the other one didn't. And if you two joined forces, you would be an unbeatable team."

"Thank you, Ms. Hunsley." I looked out the window, wondering where Mario was, and why the Mario and Harold team seemed so beaten.

"Is everything all right between you two boys?"

I refocused. "Why do you ask?"

"You two were like molecular bonds. The positive energy between you two was atomic. Now I rarely see you two together. What went wrong with my experiment?"

"I guess the atoms split." *Thanks to Tommy and Keith.*

"Care to talk about it?"

"I don't know if that's a good idea."

She put a hand on my twitching knee. "You can trust me, Harold."

I feel that I can. "As you know I was tutoring Mario, and we became close... friends. After the thing with Tommy and Keith, Mario got frightened, and things with us... cooled off."

"That's what I thought." Ms. Hunsley went to her desk, opened a drawer, and brought back a small gold plaque. "Don't tell Mr. Ringwood I'm doing this." She put the plaque in my hand. "I want you to have this, Harold."

I was speechless, literally.

"There's a quote on it from a poem by Percy Shelley. Like you, he was... *different.*"

I read the words on the plaque.

Nothing in the world is single;
All things by a law divine,
In one spirit meet and mingle.
Why not I with thine?

I looked up at Ms. Hunsley, not knowing what to say.

"You're wondering why a chemistry teacher is quoting Shelley? There's a lot about me my students don't know, Harold."

"Ms. Hunsley, the plaque is beautiful, but why are you giving this to *me?*"

She sat back down. "Harold, that plaque was given to me by someone very special to me... many years ago. A man... that I loved a great deal." She smiled in fond recollection. "He was like Mario in some ways. A sportsman. Rugged, strong, and determined on the outside, but soft, tender, and very much in need of love on the inside." She looked out the window.

I noticed a tear form in the corner of her eye. "He hated chemistry. I hated sports. We were total opposites, but we were an unstoppable pair. We were very happy."

"What happened, Ms. Hunsley?"

"Other people weren't so happy."

"I don't understand."

Ms. Hunsley wiped her eye with the sleeve of her lab coat and faced me. "Some people didn't like the color of his skin."

"So they made trouble for you, because he was black?"

She nodded. "And he got frightened."

"Ms. Hunsley—"

She shrugged away my hand. "I didn't tell you this for sympathy."

"I'm sorry."

"Don't be sorry. More importantly, don't be afraid. And don't let people like Tommy and Keith decide who you can *or can't* love. Because when you are alone at night, it's only love that matters. Tell that to Mario too. Will you promise me that you will?"

I nodded, feeling the tears brimming in my eyes.

She squeezed my knee. "You're a good boy, Harold. Don't let anybody tell you any differently. Including Mario." She stood and went back to her desk. "I've said too much. Thank goodness for tenure. You can go now."

I stood and walked to the door. "Thank you for the gift, Ms. Hunsley."

"It's only a little plaque."

"That's not the gift I meant." I smiled at her and left the classroom.

CHAPTER FOUR/20 YEARS AGO

I WENT home and put the plaque under my pillow. I phoned Mario, but thanks to my college application essays, he was out visiting colleges. I didn't see him for a whole week. That hurt more than my bruised nose and stomach.

My heart leapt one afternoon when he walked into my bedroom, threw his leather jacket onto my desk, and kicked his black work boots off under the bed. After our tutoring session, which just happened to end with us sitting at the edge of my bed, I started to reach under my pillow to show Mario my new plaque. Before I could retrieve it, Mario took my clammy hands in his and destroyed my life.

"Harold, I have some good news."

Your school ring on a chain around my neck?

His smile was crooked, and his focus was on the rug. "I'm in love."

Me, too.

"And considering… what's been going on… I think this is the best thing… for everybody."

Wedding bells? "Mario, I'm in—"

"It's Barbara Babinsky," Mario blurted out as if vomiting. I nearly joined him.

So my cozy twosome has become a messy threesome. "The cheerleader?"

Mario sounded like a cult member at the pink lemonade table. "That's not the only reason I love her. She's beautiful. She's sexy. And she don't stuff her blouse with tissues like the other cheerleaders." He hit the literature book against his head. "I mean, *doesn't.*" Mario continued his diatribe like a job interviewer with a fabricated resume. "I thought of you when Barb and I made out for the first time. It was in the *coach's office.*"

How nice of you.

He walked to the bookcase and held up the books that *we* studied together. "Me and Barbara…. Barbara and *I*… are like Romeo and Juliet, or George and Emily."

Yeah, and look where they all ended up.

Like a first-time visitor to a mental institution, I approached Mario and rested a shaky hand on his broad shoulder. "Mario, it's me. You can stop this. You can tell me the truth."

Mario's shoulder contracted and my hand flew back to my side. "I know it's really soon. But I can tell. I love her, Harold. My hand to God."

"But what about *us*?"

He sat at my desk like a child playing teacher. "I've been doing some reading, Harold."

Since when?

"I read a pamphlet… from church."

Ah, a highly regarded psychological study.

"A lot of guys, at our age, go through… what we went through."

"And what is that?"

"You know, messing around a little, experimenting with each other."

Before I could faint, I sat on the desk.

"But, Harold, don't worry."

And why is that?

"Just because we… *experimented*, that doesn't mean we are gay. It's actually pretty normal, because at our age our hormones are raging."

I'm raging all right. I somehow got out, through a mouth as dry as the Sahara, "Who told you this?"

Mario looked at me for the first time all evening. "Father Ryan at church."

"Did he touch you or…?"

"No, Harold, I went to see him. He was really nice. He explained everything to me."

"Well, I hope you can explain *everything* to me."

Mario paced the room like a college professor in front of the tenure committee. "See, God has a plan for all of us."

"Which is?" I knew I wouldn't like the answer.

"As Father Ryan explained it, the plan is for us to get married and have children."

Sounds good to me. "So why can't you marry a man and adopt children?"

"Because, as Father Ryan explained, that's *unnatural*."

"So is using a computer and driving a car, but Father Ryan does both."

"Harold, two men together. It's against God."

"You've talked to God lately?"

Mario sat me on the desk chair and kneeled next to me with a pious look on his face. "Father Ryan showed me in the Bible. It's an *abomination*."

"We're Catholic. We don't read the Bible."

"Can you be serious, please?"

"You want to be serious? Okay. Many people believe the anti-gay line in Leviticus is a mistranslation for a pagan prostitution ritual with eunuchs."

"What's a eunuch?"

"What Father Ryan is trying to make you."

"Stop talking shit about a priest. He's a man of God."

"Tell that to the altar boys."

"Stick to the subject, Harold."

"Okay, the Bible says a lot of things are an abomination: eating shellfish, women wearing jewelry, women not lying outside in the fields during menstruation, not stoning to death your unbelieving neighbor, wearing clothing made from more than one fabric."

He stood and glared down at me. "Stop confusing me, Harold."

"You're confused all right. The Bible is various books written thousands of years ago in different languages about a different place and time, and rewritten by many people over the centuries. It isn't a rulebook. It's meant for spiritual reflection. People who pick out and parrot certain verses to hurt other people are hateful, whether it is to support slavery, decline women the right to vote, or ban interracial or same-sex love and marriage. How can harming other people be godly? Didn't Jesus say not to judge one another, and to love your neighbor as yourself?"

He put his hand over his ears. "Stop it!"

"Jonathan and David were a couple. On the cross Jesus told his mother that John, his most *beloved* disciple, was her *son* too."

"Shut up!" Mario had fire in his eyes.

"If being gay is so abominable, why didn't Jesus say anything about it in the Bible stories? Why did he eat with, preach to, and love everyone, *everyone*, Mario, even the outcasts… like *us*?"

Mario pushed me onto the floor. He quickly sat next to me to make sure nothing was broken. Everything was in one piece, except my heart. "Harold, I'm sorry. I'm a piece of shit. Sometimes you make me so crazy."

I sat on the rug next to him, wishing I had a magic wand to bring back my Mario. "Mario, don't mess up your life because of what some priest said."

"I'm not." He looked so cute when he pouted.

Trying a different tactic, I asked, "Mario, do you remember Kinsey from psychology?"

"No, does he go to our school?"

I wish then he could help me here. "Kinsey is a famous psychologist who conducted a study with lots of people, then created a scale."

"Who cares about some guy who weighs people?"

"He's famous. The Kinsey Scale."

"He named a scale after himself?"

I sat up on my knees so we were eye to eye. "Mario, Kinsey studied people's sexuality."

"So he was a pervert?"

"He was a social scientist who theorized that every person's sexuality can be categorized on a scale of zero to six; zero being totally straight, and six being totally gay."

"So he *was* a pervert." He turned away.

I grasped his shoulders so he would face me again. "No, Mario, Kinsey believed that not everyone is a zero or a six. That some people fall *in between.*"

"You mean they're bi… confused?"

"Maybe. Or maybe not. Perhaps with all the different factors that make up our sexuality… nature, genes, nurture, hormones… sexuality isn't as simple as we think."

"Or maybe he's full of crap and got rich off gullible nerds like you." He stood up.

I jumped up. "Or maybe sexuality isn't only about gender. Maybe there's a possibility for *any* two people to.…" *Say it.* "…fall in love." I took out Ms. Hunsley's plaque and read Shelley's poem to Mario.

After a pause, he said, "Harold, I agree with you, and with *Shelby.* I fell in love. It's the real thing, Harold. Grover's Corners stuff. Heading down the aisle material."

I'll ask my father to give me away. We know he'll be on time. And Hannah can be my Best… Hannah.

"That's what I've been trying to tell you, Harold. I know it's fast, but I fell in love… with Barbara. And someday I want to marry her."

My stomach dropped to the floor. I grabbed onto his arm like a life raft. "I don't believe you."

"Believe me, Harold… if you want to be my friend."

"You're just trying to prove you aren't gay."

"I'm not gay, Harold. We're different. I'm not like you."

A tear landed on my cheek.

"Please, stop trying to psychoanalyze me, Harold, and just be happy for me. Be happy for me… and Barbara."

"Why?"

"'Cause I don't want my future best man looking sad." He smiled like a cartoon character before a great fall. "When the time comes, I want you to write out the invitations for our wedding. You're a good writer. You can help us pick out the food too. I want my favorite, Italian. We can give the caterer my Nonna's old recipes. We'll play bocci ball at the wedding. And everybody will get drunk off their asses." Mario brought me into his massive chest for a tight hug. "Harold, you're my best friend. You're my Rock of *Gibraltic*. Believe me. Be happy for me. Support me in this, please."

"What if I can't?"

"Then I'll make you." Mario swung me in a circle, and kissed my cheek. *So that's how Jesus felt with Judas.* "I'm in love, Harold. I'm really in love… with Barbara Babinsky."

Wait, it gets better. The next day in the courtyard at school during lunch, Mario looked happy to see me. I wanted to throw myself into his arms.

"Harold!"

"Mario. Hi."

There was so much electricity between us, Ben Franklin could have put a kite and a key on us. Then I noticed Barbara Babinsky, channeling Hester Prynne, as she clutched onto Mario's arm like an albatross in heat.

"Hi, High." Barbara tugged at the underpants under her cheerleading skirt to make sure her lower butt cheeks were visible, then rested her bleached blonde locks on Mario's glorious dark curls.

"Hi, Barbara. Good game, Mario," I said, as if I paid any attention.

"I threw that last pass for you, pal."

"We played 'We Belong Together' for you, Mario." *If I ravage him in public, there will be too many witnesses.*

Barbara spit out her bubble gum and replaced it with a new supply. "The band sounded good, Harold."

Feeling obligated, I responded, "Nice cheers out there too, Barbara."

"Oh, I don't know." Clearly Mario was expected to respond to this. When he didn't, Barbara turned to stone, like Lot's wife in Sodom.

Mario finally took the hint. "Barb, the cheers were great. You stole the half-time show, as usual."

"Thanks… I guess." In an effort to pout, Barbara raised her berry-glossed lower lip toward her surgically altered nose. When Mario didn't get the message, Barbara bit her cheek and a tear formed in her eye.

"What's wrong, babe?" Mario asked, finally catching the hint.

Barbara rolled her eyes. "You know I don't like to complain, honey."

"Barbara's got a lot on her plate right now," Mario explained to me.

Yeah, you.

Hearing her cue, Barbara said, "More than a lot. I have to teach all the cheers, keep our advisor away from practice, ensure the uniforms are sweat-mark-free, share makeup and hair tips with the other girls, and check out other school's squads to make sure their girls aren't better than we are."

"I know, honey," Mario responded, trying to sound concerned.

In an attempt to end my agony, I said, "Well, I better go. I got a job at the fruit market after school."

"That's appropriate," said Barbara, stifling a laugh.

Ignoring her, I asked Mario hopefully, "Are you coming over to study tonight? We have a government test tomorrow."

Barbara cuddled up to Mario like a snake released from its basket. "Mario, do you want to give Harold the good news… or should *I*?"

Yippee. More good news.

Mario shuffled his feet back and forth. "Ah, yeah, Harold, Barbara's tutoring me now. So I'm okay."

You are definitely not okay.

Barbara turned her attention to me… briefly. "Marci from the squad has an aunt who works in the office at school, and she gave Marci a copy of the upcoming tests. Of course Marci shared them with the rest of the girls. It pays to have friends in high places." Barbara's laugh sounded like a goose caught in a blender. "So Mario won't be needing your help anymore, Harold. Isn't that good news?"

Thrilling.

"Now you can have more time to play the tuba, be with Hannah, and do… whatever else you do."

Do I see a slight look of guilt on her made-up face?

"And of course you can always visit *us* if you get lonely."

I'd rather be in solitary confinement.

Having done her civic duty, Barbara focused her attention back on Mario. "Come on, hon, let's go to my house and relax in the whirlpool."

"What about the government test, babe?"

"We can look at the test later. Who cares about the UN and the Middle East anyway? What could possibly happen way over *there* that could affect us in any way *here*?"

As Barbara pulled him away, Mario called over his shoulder with a sad tinge in his voice, "Catch up with you later, Harold."

"Bye, High," Barbara sang as she waved Mario's senior ring on a chain around her neck then walked away with her tongue down his throat.

Hope Mario's allergic to bubble gum.

I walked away in disappointment with my chin practically hitting the ground, and I accidentally bumped into Hannah.

"Hi, Harold." Hannah's fire engine red hair, silver braces, and oily skin sent the reflection of the sun straight into my squinting eyes.

"Hi, Hannah."

At first I thought it was her flute case, but I realized Hannah was carrying a pink book bag.

She followed my gaze. "It's Barbara's. I'm carrying it for her."

"How come?"

"In exchange for a tryout as a cheerleader," she responded with embarrassment flooding her round face.

"Good luck, Hannah."

"Thanks."

I started to leave but Hannah grasped my arm.

"Are you coming to the YA meeting tomorrow?"

"I can't. I have to work."

"Okay. But if you want to know what you missed, or if you want to practice, give me a call."

"Thanks, Hannah."

Again I started to leave, and again Hannah grasped my arm.

"Harold, you know that I'm here if you need a friend."

"Yeah, friends. I had more than one once."

Sensing my pity party, Hannah took me by the arm. "Come here."

We sat on a bench under an evergreen tree. With our red hair against the leaves, we looked like a Christmas decoration.

She pulled a leaf from the tree and smelled it. "I always liked this smell. Don't you?"

She gave me a whiff.

"Sure."

She threw the leaf onto the ground. "Harold, just like that leaf is smaller than this branch, and this branch is smaller than this tree, there's a pecking order in high school too." Hannah fluffed her curly red hair. "Do you understand what I mean?"

"Not really."

She cleared her throat and spoke like a kindergarten teacher instructing her pupils on the color chart. "Mario and Barbara are like the sun. They are the popular kids who sit mightily on top of the world, deciding if the days will be sunny or cloudy, while the rest of us bask in their glorious light, or sit in darkness and think about them. Then there are the other kids. Some are like the sky. They're attractive, always around, and nice to gaze at now and then. Other kids are like this tree: functional, solid, but easy to forget. The rest of the kids are like the branches and the leaves. Nobody really notices them. And the teachers are like the water that keeps it all growing, and keeps the hierarchy in place."

I shrugged. "I guess that makes me the dirt under the tree."

After a laugh, Hannah answered, "But only for *now*. You see, Harold, these, our high school years, are *their* glory days." She pointed to Barbara's pink bag sitting next to her on the bench. "Their best days. *Ever.* Life will never be as good for them." She grinned from ear to ear. "But for *us*. These are our hell years. We just need to survive them, so we can get the hell out of high school and move on to doing amazing things in the real world."

I rested my arm on the back of the bench. "But the sun, the sky, the trees, the water, and the soil are all connected. When a leaf falls, it eventually merges with the water and the soil, and they nourish the trees, and the trees take in the sunlight, and are matted against the blue sky."

Hannah had an answer for everything. "And what happens to everything on a dark, snowy day?"

I thought about it. "Everything disappears, except for the white snow and the grey sky."

She pointed her finger at me as if I'd answered a question correctly in class. "Right. With each season, the landscape totally *changes*."

I scratched my head. "I don't understand."

Hannah pressed her glasses against her nose and ran her tongue against her braces. "One day soon, when we graduate, the seasons will *change*. Then people like Mario and Barbara will be as insignificant as dead leaves for the compost. High school is *their* time. After high school, it will be *ours*."

"How do you know that?"

She nodded as if moving on to the next chapter in the lesson. "Their good looks will fade. Their self-centeredness will turn people off. And their ignorance will make them unemployable. They'll be working at the mall, if they're lucky, talking about *the good old days* in high school while we run corporations, create great art, and patent new inventions."

I laughed. "It's amazing how you have everything figured out."

"Trust me, Harold, I'm right. You'll see." She rested back against my arm. "I'm sorry you and Mario aren't good friends any longer."

Me too.

"But you'll come out better in the end. As my mother always says, 'It's not where you start, it's where you finish.'"

I looked up at the blue sky, and thought of one of Mario's T-shirts. "Well, Mario seems to have moved on with Barbara."

"Yes, like all A-listers, now that they have each other, they no longer need their friends. So you, and I, need to move on too." She looked at me and batted the short eyelashes over her small green eyes.

"What do you mean?"

Hannah took my hand in hers. "I think we make a great team, Harold. Don't you?"

"Sure. We play well together, and I like our club."

"That's not what I mean, Harold." She giggled naughtily.

"What do you mean?"

"Wouldn't it be a riot, I mean, wouldn't we just show *everybody*, if you and I went to the senior prom *together*?"

I wiggled in my seat. "I don't know, Hannah. I didn't go to the junior prom. Things like that freak me out."

"Me too. That's why I think it would be a total hoot if we went… together."

"You mean… as friends… just to go?"

She squeezed my hand. "Of course we're friends, Harold. And the prom will be *fun*."

"I don't think so, Hannah."

"Harold, do you want to be an old man sitting and wondering why you missed out on your own prom?"

"Hannah, you're my only friend right now, and I'm really thankful for everything you've done for me. You saved my life."

She smacked her lips and one of her rubber bands flew out of her mouth. "Then it's settled. I'll make the reservation for the limousine, buy my dress, my corsage, your lapel flower, and make the reservation for the prom tickets. Can you rent your tux, or do you need me to do that too?"

My head was spinning. "Hannah, whoa, slow down."

"The prom will be here before we know it, Harold."

I released her hand and sat up straight. "Hannah, I like you, a lot. You're a great girl. But I don't think this is a very good idea."

"Why not?" She scratched at the training bra underneath her white blouse, then adjusted her cranberry skirt.

I deliberated until it suddenly came to me. "Two reasons, Hannah. First, you're too good for me. You're like the sun, and I'm like the soil."

"Well, that's very flattering, Harold, but as I said, things—"

"And second, I like someone else."

Hannah seemed genuinely surprised. "You do?"

Can she really not know? I nodded.

She digested that as we both digested a tuna sandwich she'd taken out of her purse. "Is it someone I know, Harold?" Another rubber band flew through the air.

"I'd rather not talk about it, Hannah."

"Okay, be mysterious if you like."

"So do you understand now why I can't go to the prom with you, Hannah?"

After we split her grapes, she responded, "I guess so."

I smiled. "Good. No hard feelings, Hannah?"

She returned the smile. "No hard feelings."

"Can we still be friends?"

She nodded. "Friends it is."

As we rose to walk back to school, Hannah said, "I'll tell you one thing, Harold. Whoever she is, she's a lucky girl."

Taking a play from Mario's book, I kissed her on the cheek. As I walked away, I noticed Hannah touch her cheek and grin from ear to ear.

I felt as if I had moved from the romantic lead opposite Mario to a supporting player opposite Hannah. Barbara waved Mario's class ring and I instantly became the gay best friend. Hurricane Barbara turned my sunny skies to gray, as every time I talked to Mario at school, Barbara ran interference. So after I got home each day, I stared at a picture of Mario that I'd secretly taken when he fell asleep one night while we were studying together. I also sulked, cried, and threw books at the wall. Until one night during winter break.

Mario walked into my bedroom as if in a time warp. "Your dad let me in."

I hid his picture under my mattress. "Mario, what are you doing here?"

"I was driving around... and I ended up here." His eyes looked glazed over.

"Are you all right?"

"No."

I sat on the edge of my bed, and Mario sat next to me with his knee pressed against mine. *Just like old times… except for the smell of liquor on your breath.*

"Were you and Barbara at a party?"

He let out a pitiful laugh. "Right, some *party.*"

"Tell me what's wrong?" *Besides you dating Barbara.*

Mario looked at the book next to me. "What are you studying?"

"About Amelia Earhart, for history."

"I know. She was secretly gay, but it's not in the textbook, and it won't be on the test."

I taught you well. "Did you study?"

"What's the point?" He looked at the far wall of my bedroom as if he was watching a sad movie.

"The point is that you graduate and go to your Ivy League college on a football scholarship."

"Who gives a shit?"

"I do."

"Then you're the only one."

Probably true. "How come you're not with Barbara?"

He laughed. "She and the other girls are having a *face masque night* at Cindi's. No boys allowed. Ironic huh? 'Cause nobody wears a mask better than me."

"Mario, what's going on?"

He lay back gently on my bed and looked up at the ceiling. "What's going on, Harold, is that I don't live in a happy home like you do."

I lay on my side next to him. "Mario, will you please stop talking in riddles and tell me why you're so upset?"

"Why am I upset? Let's see. Maybe it's because my father got piss drunk tonight. Not that that's unusual though. Maybe it's because he called me screwed up. Come to think of it. That's not unusual either."

I noticed a tear flow from the corner of his eye. I took a chance and rested my arm on his shoulder. He winced in pain.

Mario began to laugh, a guttural, pained gyration. "You'll love this one, Harold. My father told me tonight that his brother was gay, or as my father said, his brother was *a piece of shit faggot*. He told me they were close friends growing up. My father always looked out for him. But when they were young guys, before I was born, my father caught his brother with another guy… in the back of my dad's car. So my father disowned him.

His own brother. And my uncle locked himself in the car and turned on the engine. My father said it was *for the best*."

"Your uncle committed suicide?"

"Evidently."

"Why did your father tell you this now?"

He rested his forearm over his eyes. "Because he found a letter that I wrote."

"So?"

"To another guy?"

"To me?"

"You always were an A student, Harold."

I moved his arm away from his eyes. "What did the letter say?"

"It doesn't make any difference."

"It does to me."

Mario sat up on one elbow. "I apologized to you for being such a dick with Barbara. I asked if we could study together again."

"What's wrong with that?"

"Nothing. Nothing is wrong with that." Another tear escaped. "It was the part I wrote about missing you, and the part about the good times we had in your bedroom. Something is wrong with that. Something is *very* wrong with that."

"I'm sorry about your father, Mario. But it's good that you got everything out into the open. Now we can go back to being friends and to studying together."

"No we can't, Harold."

"Why not?"

He looked at me as if I didn't speak English. "Don't you get it? Don't you understand?"

"No, explain it to me."

"My father told me tonight that if I'm a faggot I shouldn't come home. I should kill myself in my car, like my uncle."

"Mario…."

"And when I called him a son of a bitch, he took off his belt and beat the shit out of me. When I called out to my mother for help, she left the room."

Mario's tears flowed freely. I held him in my arms and he winced from the pain. I took off his T-shirt and gasped at the welts on his shoulders and back.

"Oh, God, Mario, you have to tell someone about this."

"Who?"

"Tell the police."

"No."

"Someone at school."

"No."

"We can tell my parents."

"Stop, Harold. I don't want to tell anybody. This is *my* problem."

I examined his bruises closer. "Let me put some cream on them."

"Harold, please stop."

"You really should—"

"That's not what I want."

We were lying on our sides, facing one another. "What do you want, Mario?"

Mario looked at me like someone dying of thirst facing a gallon of water. He kissed me hard on the mouth. I tasted the alcohol. He kissed me again even harder, and the stubble on his face rubbed against my skin like sandpaper. He practically ripped off my shirt and pants, kicked off his jeans, and lay on top of me.

"Mario, what are you doing?"

"What you want me to do."

He yanked down my underpants, then threw off his own. Next, he pushed me down onto my back, and forcefully lifted my legs into the air.

I experienced flashbacks from Tommy and Keith. "Mario, no, stop!"

Mario looked down at me as if he couldn't believe his ears. "Stop? Isn't this what you wanted, what you've been begging for, ever since I first came here? Don't you want to play George and Emily, or Tennessee Williams and Alexander the Great?"

"Please, Mario. Not like *this*."

"Isn't *this* what gay people do? I thought you and Kinsey wanted me to be gay? Am I the wrong number on the scale, Harold?"

I started to cry. He released my legs, and they fell to the bed.

"I can't make anybody happy, my father, my mother, Barbara, or even *you*."

I continued to cry. As if a comatose man becoming conscious, Mario took me in and cradled me in his arms.

"Harold, I'm so sorry. I don't know why I did that. I can't believe I did that. Please forgive me."

"It's okay." I couldn't stop crying.

"No, it's not okay. Harold, my little Harold. How could I hurt you?" He kissed away my tears and held me close into his chest. "How could I hurt *you*?"

Then he got up abruptly, vomited in my bathroom, put his clothes back on, and left.

During the next few months, I went to school, club meetings, and work. When I ran into Mario at school, he apologized for his behavior at my house, blaming it all on the alcohol. I knew better. Though we spoke occasionally at school, Mario never visited me at home again. He spent most of his time with his football friends and, of course, with Barbara. His father must have been proud.

While Mario made arrangements for Ivy League college life the following year, I worked at the fruit market. My part-time job consisted of lugging boxes of fruit from a truck into the store, unpacking it, washing it, killing any bugs on it, and turning it so the bruised sections were not visible to the customers. The customers complained about the prices, the manager complained about the customers, and I thought about Mario.

CHAPTER FIVE/20 YEARS AGO

ONE SPRING Saturday after a long day at the fruit market, I came home to find Mario's little brother, Vincenzo, sitting on the sofa in our living room. He resembled a pubescent Mario, surrounded by baby fat. Afraid to leave Vincenzo with his father, Mario had brought him over on a number of our past tutoring sessions. While I tutored Mario, in the good old days, his brother would read one of my old books or play one of my old games. His little brother was so quiet that Mario and I often forgot he was there. That Saturday my mother had let Vincenzo in to wait for me before she left for her breathing and chanting class. She had evidently given him a piece of chocolate cake and a glass of milk before she left, the remnants of which adorned his chubby cheeks. As I stood over Mario's brother, I also noticed a purple mark between his right eye and cheekbone.

"Is Mario okay?" I asked.

"Yeah, he's fine. I thought he might be here." He looked out the bay window.

"He's not. What happened to your face?"

He continued to avert his eyes. "I got into a fight."

"With who?"

"Some kid."

I sat next to him on the sofa. "Vinnie…."

"Mario's the only one who calls me that."

"Sorry."

He smiled for the first time and unveiled two adorable dimples. "No, I like it."

I returned the smile. "Okay. Vinnie, why are you looking for Mario?"

He looked down at his worn sneakers. "I can't go home right now."

"Why not?"

"It's complicated."

I sat at the edge of the sofa, feeling like a therapist. "Vinnie, Mario told me about the… problems at home… with your father."

"I figured."

"Did your father *hit* you?"

Vinnie looked out the window again, and a tear fell down his pudgy cheek.

"Is your mother home?"

He nodded.

"Can't she help?"

He shook his head, and the tear landed on his sweatshirt.

I felt a connection with this kid. Perhaps it was because I'm also a younger brother, or maybe it was because he shares Mario's genes. "Vinnie, you know it's not right for your father to hit you?"

He nodded.

"And you know you should tell your mother."

"She knows. She don't care."

Italian tempers and bad grammar must run in the family.

"What about your brother?"

"He takes care of me, but he ain't around so much no more."

I put a hand on his shoulder. "Vinnie, Mario's not coming here tonight. We don't study together anymore. He's probably at Barbara's."

His lower lip doubled in size. "I hate that bitch. She treats me… and Mario like shit."

He's obviously smarter than his brother.

"Do you want me to call Mario at Barbara's house?"

He shook his head vehemently. "She won't let him come home."

"Is there somebody else I can call? A relative, a teacher, a friend?"

"I ain't got nobody else." Another tear appeared. "I didn't even do nothin'."

Let's fit in a grammar lesson while you're here.

He looked at me sadly. "I don't get why he hates me."

Your father is a real piece of work, kid. "Vinnie, sometimes the people we love can hurt us the most. They don't mean to, but they do."

"But why?" He looked up at me as if I was a wise guru.

"Maybe they find out something about someone they love, or about themselves, that scares them. Maybe they realize that what they always thought was true… isn't. They get so frightened that they might lose the people they love that, without knowing it, they push those same people away."

Vinnie hunched his back into the sofa. "I don't get it."

"Neither do I."

"Some people are nuts."

I laughed. "Vinnie, I totally agree with you there."

To my surprise Vinnie rested his head on my shoulder. I instinctively put my arm around him and rocked him back and forth. After sitting like that for a while and telling him that everything will work out, he got up and walked to the front door. Once there he stopped, looked back at me, and said, "Mario shouldn't be with Barbara. He should be here with you." With that he walked out.

The next evening, after reading a *Wonder Woman* comic book, I summoned up the courage to call Mario. Happily he answered the phone on the first ring. Unhappily he thought it was Barbara. She had given him instructions to wait by the phone that night for her call. I begrudgingly offered to hang up, but Mario seemed to want to talk.

I asked, "Is your brother all right?"

"Oh, yeah, he told me he was looking for me at your house. Sorry he bothered you."

"It wasn't a bother, Mario. Vinnie's a sweet kid."

"Thanks for looking after him, Harold."

I asked, tentatively, "Why did your father hit him?"

He sighed. "Who knows why he does anything? Vinnie might have done or not done something around the house, my mother could have burnt the dinner, the mail might have come late. It could be anything to set him off."

"Can't you call the police?"

"Right. Then he'd kill us."

Uh-oh. "Mario, I have to confess something."

His voice tightened. "What?"

"I was worried about you… and about your brother. So I told Hannah… about your father."

"And?"

"And she told her mother."

"Holy shit."

"And her mother might have called some agency."

"Damn. Harold, why the hell can't you mind your own business?"

"I was worried."

"Well now *I'm* worried."

"It's not right what your father does, Mario."

"Well, it's not right that some nosy social worker will come here and ask us questions, then leave my father to kick our asses worse than before."

"Hannah said the woman from the agency will talk to you and your brother."

"Good. We'll tell her that everything is fine, and that she should leave us alone."

"Your brother is just a kid."

"I protect my brother, Harold."

"Obviously not enough."

"I take care of things."

"Right, Mario. By trying to be the son your father wants you to be."

"What's *that* supposed to mean?"

"Mario, when he was here, Vinnie said something."

"What?"

"That you should be at my house, not at Barbara's."

"So? He hates her guts."

I was on a roll. "I think Vinnie meant more than that." After a pause I finally said it. "I've missed you."

After a long exhale, he said, "Harold, please don't start this again."

"Do you want to cram together for finals?"

"Harold, I've been really busy finishing up the school year and planning for college."

"I can help you with that."

"I've... rather, Barbara has been writing my speech for graduation."

"I can help you with that too."

Mario sounded like Pinocchio. "Harold, you have to understand. I can't spend as much time with my guy friends as I did before Barbara and I got together. She's really a handful." He added, "In more ways than one."

I blurted out, "I've been going to the YA meetings. There's a guy there who likes me."

After a tense pause, Mario asked, "Who?"

"A new kid. You don't' know him." *Mission accomplished. He's jealous.*

Mario cleared his throat and talked like a used car salesman with a lemon. "That's good, Harold. You deserve somebody nice."

I'd finally had enough. "Stop it!"

"What?"

"I can't listen to this shit anymore."

"Did you curse? You never curse."

"Mario, we are both lying, and for what? Because of something a priest said to you? Or something your father, who let his own brother die, supposedly believes?" *It's now or never.* "I love you. I thought you loved me too."

After a lengthy inhale, he asked, "What do you want from me, Harold?"

To go back to the way things were. "Tell me something, Mario. Honestly. Did you ever care about me? Do you now?"

"I can't do this, Harold."

"Please. Mario. I want to know. I think you owe me at least that much."

After a long pause, he asked, "Will you let this go if I tell you the truth?"

"Yes."

"Okay. I'm not bi like your Kinsey thinks. I understand that you are gay, and I accept you for who you are. But you have to accept me for who I am too. And you have to accept that Barbara is my girlfriend. And you're my friend."

"I don't believe you. You're saying this due to internalized homophobia."

"Harold, this has to stop."

"Then you'll have to stop it, Mario."

"All right. You want the truth? I'll give you the truth, Harold." Mario's voice was thin and quivering. "I never had romantic feelings for you. I knew you were gay. I played up to you so you would help me get good grades and get into a top college, and you did both."

"I don't believe you." My voice broke.

So did Mario's. "I'm sorry, Harold. You wanted the truth. That's it."

I hung up the phone and wept into my pillow for what seemed like hours, but was only fifteen minutes. When my sobs became heaves, I looked up and saw my mother standing over me.

"I miss your sister too. She'll be home from college for break soon."

I sat up on one elbow. "That's not why I'm crying. Actually it's been nice having a break from Karen."

My mother smiled and sat on the edge of my bed. "What's going on?"

"Nothing's going on. That's the problem."

"Care to elaborate?"

I sat up next to her. "When you and Dad were expecting me, were you hoping I'd be different?"

She ran her manicured fingers through her streaked blonde, short hair. "Different from who?"

"From me."

"Is this because I go to the meditation center? I told you that you're welcome to come any time."

I held her hand. It took me back. "Why do people love us, or not love us?"

"Are you going to make fun of me for my beliefs?"

I shook my head, having no intentions of keeping my promise.

"Okay, Buddhists believe we choose everyone around us, our parents, our children, our friends."

"So you think I chose you and Dad?"

"And that we chose you."

"Why did you choose me?"

She pulled at my brown and yellow shirt. "Because we love flannel."

"I always suspected."

After we shared a smile, Mom pulled the zipper of her jumpsuit down off her neck and said thoughtfully, "I believe we choose people who can teach us something."

"Please don't teach me how to meditate again. We live in New Jersey. All that breathing is toxic."

She hit my arm playfully. "We also pick people who help us build good energy or, pardon the word, karma."

"So if we do something good for someone, we store up good karma. If we hurt someone, we store up bad karma?"

"Only if it's intentional."

"So say somebody hurts you, hurts you really badly. But he didn't mean to do it. He only did it because he was scared."

"Okay?"

"Does he build up bad karma?"

"I'll have to look that one up, Harold."

"And when you get hurt, what should you do?"

"Forgive him, and let it go."

"What if you can't?"

"Try harder." Mom put her arm around me and the scent of incense filled my nose. "Harold, I believe our lives are like… patterns. We connect with the same energy, often the same people, again and again. It's our job to love each one of them, to learn from them, to learn from our mistakes, and not to make them again."

"So if I love somebody who goes away, you think I'll see him again someday?"

"In this life or the next." She squeezed my shoulder. "Does that make you happy?"

Even after he hurt me. "Yes."

After we sat for a few moments in silence, I said, "Mom, I'm glad I chose you and Dad to be my parents."

"Me too." She kissed me on the forehead. "It's ten o'clock. Your father will want to go over tomorrow's schedule with me, then say good night." She winked at me. "Do some deep, cleansing breathing. Tomorrow's another day." And she left my room.

After many deep breaths, each without Mario, graduation day finally arrived. As my launched cap was lost in a sky of dark clouds, so was Mario, out of my reach.

I worked at the fruit market over the summer, and Mario went away to football camp. I wrote him a number of letters, but never mailed any of them.

Fall came and we attended our separate colleges.

CHAPTER SIX/18 YEARS AGO

IT WASN'T until two years later on June 28th, at 1:16 p.m., in front of the town deli, that my high school infatuation raced by. He was wearing bicycle shorts, a tight T-shirt (purple), and he held a paper bag. His hair was combed back off his face. If it was humanly possible, he looked even more muscular and handsome than he did in high school.

"Harold."

"Mario?" *When did I become a soprano?*

He looked like a parent finding a lost child at the mall. "I haven't seen you since… graduation."

"Has it been that long?" *Is my nose growing? No, but something else is.*

Mario took me in like rain in a desert. "How *are* you?"

"Great. Great. Great." *How do I stop saying great?*

"What's up?"

Something is definitely up. "I'm in college. State. How about you?"

"I flunked out of Yale." His eyes glowed. "I needed my tutor."

I'm going to rip my pants. "Are you working?"

Mario looked down at his sneakers. I looked at his muscular thighs peeking out of his shorts.

"I'm… between jobs right now."

"How's Barbara?"

Mario smiled like a jack-o'-lantern. "Harold, we're gonna have a baby… twins. I knocked her up. Twice!"

Obviously he doesn't have birth control in the bag.

Scratching the eight-pack under his T-shirt, he asked, "You… married… or anything?"

"I'm… not married." *Why can't I tell him about Stuart?*

Our eyes danced a tango. Finally Mario said, "I better get going." His biceps flexed as he held up the bag. "Barbara's got a craving for candy."

I'll bet.

He started to go but stopped and turned to face me again. "Hey, let's get together sometime. You can read a book to me like in the old days."

I'm sure Barbara would love that.

"Harold, it's really good to see you. I'll give you a call." He ran away.

You don't have my number. But I have yours. And it looks like it hasn't changed.

True to course, Mario ran out of the street and out of my life… until eight years later.

CHAPTER SEVEN/10 YEARS AGO

I WAS a grade school teacher at the time. I got home before Stuart, and opened the mail on our maple wood table in our glass-enclosed kitchen nook that Stuart had designed when he was eight years old. Bills for Stuart. Letters for me. The first letter intrigued me.

You are cordially invited to attend your ten-year high school reunion at the (renamed) George W. Bush High School's gymnasium. This is a problem. Not only Bush. Not only the gymnasium. Mario will no doubt be at the reunion.

"Harold, don't be nervous about your high school reunion. We'll snub the doctors and lawyers and make a beeline for the other failures." Stuart always knew how to make me laugh. We were eating dinner in our dining room with its bay window, chair railing, chandelier, mahogany table, and built-in cherrywood hutch with a carved-out space for Stuart's monthly schedule.

"Stuart, does it bother you that I will probably be seeing Mario again at the reunion?"

"No, why should it? Everybody has a childhood crush."

"So you aren't jealous?"

"Actually I enjoyed hearing all of your stories about the *infamous* Mario. I can't wait to meet him in person. That is, if he's really human." He took my hand. "Harold, maybe it will be good for you to see Mario again. Get this out of your system. Put a period on it."

"What did I ever do to deserve you, Stuey?"

Stuart spooned some organic green vegetables onto my plate. "You sat next to me at college registration."

I hid a piece of kale under my free-range chicken. "Do you remember the first thing I ever said to you?"

"Help me."

"After that."

"You said I was your guardian angel."

"And you are." I kissed his cheek.

"Nah, I just told you to take mythology and literature so you could read about all those half-naked Greek gods casting spells on each other and get hot for me."

We shared a smile. "Thanks for agreeing to come to my reunion, Stuey."

He looked at me adoringly. After all our years together, that look still gave me butterflies. "Why wouldn't I come, Harold? I'm not ashamed my husband played tuba in the school band."

"If anyone brings that up, I'll ram a tuba up—"

"Oww, I love it when you talk rough." He squeezed my hand.

I squeezed back. "I love you, Stuey."

"Tell the readers that I love you too."

"They know."

Stuart looked at the built-in clock on the dining room hutch. "Harold, it's 7:00 p.m., time to do the dishes and make our lunches for tomorrow." And so we did.

That night, at precisely 10:45 p.m., after Stuart had laid out our clothes for the next day, we brushed our teeth in our his and his bathroom. At exactly 11:00 p.m. we went to bed, made love for fifteen minutes, then Stuart spooned me, his long, thin arms and legs wrapped about me firmly. As he did every night, he told me how much he loved me, until we drifted off to sleep.

My dreams were racked with fears about the reunion. In one nightmare my nametag read, *Nerdy Gay Guy Who Makes Way Less Money Than You*. In a spookier dream, the gymnasium was decorated with medicine balls that slammed into me whenever I tried to leave. In another dream the football players hung me from the rings and burned me at the stake. Barbara strangled me with Mario's class ring on a chain in yet another. The longest dream involved Mario arriving with a bald head, pot belly, three wives, and ten kids, offering me a Mormon tract. The most horrifying dream, Tommy and Keith pummeling me on the pommel horse, left me screaming and shaking in Stuart's arms. My husband rocked me back and forth, kissed my forehead, and scared away the bogeyman until exactly 7:00 a.m., when we rose to start our day.

That rest of the week at school was full of complications as Juan's nose wouldn't stop bleeding, Kenisha accused everyone—including me—of stealing her designer book bag, and Samantha kept insisting that John Adams was a Communist—courtesy of Fox News. As I led my students through their studies, the curriculum took a backseat to my thoughts about the reunion, and of course about Mario.

The night before the reunion, Stuart made dinner, did the dishes, ironed our shirts, steamed our suits, shined our shoes, put gas in his car, and made me chamomile tea.

The day of reckoning finally arrived. Since my hands were shaking so hard, Stuart drove, parked, and led me to the school entrance, like a parent bringing his child to kindergarten on the first day of school.

Stuart and I entered the gymnasium like Dorothy and Toto in the *Land of Oz*. He commented on the old pictures table, as I secretly waited for Mario to enter my field of vision like the red ruby slippers. As my eyes adjusted to the fluorescent lighting, gold banners, and sequined dresses, I heard one woman threatening another woman not to *drop the banner, spill the punch, or knock over the nametags*. When we reached the check-in table, I smiled at a familiar round face. With her cream-colored blouse and peach skirt, Hannah looked like a sundae.

"Harold High. I'm so glad you could make it." Hannah checked my name off her list, and checked me out head to toe. "We just finished setting up. Rather, *I* just finished setting up." She grimaced like a BSA CEO facing a gay Scout leader. "Barbara *supervised*, then left to put on her makeup."

Let's hope Barbara is divorced and making up her face to hook one of the boys in the band. "Hannah. It's nice to see you." The glasses, braces, and training bra were gone, but the curly red hair remained.

Stuart cleared his throat.

"Hannah, this is Stuart."

"Are you in the orchestra?" Hannah searched over her shoulder for the orchestra leader, already on his first break.

"*I* never played a musical instrument." Stuart patted me on the back, then mimed the word *tuba* with a finger over lips.

Hannah checked her list and came up empty. "Stuart, what? I don't remember you from high school."

"I cut all my classes."

After elbowing Stuart's side, I said, "Stuart is my partner."

"Oh. What kind of business do you guys do?"

Stuart was enjoying this. "Yeah, Harold, what kind of business do we guys do?"

"Stuart is my life partner, Hannah."

"Oh, a life coach! I went to—"

"Hannah, we're *married*."

"Oh. Where are your wives?" She checked her sheets again.

"To each other." *She obviously hasn't changed.*

Hannah blushed. "Oh." She let out a familiar giggle. "That's fine."

Stuart couldn't resist. "It works for us."

"Me too." Her face was a tomato. "I mean, you two make a nice couple."

Stuart was on a roll. "I think I'll keep him." He pinched my cheek.

Hannah couldn't stop herself from rambling. "I was the President of the Young Democrats Club back in high school. I should have known about you, Harold. You had all the signs back then. Oh, I didn't mean that you were effeminate… or that you are now. Not that there's anything wrong with being effeminate, or that every gay man is effeminate. I have gay friends and you would never know that *any* of them are gay. Well, some of them you would know. But most of them you wouldn't. Unless you were gay and had gaydar. But I guess not every gay person has gaydar. In any case you would never know my gay friends were gay… unless you met their spouses. I mean they have one spouse each. But in every case, their spouse is gay… like *them*. Because somebody who isn't gay wouldn't have a gay man as his spouse. Or *any* man for that matter. Unless he was transsexual, but then he wouldn't be gay, he'd be transsexual. And then he would be a *she*."

This is like watching a rabbit in a minefield.

She kept going. "Stuart, I have to admit I had a crush on Harold when we were in high school."

Stuart put his arm around me and grinned like the Cheshire cat. "My little playboy."

Hannah was unstoppable. "I even asked Harold to go to the prom with me. But it didn't go anywhere. How could it, right? I guess the joke was on me." Hannah's giggle put Anderson Cooper's to shame. "You may not know this, Stuart, but Harold and I played in the high school band. I played the flute. Harold played the tuba."

Stuart squeezed my hand. "I think I heard something about that."

"But I believe Harold played in the band to be near his friend, Mario. Has Harold told you about Mario, Stuart?"

Stuart laughed. "I've heard one or two of the Mario tales, right Harold?"

I squeezed Stuart's hand until it turned bluer than a Democrat. "Hannah, is Mario here tonight?"

"Not yet. But he should be here soon." Hannah seemed to understand. "I'm glad you found someone, Harold." She smiled at Stuart. "Someone nice."

"Thanks, Hannah." We shared a knowing smile. "How about you? What have you been up to these ten years?"

Hannah answered as she pinned on my nametag. "I went to Vassar College. Now I manage an HMO. I'm the one who decides whether or not you can see a certain doctor that you want to see, which is funny because I'm married to a doctor. And I never see him either." She giggled again, and my ears rang. "See, Harold, I was right back in high school. I told you we'd amount to something. I make great money, and I have a great medical plan… and it isn't an HMO." She whispered, "I have to admit that the work can be a bit of a drag, not drag like guys in dresses. Oh, I didn't mean you guys wear drag because you're gay."

"Only at home and only on a Saturday night." *Who knew Stuart was such a comedian?*

After more giggling, Hannah said, "I know all gay guys don't dress in drag. As I understand it, most cross-dressers are straight. But that doesn't mean my husband dresses in drag. At least not that I know about." The giggling continued like water breaking a dam. "How about you, Harold? I don't mean do you dress in drag, I mean what do you do for a living? You were always such a good student."

"I'm a grade school teacher."

Hannah released a warm smile. "A gay grade school teacher. That's great. Gay kids need role models in schools nowadays. I don't mean that you tell them you are gay. Not that there's anything wrong with kids knowing their gay teachers are gay, or married for that matter. They know their straight teachers are married."

I rescued her. "Stuart designs computer games."

More giggling ensued. "Don't tell anybody, but I play them all the time at work. Somebody will be on the phone telling me about their sickness or uncovered medical bill, and I'm creating magical fawns in a medieval kingdom, gathering sweets in a candy forest, or shooting at pimps in a car chase."

As Stuart beamed proudly, I again scanned the room, looking for Mario. Though my hero was nowhere in sight, I spotted my adversaries at the picture table. Except for the receding hairlines and too tight suits, Tommy and Keith looked just as I remembered them.

Hannah followed my glare. "I'll never forget what those guys did to you in high school, Harold."

"But you and Mario saved the day."

Hannah shook her curly red locks from side to side. "One week's detention was a slap on the wrist. They should have been expelled."

"I assume they are the illustrious Tommy and Keith." Always the optimist, Stuart added, "That was ten years ago, Harold. Maybe they've changed."

As if on cue Tommy and Keith motioned me over to the picture table.

Stuart whispered in my ear. "We don't have to go over there."

I whispered back in his. "They can't scare me any longer. I'm a teacher."

Hannah chimed in. "They'll turn out to be losers, just like Barbara and Mario. Mark my words, Harold."

We told Hannah we would catch up with her later. At the picture table, the portal to the past, I again faced my enemies. After checking out my old high school yearbook picture, Stuart understudied for Mario as my bodyguard.

"Harold, that's your name, right?" I nodded to Tommy, hoping he didn't have the medicine ball hidden under the picture table.

"Right, Harold." Keith echoed Tommy as if ten years hadn't gone by.

True to form, Tommy took the lead. "Harold, have you seen Mario?"

I croaked out, "No."

"If you see him, tell him his old buddies are looking for him. Okay?"

"Will do." *Is it possible to sound like a frog with a frog in his throat?*

Keith grinned at me. "I remember you and Mario were pretty tight back in high school."

I didn't grin back. "You remember that, do you?"

"Hey, Harold, I hope you aren't angry about our prank back then. We were just playing with you, hoping to get a week off from school."

"And we did," added Tommy.

They slapped hands and laughed, which sent me back to my attack. "As I recall, you two also got thrown off the football team."

Tommy retrieved the fumble. "We were tired of playing football anyhow. Right, Keith?" Tommy slapped Keith's back.

"Right," Keith replied obediently. "I think I had an injury anyways."

Yeah, in your brain.

"What are you doing now, Harold?" Tommy and Keith asked in unison.

"I'm a grade school teacher."

They smirked at one another. Tommy again took the lead. "Really? I thought that was for women."

Stuart pointed to my pants. "Last we checked he was definitely male."

Tommy laughed. "That's a good one." Assuming Stuart was another nerdy classmate too insignificant to remember, Tommy asked, "What's your name again?"

"Stuart."

Tommy pretended to remember. "Right, Stuart. What do *you* do now, Stuart?"

"I'm a designer… on the Internet."

Tommy and Keith looked like sharks at a water park. "Really?" they said in unison.

Keith picked up the ball. "You must make good money doing that."

I noticed a gleam in Stuart's eyes. "Yes, very good money actually. Hannah was just telling me she never leaves my sites."

I disappeared from his cosmos as Tommy unsuccessfully turned the charm on Stuart. "How interesting." Tommy pretended to get an idea. "Hey, maybe we can work together sometime, Stuart."

Keith proved he was no wordsmith. "Stuart. I like that name. It sounds really… smart. I bet you were smart back in high school."

Stuart was having too much fun. "One of the smartest. Right, Harold?"

Before I could answer, Tommy put his arm around Stuart. "Stuart, Keith and I are looking for donors, like yourself."

"Like *me*?"

"Yeah, guys who want to do their civic duty, help their fellow man, give their company a good reputation.

Keith added, "And have some political *clout*."

Stuart pretended to consider the offer. "Really? What is it that you gentlemen are selling?"

Keith displayed a grin that looked like a toothache. "Tommy and I are selling…. America."

Allowing his hand to move down Stuart's back, Tommy explained. "I'm running for Congress, Stuart, and Keith is my campaign manager."

Anybody have two tickets to Canada?

"What's your platform?" asked Stuart with a cautioning look for me not to laugh.

"Ending the over-taxation of America," Keith answered as if he was Hitler himself. "Stopping the insanity of the government's endless payouts."

I couldn't resist. "So if you win you won't be taking the salary, medical insurance, and pension?"

Ignoring me and rubbing Stuart's back, Tommy said, "We want to give our old classmates the first shot at being partners in our campaign."

Stuart further lodged his tongue into his cheek. "That's very kind of you, Tommy."

"We think so, Stuart."

Keith added, as if sharing the location of Al Capone's vault, "And once we win, we'll unveil our *real* agenda."

Stuart pretended to be mesmerized. "And what is *that*?"

Tommy whispered in Stuart's ear. "Can we trust you?"

"Of course," replied Stuart piously. "We're old school chums, aren't we?"

Looking satisfied, Tommy announced with the sincerity of a televangelist, "Saving the American family…."

From environmental pollution, war, homelessness, illiteracy, hunger, joblessness?

"…from the liberal, atheist, gay agenda that wants to take away your gun, your faith, and your family," Tommy said, as if a US fundamentalist visiting Africa.

Stuart asked, "What about liberal, atheist, gay, gun-hating American families?"

After a pause where my heart skipped three beats, Tommy and Keith burst out laughing.

Tommy slapped Stuart on the back. "Good one, Stuart."

Keith motioned to me and I flinched from force of habit. "This guy is still a riot. Just like in high school."

Stuart gloated. "Glad you remembered."

After the laughter died down, Tommy pointed to the bleachers and said, "Seriously, Stuart, look over there at those two beautiful ladies."

Stuart and I noticed two overweight, masculine women with short haircuts and mismatched pants suits, sitting on a bleacher. They were drinking beer from the bottle and appeared more interested in one another than in the reunion.

"That's why we are doing this," explained Tommy.

For a women's tennis team?

Tommy squeezed Stuart's back. "For our *wives*. For our families. For *your* family. For *America*."

With liberty and justice for all.

Keith rested his hand on Stuart's shoulder. "You married, Stuart?"

"I am."

"You have kids yet?"

"Not yet."

"Think about this. Whose values do you want your children to have?"

Stuart asked, with a wink in my nervous direction, "I don't know. Harold, whose values do we want our children to have?"

Not getting it, Keith asked, "Do you want your kids, and your buddy's kids, to be influenced by the liberal agenda?"

Rehearsing his campaign speech, Tommy said, too grandly, "Or do you want your kids to grow up in a Christian nation, where nobody gets a handout...."

Didn't Jesus preach to house the homeless, feed the hungry, and help the downtrodden?

"...a world where the institution of marriage never changes..."

Back to one white, landowning man with many women as his property.

"...and every man, woman, and child has the right to carry a gun...."

What happened to turn the other cheek?

And turn it did when a young, good-looking waiter walked by us carrying a tray of crab puffs.

After the waiter passed, Tommy gave Stuart his card, which surprisingly didn't have a swastika as a logo. "Here's my card, Stuart. Give me a call. We'll talk about how you can play a role in the campaign. I also want to hear more about your business, and see what I can do for *you* after I'm elected."

Keith took up the rear. "You have to decide, Stuart. Do you want to protect America, or don't you?"

"I definitely want to protect America," replied Stuart

"Terrific!" Tommy and Keith smiled merrily at the dollar signs in front of them.

Stuart continued. "So I *won't* be investing in your campaign."

Tommy and Keith removed their hands, and their smiles vanished like clowns in the rain. Tommy spoke first, as usual, as he looked after the waiter. "You might change your mind, Stuart, when this nation is run by the liberals and the homosexuals."

"I doubt it." Stuart winked at me.

Realizing Stuart was no longer a prospect to fill their campaign coffers, Keith remembered I was in the room. "How about you, Harold?"

Still glancing over at the waiter, Tommy cut Keith off. "Harold won't be interested, Keith. Don't you remember? Harold was in the Democrat Club back in high school. And as I recall, he was"—he made quotation marks in the air with his fingers—"*struggling with his sexuality.*"

I couldn't hold back any longer. "Tommy, Keith, you're trying to do to America what you tried to do to me back in high school. But no worries. You didn't get away with it then and you won't get away with it now."

Tommy took a step closer to me. "And why is that, Harold?"

"Because even with all the tax-exempt money, political power, and right-wing media channels at your disposal, the majority won't buy what you are selling."

Parroting Tommy as usual, Keith took a step closer to me as well. "And why is that, Harold?"

"Because most people aren't as misguided, greedy, and self-loathing as you two."

Tommy took another step toward me. Stuart blocked his path and said, "A nasty incident at your high school reunion could hurt your campaign, Tommy."

Realizing Stuart was right, Keith followed Tommy's gaze to the waiter and said, "My appetite is out of control. Let's leave these two losers and get something to eat."

Tommy nodded lasciviously. "Sounds good. Then I have to hit the john."

No doubt with a wide stance.

And Tommy and Keith were gone.

After I hugged Stuart for being… Stuart, he looked at his watch and realized it was 8:00 p.m., time for our evening multivitamins. So Stuart left me to get some bottled water from the drinks table, and I spotted Mr. Ringwood headed my way. He looked exactly the same, except ten years older. His bowtie bobbed underneath his smile as he gave me a warm embrace.

"Mr. Ringwood, I thought you retired."

"I did, but I never miss a class reunion. The teachers used to come. I guess now they are all too busy doing whatever they do on *social media*." He said it as if naming a deadly disease.

"Thank you for finding me, Mr. R."

"My pleasure, Harold. Tell me, what have you been up to, young man?"

"I'm a teacher, grade school, happily married to the man downing vitamins over there."

I waved to Stuart, and he waved back, nearly needing the Heimlich maneuver to cough up a vitamin.

Mr. Ringwood nodded his approval. "Very nice."

I scanned the room again in search of the absent Mario.

Mr. R. seemed to understand. "Have you seen Mario yet?"

"Not yet."

"When you do, I hope there aren't any fireworks with hubby." He raised his eyebrows naughtily.

"Mr. R., you knew I had a crush on Mario back in high school?"

"I was old but not dead."

"Did other people at school know?"

"Of course. You two were so adorable. Even the cleaning staff was rooting for you."

We shared a laugh.

He tugged at his bowtie, which brought me back to that day in his office after my attack. "Harold, I have to admit, after seeing you talking to Tommy and Keith just now, I had an ulterior motive in seeking you out."

"What is that?" *Recommend that I hide from them under the picture table? Tell me that I should beg Tommy and Keith's forgiveness for not letting them take away my civil rights?*

One of my classmates, whom I vaguely remembered, was standing at the microphone calling couples up to dance the Macarena. Mr. Ringwood motioned for me to sit next to him on chairs stationed away from the action.

Once seated, he said something that surprised me. "Harold, will you accept my apology?"

"I don't understand."

The familiar lines on his forehead made their appearance as the usual smile vanished. "I think you do." He put a liver-spotted hand on my shoulder. "Harold, I can't tell you how many times over the last ten years I've thought about you."

"Me?"

"Yes, Harold, you. And how much I regret the way I treated you after those two boys hurt you."

"It's all right, Mr. Ringwood."

"No, no, it isn't all right, Harold. It was not all right then and it is not all right now." He grasped my hand. "You were a warm, honest, open boy in love with another wonderful boy. And there is nothing wrong with that. I, of all people, should have never made you feel as if there were."

I took the high road and smiled at my old principal. "I understand, Mr. Ringwood."

He held on tighter. "No, you don't. You can't." He released my hand and looked out as if being transported to another time and place. "My generation lived through Anita Bryant's Save Our Children campaign. Gay teachers… and principals were fired left and right. We lived through the sodomy laws, where any of us could be taken from our homes, arrested, and thrown in jail. Police raids of parks and bars were the norm, with bloody billy clubs a nightly fixture. We had no role models on television. No rock stars. No mention of our struggles on the news, except to warn *decent* people to keep their children away from us *degenerates*. We were absolutely isolated. We each were the *only* one. What we were was *unmentionable*. Anybody who didn't toe the line of passing, or hiding, was beaten up... or worse."

"Mr. Ringwood, things haven't changed all that much. We have some celebrities who are out, and we've made some advances in our civil rights, but there are still gay bashings and people fired for being gay. Republican Party leaders denouncing us as villains. Lots of people with lots of money, and lots of power, hiding behind their so-called *religious beliefs*, determined to take away our civil rights and to destroy our families." Remembering Tommy and Keith, I added, "Some of them are just like us, only too afraid to admit it."

My old principal looked at me like a leprechaun finding his pot of gold. "But, Harold, there *is* something very different now. There are amazing young men like *you* who are proud to be who you are, and who demand a seat at the table." He wiped a tear away. "It's too late for me. My time has gone. But your time, Harold, is *now*."

I didn't know what to say. "Thank you, Mr. Ringwood."

"No, thank *you*. The banner is in *your* hands, Harold. Wave it proudly for the world to see, and settle for nothing less than *everything*." He squeezed my shoulder. "I've left my partner alone for too long." He waved at a tall gentleman on the far side of the gymnasium, also wearing a bowtie. Mr. Ringwood's partner smiled adoringly and waved back. "Enjoy the festivities, Harold. You deserve it."

Mr. Ringwood patted me on the arm and disappeared into the crowd. As if by magic, Stuart reappeared and handed me my vitamins and a bottle of water. After I swallowed the last one, I heard another familiar voice.

"Hannah, we need more chairs from the choir room!"

I followed the voice to Barbara, playing queen of the reunion. Before I could look away, she motioned Stuart and me over to her throne, the punch bowl.

"Hi, High."

"Hello, Barbara." *Should I genuflect?*

She kissed my cheek, and then Stuart wiped the lipstick off it with his handkerchief. "Harold, you look exactly the same. How about me?" Barbara did a spin and nearly tripped on her four-inch heels.

"You look exactly the same too." *Except for the extra twenty pounds, platinum hair, and skin-tight silver strapless dress.*

Stuart waved to her.

"Barbara, this is my husband, Stuart."

Barbara revealed three-inch silver-painted nails.

Stuart gently shook her hand, careful not to puncture a vein. "It's nice to meet you, Barbara."

As if a queen examining one of her subjects, Barbara said, "I definitely approve!" Turning her royal attentions to me, she added, "I'm glad you found someone nice, Harold." She focused back on Stuart. "Back in high school, I felt so bad for Harold. We were all partnered up, and Harold was always alone."

Stuart put his arm around me. "My little loner."

"He was. He was a little loner." Her hand grazed my arm and nearly drew blood. "Remember, Harold?" Before I could respond, she was facing Stuart again. "Mario and I were Harold's *only* friends… besides Hannah, and she didn't really count. Mario and I felt so bad leaving Harold when we'd go to parties with the other football players and cheerleaders."

I'm sure.

Barbara's painted claws reached for my hand, and I put it in my pocket for cover. "Harold, it's so nice to see you again. I bet you can't wait to see Mario too."

"Oh, is *he* coming?" *Did I just sound like a southern belle at a cotillion?*

Stuart rested a steadying hand on my back.

"Mario's outside talking to the limo driver." Barbara scrunched her tiny plastic nose, "We had a little *incident* driving over here."

"Is Mario *okay*?" *Did I sound frantic?*

Barbara waved my concerns away with her claws. "Mario's fine. I got home late from my double-booker hairdresser today." She nudged Stuart. "He's totally in demand." Back to me. "So we were running a bit late getting here. Since I'm coordinating the reunion, I asked our driver if he could speed up a tiny bit. Unfortunately, he hit a van… full of nuns coming back from playing bingo at the church."

Stuart took a small pad out of his jacket pocket and jotted down, *new game idea: hit the nuns in the van*, then he asked, "Anyone hurt?"

She raised her eyes to the ceiling. "Mario was concerned because one of the nuns said she saw white lights in front of her eyes. I don't know what the big to-do was all about. Aren't nuns supposed to see visions?" She shrugged away the unpleasant memory. "I'm sure the insurance companies will straighten it all out. So enough talk about that. You two guys enjoying the reunion?"

Stuart answered, "It's been a blast so far."

"Thank you." Barbara got back to business. "What have you been doing since high school, Harold?"

"I went to State and became a teacher."

Barbara raised her index finger, and Stuart and I ducked. "That is a noble profession, Harold." She turned to Stuart. "Even though I cut most of my classes in high school." After sharing a laugh with Stuart, Barbara said like a gossip columnist, "I'm a film producer now. Infomercials."

"Really," said Stuart.

"I know." She was back to me. "Can you believe it, Harold?"

Totally.

"I produced the combination hair dryer and deep fryer infomercial with Goldie Hawn, *and* the spinning sandwich maker infomercial with Cindy Williams."

How did I miss those?

"Mario is a stay-at-home dad… *and* an occasional male model. I'm his agent."

Makes sense to me.

"We have two children. Well, three, if you count our housekeeper." She whispered to Stuart, "She's a fifteen-year-old from Guatemala."

If Barbara's nasal laugh didn't puncture Stuart's eardrum, her shouting must have done the trick. "Mario! Mario! I'm over here!"

It's him. Black hair, dark eyes, Roman nose, olive skin, white teeth, red lips, cleft chin, huge muscles, and warm smile. As in high school, he wore a skin-tight T-shirt—red, and jeans. He evidently traded in his black leather jacket for a black blazer, and his work boots for Italian loafers. The new lines on his face gave him an erudite look.

"Harold!"

"Mario!"

As we gazed at one another, I reached out my hand to shake as Mario opened his arms for a hug. We tried again but reversed greetings. Finally we settled for a straight man's hug—a quick slap on the back. *He still smells like cinnamon, coconut, and almonds.*

Stuart took my hand. "Remember me?"

Without breaking my eye contact with Mario, I said, "This is my Stuart… other."

"Close enough," Stuart replied as he and Mario shook hands. Then, after a buzzing noise, Stuart said, "Excuse me," and held his cell phone up to his ear.

Coming back to earth, I asked Stuart, "What's wrong?"

After a brief chat, Stuart put his phone back inside his pocket. "There was an issue with one of my new games. I think we're okay now."

Barbara looked like she'd swallowed a bag of sugar. "Stuart, do you play games online?"

"He invents them," I explained.

She looked like a kid with a new puppy at Christmas. "Oh my God."

"Do you play?" Stuart asked casually.

Mario laughed. "Play? She sleeps with her laptop."

Obviously not amused by Mario's joke, Barbara whispered to him through gritted teeth, "It's better than sleeping alone."

Mario responded with clenched jaw, "I don't mind."

"Funny, Mario."

"Not anymore, Barbara."

Stuart played referee. "What games do you play, Barbara?"

To my surprise, Mario's disgust, and Stuart's admiration, Barbara ticked off a litany of games, many of which Stuart had designed.

Approaching Stuart as if he was a rock star, Barbara asked, "Can you explain to me how to get to level 19 of *Star Ships and Planets*?"

Mario couldn't resist. "Please help her, Stuart. Barbara getting to level 18 was a traumatic time for both of us."

Barbara put her arm through Stuart's and luckily didn't slit his wrist with her fingernails. "Stuart, let's go to the computer lab upstairs. You can teach me how to get to level 19."

"Do you mind, Harold?" Stuart squeezed my elbow.

"No problem, Stuart."

Barbara cackled. "Stuart, maybe you'll invent a game about a high school reunion."

Stuart glanced in Mario's direction and whispered in my ear, "Be good while I'm gone, Harold."

Before I could respond, Barbara clutched onto Stuart like a dog in heat. "Maybe you'd like to hear *my* idea for a new game, Stuart?"

Though Stuart had heard that all the time, he politely agreed.

Barbara forged on as they walked off. "It's called *Throw the Screaming Children off the Plane*."

After I waved to Stuart, I said to Mario, "Catchy title," and we both laughed.

We looked after them, and I added, "It was nice of Barbara to be on the reunion committee."

"Barbara *was* the reunion committee."

We laughed again and cased the room as I said, "It's funny how the troublemakers back in high school are all police officers now… or politicians."

After another laugh, Mario looked at me and grinned like a kid with a candy apple. "It feels good."

"What?"

"To laugh. It's been a while."

"Sorry. Stuart and I laugh all the time."

He nodded. "You two are… a *couple*, then?"

"We've been together nine and a half years."

Mario looked pensive.

"Does that shock you?"

He flinched. "No."

Liar.

"How's it going… with you and Stuart?"

I watched Stuart and Barbara leave the gymnasium. "Our life together is as wonderful as playing a computer game."

After another laugh, Mario sat on a nearby bleacher. A hardened look took over his face. "I wish I could say the same about me and Barbara." He smiled. "Barbara and me."

I sat next to him and asked hopefully, "You're having trouble with Barbara?"

He scratched his massive neck. "She's the mother of my kids. I shouldn't rag on her."

"Tell me about your kids."

He pulled out their picture faster than a black jack dealer pulling out cards with a losing player. "They're twins. They look like me. *Both* of them."

Hence the term twins. I smiled at their picture. *They do.* "I'd love to meet them."

He added, "And they talk like their mother."

But there's no rush. "They look adorable in their Catholic school uniforms, Mario."

"Don't worry, I told them to watch out for the priests."

Good advice.

Mario pointed proudly. "The one on the left is Mario, and the one on the right is Harold."

A lump the size of a baseball formed in my throat. "I'm honored, Mario."

"You were my best friend." Mario messed my hair like he did when we were kids. It felt rejuvenating.

"I wish I could have been there when they were born, Mario."

"No you don't. Barbara screamed she was going to cut off my balls and take up juggling."

We laughed again and relaxed into the bleachers.

"Harold, remember when we were kids how Barbara was so sweet?"

Isn't life a hoot?

"Sorry, Harold, I haven't seen you in a long time. I don't want to dump my problems on you, especially at a party."

"Go for it, Mario. I've already shocked Hannah, escaped Tommy and Keith, and been apologized to by Mr. Ringwood. I'm all yours."

Mario looked like the weight of the world was on his mountainous, perfect shoulders. "She's changed, Harold. You won't believe this, but Barbara's become... a real *bitch*."

Duh. "I'm sorry you and Barbara are having problems, Mario." *Not.*

He sighed. "She complains about everything I do, Harold, everything I say, what I wear, what I eat, what I watch on TV, when I go to bed at night. If I walk around the house naked, she goes crazy."

Can't blame her there.

"When I come home from the gym, she tells me I stink."

I'll take a whiff.

"Whenever I do something nice for her, it's never enough. If I get her flowers on Mother's Day, she asks, where's the chocolates?"

Looking at how Barbara has grown, she should probably stick to the flowers.

I noticed faint circles forming under his eyes. "And she's become reckless, Harold. Arguing with people in stores and fighting with waiters in restaurants. Like driving here tonight. She insisted that we rent a limo, then she went off on the driver because he wouldn't go through the red lights."

"I heard about the incident with the nuns."

Mario's head dropped sadly. "One nun has a concussion, and she's seeing double. She'll probably sue our pants off. Like the Catholic Church don't... *doesn't* have enough money with all their gold and marble. Not to mention their intake from bingo."

"I'm sorry to hear about Barbara, Mario." *Not really.*

"Ah, enough about Barbara." He put his strong, perfectly manicured hand on my fidgeting knee. "What have you been up to, Harold?"

I felt the warmth of his hand, and I tried to remain conscious. "I'm a fourth grade teacher in a public school."

He looked at me in admiration. "You were a great teacher, Harold." He smiled. "Now my taxes pay your salary, if I paid any taxes."

If it's good enough for the Catholic Church. "Barbara told me you are a model."

He shrugged. "Yeah, I did a few newspapers and magazines, and a billboard, mostly swimsuits and underwear ads."

I'll buy every one.

We sat and watched our former classmates dance to ten-year-old songs. As they, and the band, had more to drink, the music got louder and the dancing got wilder.

Mario tapped me on the shoulder and shouted over the music, "Let's go someplace where we can talk."

I shouted back, "Don't you want to talk to your old football buddies?"

He hollered, "Nah, they all look drunk."

"Don't you have to make a speech as class president?" I shrieked.

He shook his head back and forth, pointed to me, and rolled his finger around his ear.

"What about Stuart and Barbara?" I yelled, hoping I wouldn't lose my voice.

Mario shouted back, "Knowing Barbara as well as I unfortunately do, they'll be at the computer playing games for hours. Come on. Let's go."

"Where?" I hollered.

He said in my ear, "The coach's office."

His breath felt warm and wonderful on my…. *The coach's office. The sacred make-out Shangri-La, only football players and cheerleaders with nubile pom-poms dared to penetrate. I'm going to the coach's office… with Mario.*

CHAPTER EIGHT/10 YEARS AGO

MARIO LED the way around a few corridors. Once at our hallowed destination, he opened the heavy wooden door and we entered… the coach's office.

Mario smiled fondly. "It feels good to be back here."

Ah, the smell of perspiration, testosterone, and homophobia.

"Look, the old couch." Mario caressed the threadbare brown corduroy sofa, then rushed over to the knotted birch desk. "And the desk! The old plays are still here! This place hasn't changed at all." He looked just like the old, or rather young, Mario.

I felt like a patron on an historic tour with Mario as my tour guide. "You haven't changed either, Mario."

"Neither have you, Harold."

"I've changed."

"How?"

"Mel Gibson's no longer my favorite actor."

Mario laughed, then sat on the couch and motioned for me to join him.

"Am I allowed to sit here, Mario?"

He took hold of my arm and sat me down next to him. "Let's talk about the good old days in high school."

"They were good for *you*, Mario."

"Harold, they were pretty good for you too." His knee rested against mine like when we were kids studying in my bedroom.

I laughed. "Sure being beaten up and called names was a laugh riot, and having no friends was a picnic."

"You had friends. You had Horrible Hannah." He tweaked my nose. "And you had *me*." His smile enveloped me. "And *I* had the best tutor in New Jersey. You know, Harold, if it wasn't for you, I wouldn't be as intelligent as I am now."

They can put that on my tombstone.

Mario rested back on the sofa as if we were in his family room watching a game on his wide screen television. *Okay, I drove by his house and peeked in a window once… or twice.*

"Your folks okay, Harold?"

"Yeah, my mother went through a rough time with her illness, but my father was there to schedule each chemo treatment, acupuncture session, each meeting with her herbalist and nutritionist and hypnotist, every meal, every nap, and every doctor's visit."

"I always liked your parents, Harold."

"They liked you too."

"They're okay with you and Stuart?"

"My father calls Stuart the son he never had. My mother said since gay couples are okay with the Dalai Lama, she's onboard too. How are your parents?"

Mario kicked off his loafers. All he needed was a fireplace, slippers, and a pipe for the perfect picture. "My father's still a dick. My mother still takes it. I'm glad I don't have to anymore. I don't see them too much. I still miss my nonna."

"I remember."

We sat in thought for a while.

I broke the silence. "How's your little brother?"

"Not so little anymore. He's a marine."

"Ah, a stud like his big brother."

Mario nudged my shoulder with his. I put my hands over my lap and thought about something unpleasant.

"Mario, my sister moved to Florida. She runs a nursing home there."

"Good, we can move to Florida when we get old and feeble."

"I think we have to. Isn't it the law?"

We shared a laugh.

He winked at me. "This is great, Harold."

"What?"

"Us, together again. It makes me feel… *young*."

"I'm sorry we lost touch, Mario."

"I never called you."

Sure, rub it in, Mario.

"But I visited you."

"What? When?"

"One day after Barbara and me… *I* had a fight."

"I'm sorry I missed your visit."

He thought back. "Your mom told me you were at a class… in college. I had flunked out."

You needed a tutor.

"I figured you had new friends in college and wouldn't want to listen to my problems anymore."

"Mario, I wish I knew."

"How come you never contacted me over the years?"

I looked into his dark eyes. "I called you. You had already moved out of your parents' house."

"My mother didn't give you my new phone number and address?"

"She did. I didn't think you'd want to hear from me."

"You thought wrong." Mario pushed me playfully. "My mother always liked you. She said I should be more like you."

"My mother said I should be more like *you*."

"Your mother was right." He messed my hair again.

"I did call once."

"Barbara never told me."

"That's because I hung up." *And I'm admitting this because?*

"Why?"

"I wanted to hear your voice."

"But not talk to me? You're weird." Mario playfully punched my jaw.

"It was good running into you outside the deli two years after graduation."

He remembered. "Right, before Barbara crapped out the twins."

I replayed it in my head. "But it was clear you had moved on with your life." I walked over to the desk and pretended I could read the game plans.

Mario stood and faced me. "So what? Because I have a family, I can't have a friend?"

I sat on the arm of the sofa. "Well, nothing would have changed. You would have married Barbara, and I would have married Stuart."

Mario stood next to me. "I guess you're right."

"Mario, how come you didn't invite me to your wedding?"

"We eloped, with Barbara sticking out to here." He rounded his hands over his stomach like Humpty Dumpty. "It was a typical shotgun wedding."

"How come you didn't invite me to the twins' christening?"

"Barbara wouldn't let me have anything to do with it. She picked the sponsors, the christening gowns, the guests, the priest—who by the way charged a pretty penny to sprinkle a little water on the kids' foreheads."

"It was very nice." *Oops.*

Mario was bug-eyed. "You were there?"

"I read the announcement in the newspaper. Anybody can go into a church."

"Why didn't you congratulate us afterwards?"

"I think I tried, but one of Barbara's relatives elbowed me in the eye."

We shared a comforting laugh.

I sat back down on the sofa. "Confession time, Mario. As the years went by, I thought about you… a lot. When I graduated college…."

"I was there."

I hit him on the shoulder.

"What? My cousin was graduating too."

"Why didn't you tell me?"

"You were a college graduate. I thought you wouldn't want anything to do with someone stupid like me?"

"That's crazy, Mario."

He sat next to me. "Hey, who you calling crazy, tuba boy?"

When our laughter subsided, I continued. "Seriously, Mario, I thought about you when I met Stuart, when Stuart and I got married…."

"I was there."

My eyes overtook my face. "You what?"

"I heard about it from your mother. I stood in the back of that Unitarian Church. It was a little wooo-hoooo New Agey for me, but it was nice. You looked happy."

"Why didn't you say anything?"

"It was your special day. You didn't need *me* around."

"It would have been even more special knowing you were there." I meant it. "I also thought about you when we built our house."

"You have a nice house, Harold."

"So do you."

We both said at the same time, "Next time you drive by, stop in."

We laughed so hard our stomachs ached.

Mario surprised me by saying, "Let's make a pact to keep in touch from now on. Deal?"

"Deal."

We shook hands and I enjoyed the sensation of Mario's large, warm hand covering mine. He didn't let go. *Oh, he's holding my hand. That's fine. When two friends relive the old days, it's nice for them to hold hands… briefly.* I unclasped our hands, and walked over to the door. I could hear the music playing from the gymnasium.

"Remember 'We Belong Together' from the football halftime shows?"

"Sure." Mario rose and stood next to me. "Those were my glory days."

"And my tuba days."

After we laughed, Mario said, "Let's dance."

"What?"

"Let's dance, Harold."

"I don't understand."

"Dance, it's something two people do when they hear music."

Before I knew it, Mario's strong arms were around me and we were dancing cheek to cheek.

"Mario, do you and Barbara go out dancing a lot?"

"Are you kidding? With those giant heels she wears, my feet would be Swiss cheese."

He gave me a spin and we continued dancing. "How about you and Stuart?

"Not since I broke his toe at The Gay Hoedown in Jersey City."

Mario laughed and moved me down for a dip.

"Ow!" My head hit the coach's desk.

"Harold, are you okay?"

"I'm fine." *How did stars get into the room?*

"Sit down." He sat me down on the sofa.

"I'm just a little rusty."

"I think I know what will help." Mario took off his jacket and threw it over the coach's desk.

I'm feeling better already.

Next, Mario opened a desk drawer and retrieved a half-filled bottle of whiskey. "It's still here! Coach thought none of us knew about his little stash." He took off the cap and drank from the bottle. "Not bad." He held out the bottle. "Have a swig?"

"No, thanks. I don't drink."

Mario sat next to me on the sofa. "How come?"

"I have no tolerance for alcohol. I had a drink once at a party, and Stuart had to carry me out over his shoulder after I made out with a cat. He was mortified. Stuart. The cat was fine. He shortly thereafter became quite a man-magnet. The cat, not Stuart." *Did that knock on the head make me totally lose my mind?*

Mario put the bottle down on the floor next to him and turned my chin to face him. "Harold, relax. I understand."

"What do you mean?"

"It's like it was back in high school… with *us*."

"Mario, that was ten years ago."

"I know some things have changed, Harold, but not that." Mario cleared his throat like a college professor about to deliver a lecture. "When I walked into chemistry class back in high school. The day Ms. Hunsley paired us up as lab partners. I knew you were hot for me."

"You knew?"

"Hey, I wasn't *that* stupid."

I rubbed my head in an effort to understand the mystery known as Mario, and to see if I was growing a lump somewhere besides inside my pants. "Mario, you knew when I first started tutoring you that I was—"

"Totally hot for me. A blind man could have seen I got your motor running." He laughed. "I remember how you'd stutter and stammer, and say crazy things around me."

Good thing I outgrew that. "How… I… even then?" I sat forward on the sofa to analyze the situation. "And that night when we… kissed in my bedroom. Do you remember that?"

"What do you think, I got… *have magnesia*?"

"Mario, why did you kiss me that night?"

"Because I wanted to." He smiled. "Because I liked you."

"I liked you too." *Maybe I should stop this discussion and read to him like I did in high school. Right, like I'm going to find a book in a coach's office.*

Suddenly Mario looked sad. "Harold, when we were kids, the way I behaved. That day Tommy and Keith tried to… hurt you. That night on the phone, when I told you I didn't care about you. And the night I got drunk and jumped on you—"

"It's okay, Mario."

"No, it's not okay, Harold. I was scared. I freaked out. I talked to you like my father talks to my mother. I was wrong. Totally wrong."

"I understand."

He enveloped me with his smile. "You know something, I think you do." Mario rested his muscular forearm on my undeserving shoulder. "You always understood me."

"That was a long time ago."

"Ten years. Not so long ago." Mario reached for the bottle. "You sure you don't want a drink?"

"I better not."

Mario put his arm around me. *Hopefully he's stretching out a cramp.* He squeezed my shoulder with his thick hand. *I guess not.*

"Mario, what are you doing?"

"Making up for lost time."

"Mario, that was ten years ago."

"Harold, back in high school you tutored me, listened to my problems, you even filled out my college applications. You wanted so little in return. My affection. I was too afraid to give it to you. I was wrong." Mario clapped his hands and the lights went out, leaving us bathed in moon glow.

Maybe I do have a concussion. I looked up at Mario's sexy silhouette. "Mario, we were kids then."

"But we're not kids now." He tweaked my nose. "Now, looking at you. Sitting next to you. Touching you. It's clear to me you want the same thing now you wanted back then. And I'm not making the same mistake twice."

Mario took off his shirt. His strong arms drew me into him, and I felt his mountainous pectoral muscles against my sinking chest. He moved my arms to rest on his massive back, as he massaged the sides of my face with his thick, warm thumbs.

I feel like a cheerleader.

As I felt his biceps bulge on either side of me, he tilted my head up and pressed his lips against mine. As in my frequent fantasies, we shared a sensuous, very adult kiss. Next, he took off my jacket and tie. I ran my hands over his tight, olive skin, caressing his muscular back, shoulders, arms, and neck. *Am I risking my perfect marriage for a fatal attraction?*

We kissed again. *Sew the scarlet A on my shirt.*

"Ow! Harold, did you just bite me?"

"I think I nibbled on your neck."

"Why?"

"Stuart likes that."

"Stuart *likes* that?"

"Um-hm."

"What is he, a pain freak? Go easy, okay?"

"Okay. But Mario?"

"What?"

"Can we keep the lights on?"

"Why?"

"Well—"

"I know. Stuart likes it with the lights on." Mario clapped and the lights came back on. He nuzzled his Roman nose into my neck. "Zxxxxx."

I stiffened.

"What's wrong?"

"Mario, did you hear that noise?"

"What noise? Zxxxx."

"That noise."

"Zxxxx. That?"

"Yes."

"That was me, Harold."

"What were you doing?"

"I snorted."

"Why?"

"I don't know. I think Barbara likes it."

"Barbara *likes* that?" *Was she a pig farmer in another life?*

"Yeah. You got… *have* a problem with it?"

"It's a little weird, Mario."

"Okay, I'll cut it out." Mario leaned in and we shared another passionate kiss.

I pushed him away.

"What's wrong now?"

"You drooled on my shirt."

"Then take it off." Mario took off my shirt. "And get over here."

We wrapped our arms around one another. It felt like coming home.

"Harold, this feels so good, so right."

"I know. My Mario. It's just like in my fantasies."

Mario reached under the sofa cushion and pulled out a condom. "They're still here too!" He lay on top of me and began unzipping my pants. "Who says you can't go back, right, Harold?"

"Wrong." *Did I just say that?* I sat up.

Mario sat up too. "What's wrong?"

"I can't do it, Mario."

"What, you're *impudent*?"

"No, Mario, I can do it. I just can't *do* it… with you." I put my shirt back on.

"I don't get it. You've been after me since we were kids. I know I screwed it up back then, but I can make it right… now."

"Mario—"

"Harold, what you said back in high school… about the Kinsey Scale. It was true. Gender doesn't matter. We fall in love with who we fall in love with. I thought I was in love with Barbara, but I wasn't." He took my hand. "I was in love with you, but I was too chicken shit back then to admit it."

I put my hand on the side of his face. "Mario, I dreamed and fantasized about this moment for so many years."

"So the problem is?"

"One problem is that you are married to Barbara."

"I can't stand the sight of her."

"But she's still your—"

"She's cheating on me, Harold. Can you imagine? She's actually cheating on *me*! With her personal trainer."

"That is a bit cliché."

"I know, right?" Mario took another swig of whiskey. "Lots of people come on to me at the gym, at model shoots, at the mall. A lot of people are after my body."

Imagine that.

"But I didn't cheat on her, except for a few times, but it didn't mean anything." He sat back on the sofa and closed his eyes. "Harold, sometimes I feel like I'm losing my mind. Like I'm going through my life on autopilot. As if I'm watching *myself* in a movie. I don't feel anything. I'm like stone. Nothing's real." He opened his dark eyes and they engulfed me. "But something clicked when I saw you tonight. I looked at you and I felt… human again. You reminded me of who I once was. Who *we* once were… *together*, Mario and Harold." Mario stared up at the ceiling. "Harold, it's been so many years covering up my feelings, pretending I'm not… *me*. Pretending that I didn't want to be with you. Pretending that I didn't miss you. Sometimes I feel like you're the only real thing in this whole crazy world."

Is this one of my Mario fantasies, or the result of hitting my head on the desk?

Mario's grip on my wrists brought me back to reality. "Harold, I made a big mistake back in high school. You were right. I was hiding behind Barbara. She was my *mustache*. My brother was right too. You were the one back then who got *me*, who was really there for *me*. Who always saw the best in *me*. It *worked* with you. I wanted you then… and I know it's ten years later, but I want you now. And I know you want me too." He held my hands. "Harold, we were robbed of all these years together. But it's only time. We have a second chance… *now*. Let's give it a try and see what happens. Maybe it'll work and maybe it won't, but at least it will be *real*. At least I'll feel *something*." He smirked. "And you will too." He took my hand. "Don't we owe ourselves the chance to find out? What can we lose?"

I sat on the arm of the sofa. "Mario, I had a major revelation tonight too. You are gorgeous, sexy, wonderful, and perfect."

"So what was your new revelation?"

I looked at him adoringly. "You are my first love, Mario. My cherished being. I will always be yours… in an alternate reality… in my fantasies." I stood and put on my jacket. "In the real world, you don't exist."

He stood next to me. "Is it because I hurt you back in high school?"

I took his hand. "No, Mario, you could never really hurt me."

"Then why won't you give this a chance?"

"Because it's like giving a dream a chance."

"What's wrong with that?"

"Nothing, until you wake up sweating, out of breath… and alone." I released his hand. "Mario, Stuart is the prince in my life. He's my perfect partner and mate. He's my family. He's… real."

"And I'm a *phony*?"

"You are Mario the Magnificent. My prince and my perfect partner… in a parallel universe… in my fantasies."

"It's not because I smell like moth balls from so many years of being in the closet?"

I laughed. "Mario, you have a lot to work out with Barbara. And I have to make things right with Stuart."

He grabbed my arm. "So we're not gonna…?"

"We're not gonna."

He looked away. "I'm sorry."

He's sorry. I stood facing him. "Mario, if we got together it could never be as good as in my fantasies."

He flexed his biceps. "Even though I am still pretty hot, right?"

"Right." We laughed.

He took my hands. "Harold, you still love me?"

I squeezed his hands. "Like I love every fairy tale my mother ever read to me as a child."

Mario put on his shirt.

"Mario, I don't want to ruin your marriage with Barbara."

"It's already ruined."

"And you don't want to end my marriage with Stuart."

"I don't know. I'm a Republican."

We shared another laugh.

"Most of all, Mario, I don't want to destroy my memories of *you*."

He handed me my tie. "I'm disappointed."

"Maybe someday you'll meet somebody new."

He thought about it. "Maybe I'll meet someone like *you*."

"If so, don't tell me about him."

Mario smiled and put on his jacket.

"Well, Mario, I never thought I'd say these words—let's go back to the gym."

Mario blocked my way to the door. "Hey, Stuart's a lucky and a terrific guy."

"He sure is. And Barbara is… Barbara."

"Harold, I'm really sorry we didn't give this a shot."

Me too. "Nothing's changed, Mario. We still have our fantasies."

Mario smiled and opened the door. "Harold, this reminds me of that poem you taught me about in high school by Robert what's his name. Remember the red, red rose? Even though it goes away, after the snow and shit clear up, it comes back again in June… every ten years." He messed my hair like he did in high school. "Even though we can't be together, Harold, you'll always be my red, red rose."

I told you he was the best.

Mario and I walked back to the gym, where Barbara chewed out Mario for not telling her where he and I had gone. He told her they needed to talk and they left. After saying good-bye to Hannah, Stuart and I left as well.

On the drive home, as my heart pounded out of my chest, I confessed everything to Stuart. My wonderful husband's response? "At first I was jealous, but I knew you'd pick me over him. I'm glad you got that out of your system, Harold. I love you and I always will."

When we got into bed that night, I asked, "Stuart, have you ever had an infatuation?"

He turned to me and said, "Yes. You. It's 11:00 p.m., Harold, so lights out."

Isn't he the best? As we cuddled under the covers awaiting peaceful sleep and pleasant dreams, I felt totally content.

My concerns about the reunion were all for naught. Stuart is the best husband on the planet. And he is all mine. But in the world of my fantasies, I have Mario, my infatuation. Two really is better than one.

CHAPTER NINE/7 YEARS AGO

OVER THE next three years, there was an occasional e-mail or phone call—some hang ups—and a holiday card here and there, but basically Mario remained my fantasy.

When I read in the newspaper that his brother had died in Iraq, I stood in the back of the funeral home while Mario greeted a long line of hysterical relatives. At the burial site, he asked me to put the last flower on the grave, and I did.

Mario was there for me when my mother passed away. We never spoke, but right after the Buddhist monk said his prayer, Mario blew a kiss to me and left.

The last time I'd spoken to Mario was on a Sunday evening three years after the reunion. In honor of my mother, Stuart was creating a schedule for his—and my—new meditation regime. My phone rang, and somehow I knew it was Mario.

"Hi."

"Mario, it's good to hear your voice." I shut the door to my study. "Everything all right?"

"Not really." He sounded distant.

"What's wrong?" I felt my pulse quicken.

"Things aren't working for me here, Harold."

"What do you mean?"

I heard the clinking of ice in a glass. "I can't find work for one."

"What about your modeling work?"

"It dried up. I'm too old, and I gained some weight. Obviously things dried up with Barbara a long time ago."

"How are the kids?"

"Getting into trouble at school and driving Barbara and me nuts."

"Mario, do you want to come over and talk?"

"No… thanks." I heard him gulp down his drink.

"Mario, what is it?"

"I miss my brother."

"I know. I miss my mom too. How are *your* parents?"

"My mother's always bitching about something. And my father's more of a piece of shit sick than when he was well... if he ever was *well*."

"I'm sorry, Mario."

"Me, too." After a pause with more clinking of ice against glass, he added, "Harold, I'm moving away."

No! "Where?"

"LA."

"Why?"

"Fresh start. Fresh air."

Really? "Do you know anyone there, Mario?"

"I met some people in New York City who live there. I have a few... prospects for work."

"What kind of work?"

"As a photographer. For print shoots." I heard another long swallow.

"Do you like photography?"

"It's okay." After another gulp, Mario added, "Or maybe I'll open a restaurant.... *Nonna's*."

"That sounds nice." I took in a deep breath. "Anyone special in your life?"

"Yeah."

"Who?"

"You."

I wiped away a tear. "How about Mario and Harold?" I meant the kids.

"Like you said, Harold, we'll always be together... in your *dreams*."

I swallowed hard. "I'll miss you."

"I'll keep in touch."

No you won't....

After a pause, he said, "I wanted to let you know."

"Thanks."

"Harold?"

"Yes?"

"Don't forget about me, okay?"

"Never."

I never heard from him again.

CHAPTER TEN/NOW

SEVEN YEARS later, ten years after our high school reunion, one afternoon while Stuart was still at work, my doorbell rang. I opened our front double doors to Mario holding a box, looking just like he had in high school. To make me further doubt my sanity, he said, "I'm Mario Ginnetti."

When my visitor noticed the color draining from my cheeks, he asked if we could sit down inside. Unable to speak, I nodded and somehow ended up sitting across from Mario on the loveseat next to the fireplace in my great room. I stared out our floor-to-ceiling windows at the mountain view, blinking, then looked back at Mario. He was still there. It wasn't a hallucination.

Mario placed the box on the floor next to him. "I'm sorry for barging in like this. My mother says I'm impulsive, like my dad."

Oh my God. "Y-Y-You're Mario's son."

He smiled and revealed his dimpled chin. "I never liked the Jr."

After the room stopped spinning, I asked, "Can I get you something to drink, or to eat?"

"No, thanks. I can't stay long. My boyfriend's coming over to my house to study." He rubbed his Roman nose. "I don't know how much studying we'll get done though."

Like father, like son. "Are you in high school?"

"Soon to enter college... on a football scholarship."

Definitely like father, like son.

"I won't flunk out like he did though."

I looked into his dark eyes and remembered. "I used to tutor your father... when we were in high school."

"I know. Dad talked about you all the time. He showed me your picture in his yearbook."

"I got older."

"Yeah."

Thanks.

Mario Jr. looked around. "And you married well."

"Stuart, my spouse, is a dot-com executive."

"And you're a grade school teacher, right?"

"Was. I'm the principal." *And I'm on the national board of the Gay Lesbian Straight Education Network. I'm carrying the torch, Mr. Ringwood.*

He leaned his elbows on his knees and his biceps doubled in size.

"Mario, are you sure I can't get you anything?"

"I'm cool." After an awkward pause, he continued. "Harold—can I call you Harold?"

"Please." *I'm eighteen again.*

"Harold, my dad said you were his best friend... his only *real* friend. He named my brother after you."

"I'm sorry we haven't met before this. I sort of lost touch with your father."

"You and everybody else."

I sat on the edge of the sofa. "Didn't your dad move to Los Angeles seven years ago?"

He nodded. "It was after he and my mom got divorced. Except for an occasional e-mail or text message, we didn't hear much from him... until last week."

"What happened last week?" I felt a line of sweat dripping down my back.

"My brother, and of course my mother, are really bitter. But I can't hate my dad, no matter how hard I try."

"Why is that, Mario?"

"Maybe because like you... and I guess like him, I'm gay."

My heart raced. "Mario, please tell me what's going on."

"I don't know everything."

"Then tell me what you know, please."

His rosy cheeks got redder. "Harold, were you and my dad lovers?"

My palpitations had palpitations. "No. Yes. It's really complicated."

He shrugged his massive shoulders. "Okay, I get it. It's none of my business."

"No." I took in a deep breath. "I loved your dad, Mario."

"He loved you too."

"How do you know that?" My hands were soaking wet.

Mario Jr. picked up the box at his feet and handed it to me. "Before he died, my dad wanted you to have this."

I dropped the box on my lap like it was on fire.

Mario Jr. sat closer to me. "Are you okay?"

"No."

My body was shaking. Mario Jr. hurried to the kitchen, poured a glass of water, and brought it to me. After a sip, I croaked out, "Please tell me what happened."

Mario Jr. sat back down on the loveseat. "Well, my father became a photographer in LA. I think he got mixed up with a wild crowd, parties, liquor, drugs, sex."

"But how did he…?"

"They think it was an overdose."

"Accidental?"

"They don't know."

I took his hand. "Mario, I'm so sorry."

"Thank you."

It suddenly occurred to me. "Mario, are you, and Harold, and your mom okay with money? Do you need…?"

"We're fine. Harold and I got scholarships to college. My mom remarried a guy in the mob."

"I don't know what to say. You must miss him."

"I miss my *old* dad. The guy who used to play football with me, bitch with me about Mom, make my brother and me laugh by making funny faces, and tell us about his glory days in high school… with *you*."

I sat back and stared at the ceiling, too in shock to cry. I suddenly remembered the box on my lap. "What should I do with this box?"

"Open it."

"Now?"

Mario Jr. nodded. "My dad lost everything he had. All we got were his clothes. My mother wanted to burn them. I took them." He raised his palms upward. "He was my dad."

Words were coming to me slowly. "How do you know your father wanted me to have… this?"

"A neighbor in LA found him and called the police."

I opened the box and held up a letter in an envelope, addressed to me.

"The police looked through his apartment, it was just a room. They found that letter. We had it sent, along with his clothes, his will… and his body, to us."

"Why did you put this letter in a box?"

Mario Jr.'s huge pectoral muscles heaved up, then rested back in place. "Read the letter, Harold."

"Out loud?"

"If you don't mind."

I slowly opened the envelope and held the letter. My voice, and hand, shook as I read. "Harold, I've been sitting here thinking about the old days. Thinking about how I went from something so right to something so wrong. Everything made sense back then. And nothing makes any sense now. Maybe your mom was right, and we pick our family members and friends to learn something from them. If so, I know why I picked you to be in my life. You looked at me and showed me all the good things I could have been. To you I was perfection. No matter what I was or did, you loved me unconditionally. I wish I could love someone like that, Harold. I wish I could have been the guy you thought I was. I wish I could have been the hero. I hope we will be together in another life, Harold. And if so, the next time around, I hope I'm half the man you are. I hope I have your strength, courage, and ability to love and to be loved. You were right to choose Stuart. I'm glad you are happy with him. And I hope you still think about me sometimes. I'm putting my will next to this letter so my family knows what I want. Never forget me, Harold. I love you. See you in another place and time. See you in your dreams."

Mario Jr. wiped his eyes. "Dad's will stated that you should get his ashes."

I opened the box and picked up a small urn. My tears flowed freely.

Somehow I managed to see Mario Jr. to the door, thank him, and ask him if I could be a part of his life. Thankfully he agreed, and thankfully he's kept his promise so far.

Now, a month later, as I conclude where I began, I stare at Mario's urn on my fireplace mantel, next to Ms. Hunsley's plaque with the quote from Shelley. I feel so lucky, so blessed to have had my passion, my flame, my cherished one, my infatuation. And to still have him… in the world of my fantasies.

Stuart has just come down the stairs to tell me some good news. Our surrogate mother is in labor… with our son. *We're going to be parents!* I think of my mother. Stuart and I embrace, and we share a number of happy kisses.

As we rush out the door to drive to the hospital, I think of Mario. Stuart takes out his car keys, turns to me, and says, "I know. We're naming him *Mario*." I kiss Stuart's cheek.

Isn't he the best?

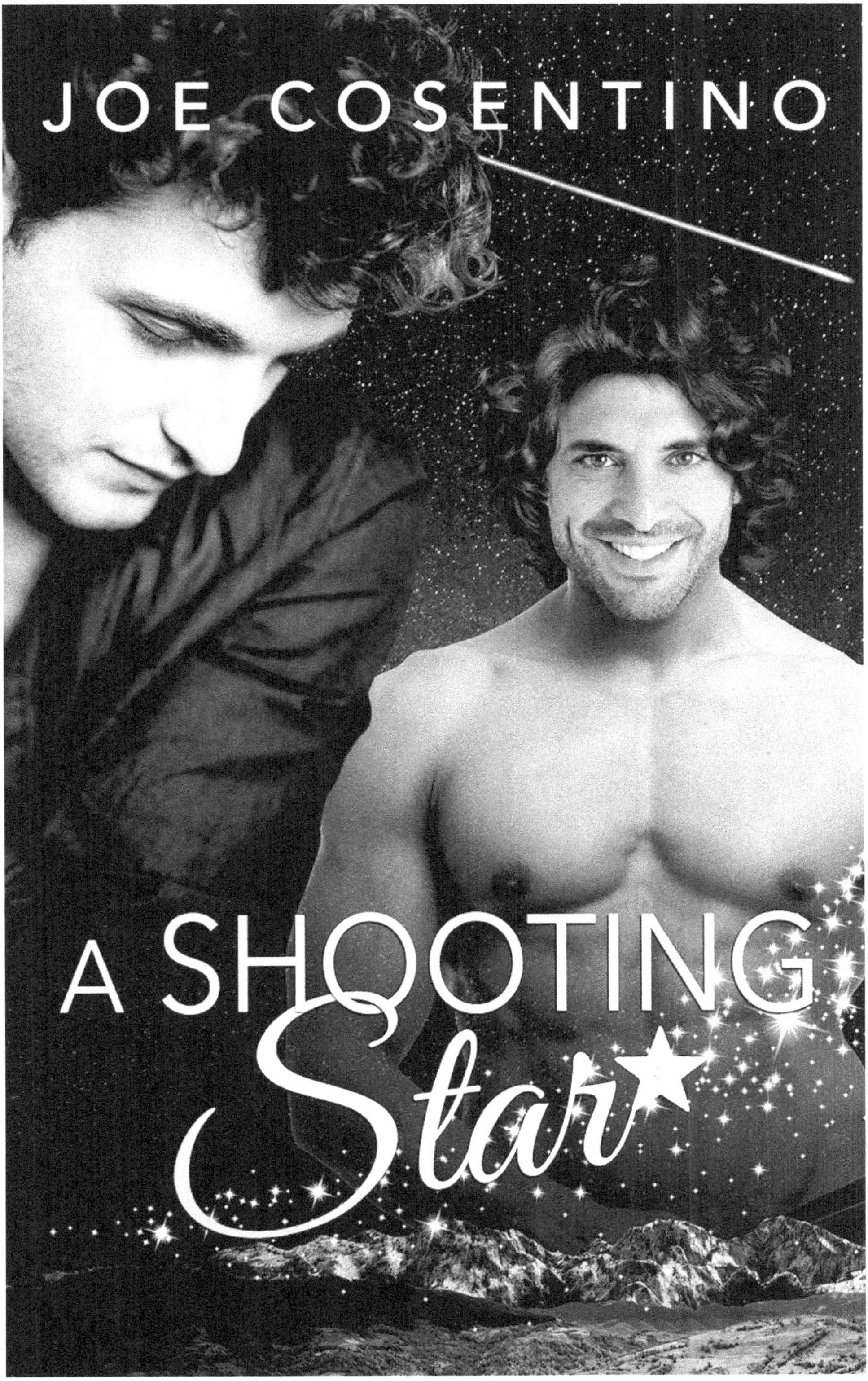
JOE COSENTINO
A SHOOTING
Star

To Fred for everything over all these years,
to the staff at Dreamspinner Press,
and to everyone who follows a shooting star.
Special thanks to all the readers who loved *An Infatuation*
and asked for another Bittersweet Dreams novella.

"If any one faculty of our nature may be called more wonderful than the rest, I do think it is memory. There seems something more speakingly incomprehensible in the powers, the failures, the inequalities of memory, than in any other of our intelligences. The memory is sometimes so retentive, so serviceable, so obedient; at others, so bewildered and so weak; and at others again, so tyrannic, so beyond control! We are, to be sure, a miracle every way; but our powers of recollecting and of forgetting do seem peculiarly past finding out." Jane Austen, *Mansfield Park*

PROLOGUE

As I stand in the double-story, all-glass great room of my Malibu beach home on this amazing night, I stare at the new statue on my bookcase. With my eyes fixed on my Oscar, I think about another man who was with me when it all began.

Like David, my memories of him are enigmas, magical manipulations of my mind. What is real and what is fantasy, I can no longer remember. Yet somewhere in all the mirth, drama, affection, and adoration lies my truth. My David Star.

CHAPTER ONE

IT RAINED on every first in my life: my baptism (so I'm told), starting kindergarten, beginning high school, opening night of my high school senior play, and my first day at college. With stars in my eyes to match the stars in the sky, I had flown from Pennsylvania to Colorado. My luggage was packed with more acting books than clothes, and my pockets were stuffed with food (courtesy of my mother) and cash (courtesy of my father).

After sitting through all-day orientation meetings in the college's gymnasium, I purchased my textbooks in the college bookstore, then walked to my new home—in the rain.

In case you haven't figured it out yet, to my parents' horror, my friends' confusion, and my delight, I was a theater major. Since I was a walking calculator, my parents assumed I would become an accountant like the other men in my family. Since I won most of my high school competitions, my gymnastics coach and team members assumed I would be the next Mitch Gaylord (no pun intended). However, after starring in my senior play as the Frog in *The Frog and the Toad* (at least I got top billing), I had a terminal case of show business bug bite.

It was such a traumatic time for everyone in my life that finding out I was gay elicited this surprisingly uneventful response, "That's nice, Johnny."

As for the theater major issue, we're Italian—we rant and rave into our pasta, then get over things quickly. So after seeing me play Stanley Kowalski (of the ripped T-shirt) in *A Streetcar Named Desire* at our local summer theater, everyone in the neighborhood proclaimed me the next John Travolta and wished me well in college.

The college was only fifteen years old, so it was modern in design. A tall iron gate opened to a winding road leading to the various academic buildings. Each building was circular, triangular, rectangular, or square, reminding me of a child's play set. A small but well-kept lawn, sporting benches and lampposts, was stationed between each building.

I made my way to my room on the third floor of the men's wing. It was the usual college dorm room—like a prison cell in double vision. The bed, bureau, bookshelf, closet, desk, and chair on one side of the room were replicated on the other. The window looked out onto enormous jagged mountains like a painted flat over a sky-blue cyclorama. (I told you I was a theater major.)

I dried off, quickly unpacked, then changed into jeans and my newly purchased college sweatshirt. Somewhat muscular from my high school gymnastics, I decided baggy clothes would help me fit in with what I assumed would be the skinny or overweight theater nerds. They're the kids who spend all their time indoors listening to Broadway show tunes, talking about the true meaning of Sondheim's lyrics, arguing if *Rent*, *Les Mis*, or *Phantom* is the best musical, and reading every play from William Shakespeare to Neil Simon.

Since my chestnut hair frizzed from the rain, I was happy my mother packed my blow dryer. As I got to work on my hair, I was surprised at how nervous I felt about attending my classes and auditioning for my first college production. Being shy by nature, I was also anxious about meeting my professors, the other theater majors, and of course my roommate.

As an Italian-American, I subscribed to my mother's theory that if someone doesn't want you to see something, he will hide it in a locked vault covered with cement. So I *inadvertently* took a quick look at my roommate's things on the other side of the room. He was incredibly neat. Numerous theater textbooks and play scripts lined his bookshelf in alphabetical order. The bulletin board above his desk displayed artistically arranged programs from various comedy, drama, and musical college productions listing the same male lead in each show: "David Star".

"Do you always look at other people's things?"

I nearly got whiplash as he entered the room.

Stammering like a kid caught masturbating by his parents, I said, "I... w-was... ad-m-miring y-your... r-room."

Though it was a fall September day, he took off his scarf (violet) and rested it on a tall coatrack, which held scarves in various colors like a department store window display. He was taller than me, with a chiseled, handsome face, and straight, shiny black hair, which fell down his thick neck. I admired his perfectly sculpted muscles, housed in a turquoise designer dress shirt. But what captivated me the most were his piercing crystal-blue eyes—and the enormous bulge in his skintight, beige designer pants.

As I went back to my side of the room, he placed the paper bag he carried onto his otherwise clear desk. After opening a bureau drawer, he removed a portable oven burner, cutting board, pan, and knife and rested them on top of his sparkling clean bureau. Next, he placed the pan on top of the burner. After emptying the contents of his bag onto his desk, he chopped, diced, seasoned, sautéed, and stirred ingredients in the pan.

Opening another dresser drawer, he pulled out a china plate with a delicate rose pattern. As if a chef in a gourmet restaurant, he plated his creation (chicken Florentine, new potatoes with thyme, and asparagus tips with shiitake mushrooms), added a parsley sprig, then rested it on top of his desk. He took a silk napkin and set of silverware from inside his desk drawer for his place setting. A wine bottle came out of his grocery bag. After using a corkscrew from his desk drawer to open the bottle, he retrieved a crystal wine glass from his dresser drawer and poured himself a glass of white wine.

Sitting at his desk and circling the wine in his glass, he asked, "Would you like a glass?"

My head was spinning from the delectable sights and scents, including David's musk cologne. "At the orientation meeting today, they said it's against college policy to have alcohol… or to cook in your dorm room."

"*Did* they?" He laughed as if sharing a private joke with himself.

Noticing the time, I said, "I should get to the cafeteria for dinner."

His clear blue eyes pierced through me. "Why?"

I scratched my head. "Because I'm hungry." Looking at the meal ticket on my desk, I added, "And I have a meal plan."

Taking another plate from his dresser drawer and placing half of the dinner onto it, he replied, "You don't want to eat industrial food with all those shouting children."

"Why not?"

He held up the plate, as if getting a pet dog to trust him.

After I took it, he opened his desk drawer and handed me a silk napkin and silverware set. "You sure you don't want a glass of white wine?"

"No, thank you."

He opened his desk drawer. "I have red… 1937. Or would you prefer fruit juice?"

Still holding the plate, napkin, and silverware, I said, "Juice is good."

He opened another desk drawer, "Apple, orange, grape, or cranberry?"

"Apple please."

After taking the bottle of juice, I put everything on my desk. Sitting behind it, I took a bite of the most delicious meal I had ever tasted. "This is amazing."

Putting his napkin on his lap, he looked over at me and said, "It's important for an actor to eat well. Our bodies are our instruments." He added with a twinkle in his eyes, "And hopefully our fortunes one day."

Stuffing my mouth with food, I asked between bites, "Where did you learn to cook like this?"

After smelling, rolling around in his mouth, then finally swallowing a sip of wine, he replied mysteriously, "People taught me."

"This is better than the restaurant food in Philly." I continued eating the mouthwatering dinner. "Are there any good restaurants here in town?"

"A few."

"I haven't walked into town yet."

"Why would you walk?" He took his first bite of dinner and savored it in his mouth.

"I don't have a car here."

"That doesn't mean you have to walk."

"Is there a bus or something?"

He continued eating slowly, enjoying each delectable morsel. "When you look like us, you don't have to walk."

Finishing my dinner and wiping my mouth with the soft napkin, I asked, "You mean you hitchhike?"

"As actors we're called on to play different roles. Hitchhiking is a great tool to study other people. Then we can use what we learn on stage."

"I guess."

He put down his fork and wine glass. "What's your name?"

"Johnny Falabella."

He looked at me like a surgeon examining a tumor. "No, it's not."

"Excuse me?"

"It's Jonathan Bello." He opened a bureau drawer, pulled out a bottle of hair gel, and tossed it to me. "You should gel your hair." He opened his closet, revealing a multitude of color-coordinated shirts and slacks, and laid some on my bed. "And you can wear these."

I looked at his perfectly pressed designer clothes. "Where did you get all these things?"

"They were gifts, mostly."

"You must have some generous friends.... Sorry, I don't know your name."

"*I'm* David Star." He took a bow.

Looking back at his play programs, I said, "You must have starred in every play at the college over the last three years."

"Guilty as charged."

"What happened to your last roommate?"

"He went to LA over the summer break and started auditioning. He got cast in a new TV sitcom. I hope it takes off. It's called *Cosby*."

"At the orientation session, they said freshmen are housed with other freshmen. How did I get a senior for a roommate?"

His eyes twinkled. "Just lucky I guess."

"Do you think it was some kind of an administrative error or something?"

"Or something." He added matter-of-factly, "I asked for a freshman roommate."

"Why?"

David came over to my side of the room and picked up the class schedule on my desk. "Theater History I, Acting I, English Literature I, Creative Movement, Voice Production I, General Math I, and Health and Fitness." He threw it down. "Those classes won't help you get cast in a play."

"What?" I stood and faced him. "I spent a lot of my… and my parents' money on those classes. I want to learn how to be an actor."

"You will, but you won't learn anything about how to audition and get a role."

"How do I learn that?"

"I'll coach you before auditions for the upcoming play." He lay on his bed. "And you can cut Health and Fitness. The professor never takes attendance. We can be workout partners in the gym. You have a nice frame, but you need to be cut to make it professionally. You won't learn that in Health and Fitness."

Feeling like I was on a rollercoaster, I said, "Why are you doing this for me?"

"Because you're my roommate."

Not knowing what else to say, I said, "Thanks."

David smiled revealing straight white teeth. Then he took a (lemon-colored) scarf from his coatrack. "After I graduate, I'm going to New York to audition for theater, then to LA for film and television. We'll talk about which is best for you." He wrapped the scarf around his neck. "I have an appointment. Get some sleep, Jonathan. That's important for an actor."

He left the room and closed the door behind him. Lying back on my bed, I pondered the enigma called David Star, and fantasized about having an *appointment* with him.

CHAPTER TWO

TRUE TO his word, David filled my mind with preparations for future stardom. In addition to lecturing me on the powers of positive thinking, he sculpted my body in the college gym—teaching me to use lighter weight with more repetitions. He insisted I get eight hours of sleep each night, and filled my stomach with healthy, homemade culinary delights. Finally, he coached me on stage presence, body language, voice, and diction. I learned how to do a successful cold (little preparation) and warm (prepared) audition by making strong and unusual choices about the character's actions, motivations, emotions, likes, dislikes, hopes, and fears.

As auditions for the first play of the semester were soon approaching, David analyzed the play script with me, going over the plot, theme, character breakdown, dialogue, and stage directions. He identified each character's history and emotional beats in every scene.

While we played each role in our dorm room, David offered an exhaustive critique of my performance in the scenes. Like Henry Higgins with Eliza Doolittle, David was a stern taskmaster, unrelentingly directing my every step. Having read nearly every book on acting, David pounded into my head the importance of listening and reacting, honesty, and performing every beat in each scene as if it were happening for the first time (though we went over every scene in the play more times than I could count). Since David had read and/or seen just about every play from the Greek period to the present, he impressed upon me the importance of understanding the play's time period and environment with all of its social implications on gender, race, socioeconomics, and sexual orientation.

Since the first college play of the semester was by Molière, David demonstrated the manner in which an educated man of wealth in 1600s France would dress, walk, talk, sit, stand, drink, and eat. It was hard for me to pick up at first, but eventually my mind, body, and voice were able to inhabit the era.

When we read the love scene between the young man and woman in the play, David was not very convinced by my performance.

Sitting next to me on my bed, he said, "Jonathan, take my hand like it's the object of your affection, not a piece of cod. Pick your head up from your script. Look into my eyes. Take your voice out of your nose. Take in a deep breath from your diaphragm. And slowly, sensuously, confidently say your line as if it's the most important sentence in the world."

Looking nervously into his handsome face and holding on to his warm, thick hand, my body and voice started to shake as I said the line.

"Try the line again. Use emotional recall from your past, Jonathan."

I repeated the line even less convincingly.

His aqua eyes widened. "Jonathan, haven't you ever been in love?"

I looked down at my cherry-red designer sneakers (actually David's cherry-red designer sneakers).

He dropped my hand like a chili pepper on fire. "You've never made love with anyone?" When I didn't respond, he rested his hand on my knee like a trauma nurse tending to a patient in a hospital emergency room. "You're a *virgin*—like Cassandra, Miranda, and Janet and Brad in *The Rocky Horror Picture Show*?"

Feeling as if I needed my own telethon, I replied, "I concentrated on my schoolwork and gymnastics in high school."

David's mouth dropped open. He sat quietly and stared at the wall for what seemed like an eternity. Then he jumped off the bed and wrapped a scarf (chartreuse) around his neck. "Let's go."

"Where?"

He placed an apricot-colored scarf around me. "Follow me, young man."

Not knowing if David was taking me to the local whorehouse or psychiatrist, I followed him out the door of our dorm room, past the dormitory lobby, and to the entrance gate of the college. David held up his thumb, and in no time a car's headlights blinded my vision.

David waved me in and we sat in the front seat of a station wagon with David where he liked to be—in the center. The driver was a pretty young woman with short blonde hair wearing a powder-blue cotton housedress. Though not that old, she had large dark circles under her eyes, and her nails were bitten down.

David said as if she were his chauffeur, "We're going to the movie theater in town."

The woman smiled, already under David's magic spell. "You two boys like going to the movies?"

"We're theater majors at the university," David explained. Then he added like a nursery school teacher pointing to a color chart, "Seeing plays and movies is part of our studies."

"You boys want to be movie actors?" she asked with a haggard look on her pretty face.

I stared out the window at the mountains that looked like charcoal cutouts against the dark sky.

David replied, "Stellar actors start out doing theater before moving on to movies."

Barely able to keep her eyes on the road, the woman took in David's handsome face. "You sure look good enough to be a movie star. What's your name?"

"David Star." David winked at her and she nearly skidded off the road. Pointing to me, he said, "And this is Jonathan Bello. Remember our names."

"I certainly will," the woman replied with a smile. "I never met any actors before."

David revealed his dimples. "And *your* name is?"

Obviously happy to be asked, the woman replied, "Sarah…. Sarah Hampton."

As if she was the only person in the world, David asked, "And what do you like to do, Sarah?"

"Me?" The woman laughed. "I'm just a housewife… two kids. My husband's a plumber. I'm going to pick my kids up from scouts."

"But what do *you* like to do, Sarah?" He said her name as if he'd known her a lifetime.

"Mostly I take care of my husband… and my kids."

"Do you like doing that, Sarah?"

She shrugged her hunched shoulders. "I haven't really thought about it."

"Think about it now."

After a pause, she replied, "Not so much lately."

"Can you remember something you liked to do before you got married?"

She giggled. "I haven't thought about that in ages."

"What did you like to do, Sarah?"

She laughed. "I liked making paper dolls."

"You mean cutting out paper to make a row of dolls?"

Her face lit up like a sunrise. "It's more complicated than that. You draw and paint the doll on paper and cut it out. Then you draw and paint different outfits with tabs to fit on each paper doll. So you can change the doll's outfits. It's so much fun."

"How come you stopped doing it?"

She scrunched her face and took some time to answer. "I guess I couldn't find the time."

"Then you should make the time, Sarah. And make paper dolls like you did when you were a kid."

She asked, "Now? At my age?"

As she pulled up to the front of the movie theater, David squeezed her hand. "Will you promise me you'll do it, Sarah? Will you make paper dolls again?"

Sarah's smile lit up her face. "Sure." As we got out of the car, Sarah shouted, "Remember me, Sarah Hampton, when you're movie stars."

David leaned into the car. "We will, Sarah. Now go and create some paper dolls!"

As we entered the movie theater, David strode up to the ticket window. Leaning on the counter with his shoulder muscles exploding out of his shirt, he said, "I'll take two tickets to *Sense and Sensibility*."

The teenage girl behind the ticket counter blew a gum bubble, took his money, then handed him the tickets.

David unleashed his pure white smile. "What's your name?"

The girl adjusted the worn collar of her drab, oversized brown sweater. "Trudy Ingham."

"David Star and Jonathan Bello."

Trudy looked confused.

David stared at her like a work of art. "Trudy, have you ever acted?"

She scratched below her dirty-blonde ponytail. "You mean like in a movie?"

"Yes."

Trudy laughed. "No."

"You should. You have a photogenic face."

"I do?" Trudy squinted at the glass partition.

David's arm muscles expanded as he pointed inside the theater. "You should be in there—on the big screen."

Trudy blew another gum bubble. "Are you kidding with me?"

"I never kid about show business, Trudy."

She thought about it. "You really think I should be an *actress*?"

"I really do. Don't you, Jonathan?"

Picking up my cue, I replied, "I do too."

David winked at her. "And we should know. We're theater majors at the college."

She scratched her nose. "You two study drama and all?"

David replied, "We do."

"You guys want to be actors?"

"That's the plan," David said.

I nodded my agreement.

"Imagine that."

"Yes, imagine that, Trudy. And after you do, come join us."

She laughed. "Maybe someday I will."

David said like an old sage, "A new future awaits you, Trudy." He grinned. "Hope to see you, Trudy."

As David led me into the theater, Trudy looked at her reflection and blew another bubble.

Since it was a late weeknight show, the theater was nearly empty. David motioned for me to join him in two seats in the back row.

"What you did for Sarah and Trudy was nice," I said.

"What did I do?" David asked ingenuously.

"You made them feel special."

"Everyone is special, Jonathan. In the arts, we not only entertain people, we help them connect with their emotions, and find that special place within themselves."

During the coming attractions, David gave me a lecture about Jane Austen's female characters losing their virginity late in life and finding true love. Then the movie theater darkened and the film began. Though it was a beautifully photographed movie taking place in an emerald-green, quaint country setting in England, my focus wasn't on the screen. Wearing tight white pants and a blue and white striped polo shirt, David positioned his bulging biceps on the armrest between us, nestled his shoulder into mine, and let his knee slide into mine. Taking in his musky scent, I shivered when David's soft hair and warm breath tickled my ear as he whispered, "The most stimulating thing about Jane Austen's characters is their refusal to fall in love… until they can no longer hold back the natural impulse to do so." He placed his hand on my knee and I nearly ripped my (rather David's) chinos. "Aren't you tired of fighting off love, Jonathan?"

"What do you mean?" I somehow got out through a hoarse throat.

"During all that studying and gymnastics in high school, didn't you ever want to just give in?"

"To what?" I croaked out.

He put his muscular arm around me. "Your natural desires to make love?"

"I haven't really thought about it."

David moved my face toward his. "Think about it, Jonathan. Don't you want to be a part of something beautiful? To be awoken, stimulated, possessed by another human being?" Leaning in with our noses nearly touching, he asked, "Don't you want to let go and experience fulfillment, passion, love?"

Sweat dripped down my back. "I don't know."

His voice was silky and masculine like a Greek god whispering in a forest. "Do you want to find out?"

I noticed I was nodding.

"Do you want to find out with *me*?"

I nodded again.

He wrapped both arms around me and pressed his toned pectoral muscles to my chest. "Do you *want* me, Jonathan?"

A frog landed in my throat. "I... I...."

David's lips were an inch away from mine. "Do you want to make love with me?"

I was speechless.

He placed my hand on his lap. "Jonathan, if you don't want me, nothing is going to happen here. Do you understand?"

I sounded like a soprano. "Yes."

"It's all up to you, Jonathan. Now, think about it, do you want me?"

Sounding like a kettle whistling, I said, "Yes."

"Are you sure?"

I nodded like a doll with a wire neck.

"Are you absolutely sure?"

Unable to stand it a moment longer, I reached out and pulled David's face into mine. Then I planted a hard, deep, passionate kiss onto his lips.

After the kiss was over, David smiled like the Cheshire Cat. "Great." He rose from his seat. "Let's go."

"But the movie isn't over."

"I'll tell you how it ends."

With my head spinning and my hand unsuccessfully pressing down my raging erection, I followed David out of the theater and back onto the street. He waved at Trudy, then raised his thumb for our ride back to the dorm.

"Now you know how to play a love scene, Jonathan," David said as a compact car stopped in front of us.

This time our driver turned out to be a middle-aged African American man. Still wearing his blue maintenance uniform and nametag from the college, Jake sat behind the wheel in the small red car while David and I rode in the back, as if we were his last fare for the evening. Since Jake's car was so tiny, David's muscular legs pressed against mine, literally making me weak at the knees. I stared out the window at the dark night enfolding us, wishing I was wrapped in David's arms.

"Whooee! I got in my car the star of the school plays!" Jake said proudly.

David put his arm around me. "And my roommate Jonathan here is co-starring in the next play with me."

"I am?" I asked.

"You are," David replied with a nod of his perfect head.

Jake smiled from ear to ear. "I won't miss that one." He scratched his curly gray hair. "What are you two boys doing off campus so late at night?"

David leaned over the front seat. "We went to a movie so Jonathan can ace his upcoming audition."

Confused, Jake replied, "Whatever you say."

"How about you, Jake?"

Jake's dimples appeared. "I just dropped off my date."

"You did?"

Jake's eyes danced. "Um-hm."

"What did you two lovebirds do this evening?" David asked like a gossip columnist.

Laughing, Jake replied, "Me and Selma went out to dinner. Maybe you two boys know Selma?"

"Does she work at the college?" David asked.

Jake nodded his large head. "She's a secretary in Registration."

David replied, "I don't believe I've had the pleasure. How about you, Jonathan?"

Not remembering anything about the whirlwind of registering, I shook my head no.

David asked, "Have you and Selma been dating long, Jake?"

Jake stole a quick look back at David. "This was our first date."

"Your first date! Isn't that great, Jonathan?"

I answered, "Sure."

"Amen to that," Jake replied with a nervous scratch of his ear.

Noticing, David asked, "Didn't things go well, Jake?"

Jake sighed. "*I* had a fine time."

David nodded at me, and I asked, "How about Selma?"

Staring straight ahead at the road and gripping the wheel, Jake said, "I've been talking with Selma on and off for years at her desk when I come in to take out the trash or bring the mail. I finally got up enough nerve to ask her out on a date."

"And?" David and I said in unison.

"She was friendly and polite like usual. The food in the restaurant was good. But being out with Selma was… different from being with her at the college."

"How was it different?" David asked, playing the role of psychiatrist.

"That's what I've been trying to figure out."

David prodded me with his elbow, so I asked, "Was the conversation strained or forced between you and Selma? Did Selma tell you she's seeing someone else?"

"Was Selma checking out other guys in the restaurant?" David added.

Shaking his head no, Jake said, "We talked about the college, our jobs, the food at the restaurant, our exes, our kids who are grown. But there weren't no… sparks. When I left Selma at her door, I reached over to kiss her on the cheek and she shook my hand." He sighed. "After all this time courting her, I feel like a guy who built a house of cards then sneezed."

David rubbed his strong hands together and got to work. "Jake, the first thing to remember is never, ever talk to Selma about your ex-wife. It will force Selma to try to compete with her. And anything that takes Selma's mind off romance with you is a bad idea."

Jake shrugged his mountainous shoulders. "Okay."

"And leave your jobs behind at the end of the day. A date shouldn't feel like an extension of work."

"Makes sense," Jake replied getting more interested.

David pronounced like a king to his court, "And every word you say and every move you make should revolve around your upcoming intimacy with Selma."

Jake looked at David with fear in his large dark eyes. "But what if there ain't no intimacy with me and Selma?"

"There will be, Jake."

Looking back at the road, Jake asked, "How do you know, David?"

As if a televangelist checking his donation count on air, David replied, "Because *you will believe* there will be."

"I don't understand."

David leaned over farther. "Jake, tonight before falling asleep, envision yourself with Selma. See you two making eyes at one another over dinner, that warm and wonderful kiss at her door, the drink you two share in Selma's kitchen." David's eyes twinkled. "And watch that passionate, earth-shattering, life-changing lovemaking in her bed."

Jake laughed. "I can't do that, David."

"Yes you can, Jake. Don't you think Jake can do it, Jonathan?"

I slid to the edge of my seat. "I definitely think you can do it, Jake. And imagine how much fun it will be."

Jake laughed louder and adjusted the growing lump in his pants.

David spoke like a football coach addressing his team in the locker room before a game. "And when *you* believe it, *Selma* will believe it." He leaned over the seat even farther, moving his round, muscular bottom inches away from my face. "Then on your next date with Selma, don't think about your ex-wife, your adult kids, your job, or even the food at the restaurant. Think about Selma. Taste her lips on yours. Smell the scent of her perfume. See her breasts resting in your hands. Feel the warmth of her body sculpted into yours. Hear her moans of delight as you become one. Arouse Selma. Enter Selma. Please Selma. And release your love into her welcoming body. Concentrate on those things and *only* those things during your date. Will you do that, Jake?"

Looking postorgasmic, Jake wiped the sweat off his forehead. Then like a man with a new gym membership card, he announced, "I'll do it!"

After Jake dropped us off at the entrance to the college, David and I walked back to our dorm.

"Jake's a really nice guy," I said. "I hope things work out with him and Selma."

"Did you study him?" David asked.

"Study him?"

"You may play a character like that someday, Jonathan. Whenever you're with someone, watch how he walks, talks, dresses, reacts. And remember it."

The moment we arrived back in our room, David sat next to me on my bed, and placed the play script in my hand. "Now think about the woman losing her virginity in the movie, Jonathan. Remember Sarah's passion for her paper dolls, Trudy's joy over being admired by us, and my advice to Jake about making love to Selma. And let's try the scene again."

As we went through the scene, arousal grew inside me like wildfire. I heard bells chime. The heat between David and me rivaled the great fire of Chicago. With each of my lines, I teased, seduced, and spewed passion. David returned each of my volleys and threw a number of his own. By the end of the scene, we were in one another's arms, panting for air.

David rose from the bed. "Good work, Jonathan. I knew you could do it." As he wrapped a lime-colored scarf around his neck, he said, "Keep reading the play. I have an appointment."

Coming up for air on my bed, I crossed my leg over my erection. Using my newfound acting skills, I asked casually, "Who are you meeting?"

He smiled. "You've learned enough for one night, Jonathan. Get some rest." Then he left the room.

CHAPTER THREE

IT WAS the night of auditions for the first production of the school year, Molière's *Tartuffe*. The sun had set, spinning a bouquet of coral, indigo, and scarlet ribbons through the mountains. David led me across campus like a parent taking a child to kindergarten on the first day of school.

Unlike my high school's makeshift theater in the cafeteria, the college's theater included a large lobby with sofas, a snack bar, and a ticket booth. Backstage at my high school was the kitchen. The backstage area at the college included six dressing rooms with vanities, a green room (waiting room for actors), a scene shop, a costume loft, a props closet, and a rehearsal room. My high school theater was painted canary yellow with two hundred metal folding chairs for seating. The walls of the theater proper (or improper—according to stories from the tech students) at the college were painted a cocoa color and surrounded five hundred ruby-red upholstered seats for the audience members. Unlike the open platforms at my high school, there was a proscenium stage with a dark red brocade front curtain and orchestra pit. Behind the first floor seating was a lighting booth, and a balcony hung over the rear orchestra.

Upon entering the theater, David instructed me to sit in the front of the house with the other nervous students who were auditioning, as he strutted up to the director.

Professor Seymour Katzer stood in the orchestra pit mumbling to himself and rummaging nervously through various photocopied scenes from the script. Having suffered three heart attacks and more nervous breakdowns than his students could count, Professor Katzer was embarking on his "last directorial stint" for the tenth time. Pushing seventy years old, the acting professor had taught at three different colleges, threatening retirement since the day he turned fifty. Weighing about a hundred pounds wet, Professor Katzer, who wore a black shirt, pants, and blazer, looked like a bald head hovering over a red bow tie.

Throwing his small arms around my roommate, Professor Katzer exclaimed, "David, thank goodness you're here!" I noticed the professor's hands linger on David's perfect, V-shaped back.

After giving the professor a hug, David asked with concern on his handsome face, "Are you all right, professor?"

Professor Katzer flailed his arms in the air like an airport flagger during a hijacking. "Am I *all right*? How can I be all right? I had the selected scenes for auditions in piles by character until I dropped them all over the orchestra pit." His small fingers fluttered through drawings. "Professor Herrington left me the set designs, but I can't understand all his technical mumbo jumbo." He raised his brown eyes to the catwalk. "You know straight men and their renderings." He kicked a box loaded with fabric swatches and sketches. "Professor Joy left me this costume paraphernalia, which looks like a secondhand store's trashcan." Tears stained his sunken cheeks. "Karen, the student technical director, and Helen, the student stage manager, are both out tonight." He added under his breath, "No doubt setting up house together in flannel bliss." He leaned into David. "As you know I don't eat during a show, so my blood sugar has plummeted. I think I'm going to faint!"

Holding on to his professor, David asked ingenuously, "Would you like me to help you, professor?"

As he wiped his eyes with his sleeve, Professor Katzer tried to inhale. "Wo… uld y… ou, Da… vid?"

"Of course I will, professor."

In five minutes flat, David organized the scene pages by characters and placed them on the apron of the stage, turned on the stage lights, dimmed the house lights, sat Professor Katzer in the front row with a pillow for his back and cushion for his feet, called everyone auditioning to attention, explained the set and costume designs, discussed the play's various translations, distributed the scenes based on our individual character type, and took the seat next to Professor Katzer's.

Before the first student auditioned, Professor Katzer said to David, "Of course I want you to play Tartuffe."

David took the professor's clammy hand in his and held it next to his heart. "Professor, though I'm more than flattered, I wouldn't dream of letting you precast me in the show. I insist on auditioning like everyone else."

Katzer shrugged his bony shoulders. "All right, then. Go on stage and read one of Tartuffe's speeches for me."

After making his entrance onto the stage, David played Tartuffe as if he were the great impostor himself. David was charismatic, enchanting, and riveting, commanding the stage as if it were his domain. With his body floating across the stage like a specter, David's enormous muscles contracted and released in perfect sync with each beat of the scene. David's voice was like a violin gliding angelically from word to word. Each feature on his handsome face brought every nuance, subtext, and innuendo in the play to life tenfold.

When David finished his audition, he received a standing ovation from the enamored students in the audience. As David took his seat again, Professor Katzer said, "Wonderful work, David. You had a very good acting teacher."

"That I did," David replied, squeezing Katzer's emaciated arm.

"Who is auditioning next?" the professor asked David, as if David was the director.

David rose and faced the other students. He locked eyes with a tall, extremely muscular, Asian American young man sitting a row behind me. I felt like a paper clip caught between two magnets.

"Terrence should read for Orgon." With his eyes still on Terrence, David added, "And Samantha can audition for Elmire."

Terrence winked at David as he took the scene pages from David's hand. Once on stage, Terrence and Samantha were believable as husband and wife, and they handled Molière's wit and period style well. I also noted Terrence had no problem with Orgon's dialogue, especially the section where Orgon proclaims his admiration for Tartuffe.

The evening went on with various students auditioning for the remaining roles. After every other student had auditioned, Katzer turned to David. Losing his breath again, beads of sweat appeared on the professor's large forehead. "I was afraid of this."

"What is it, professor?" David asked with a reassuring hand on Katzer's knee.

"Mark Thomas isn't auditioning because he got a job at a local restaurant as a waiter." Katzer blinked back tears. "I hope he's good at it, because *that's* what he'll be doing for the rest of his life."

David shrugged his wide shoulders. "So, Thomas won't be in the production."

Katzer rubbed his chest. "But that leaves us with all the roles cast except Valère." He put a white pill under his tongue. "Valère has to be handsome, virile, and charming. You are already cast as Tartuffe. Terrence is our Orgon."

David smiled. "I have just the actor, professor."

Straining his eyes to peer out into the darkened audience, Katzer asked, "Who?"

As if introducing the next guest on a television talk show, David stood and pointed to me. "Jonathan Bello."

The professor looked at me, searching his memory. "Aren't you in my Acting I class?"

I stammered, "Ye… s."

"What scene are you rehearsing in class?" Katzer asked, searching my face for a hidden clue.

While most of the other students in the class had already selected scenes and partners, I was too shy to do so. "Well… I—"

A tall, thin boy with curly auburn hair and a long nose said, "Don't you remember, professor? Jonathan is *my* scene partner in class. We're doing a scene from…" He thought fast. "*Angels in America.*"

Professor Katzer's eyes glazed over. "Of course I remember." He whispered to David. "I had no idea." Then he shouted, "What is your name, young man?"

"Barry Goldman," he replied.

"Barry, of course." Katzer whispered to David. "I didn't remember that either. I hope I didn't suffer a stroke."

David replied sotto voce, "You'll feel better after you see Jonathan."

"Jonathan, please go on stage and audition for Valère. You can read with Ayisha, who I cast as Mariane."

David cut in. "Professor, Ayisha's in the ladies' room."

"All right," Katzer said as if bodily functions were an affront to the American theater. "He can read with Ling Chow, who will be Ayisha's understudy."

Again David replied, "Ling Chow is in the ladies' room with Ayisha."

"Are we doing *The Vagina Monologues* or *Tartuffe*?" Katzer fanned himself with one of the scene pages, then checked his pulse.

"Professor, I'll read with Jonathan," David said with a conspiratorial wink in my direction.

"Thank you, David," Katzer said with adoration in his bloodshot eyes. "That's very nice of you."

David nodded at me, and we went up onstage. Doing the scene exactly as we had rehearsed it in our dorm room, my Valère was full of strength, honor, and desire… for David. The heat between us was palpable. It felt as if all eyes and hearts were on us. When I reached my arms around David and shared my love for him, I heard sighing from the audience, and from me. I relished in David's musky scent, sky-blue eyes, full rosy lips, square jaw, and straight nose. I ran my fingers through his thick black locks, and rubbed my hands over his muscular arms. When the audience was near orgasm, as was I, the scene ended with me kneeling at David's feet. Again the students rose for a jubilant standing ovation. Professor Katzer wept with relief into his digitalis, then pronounced me *his Valère*, thanking David for the recommendation.

At the conclusion of the auditions, Professor Katzer handed me my script. "Congratulations…."

"Jonathan," I said.

Katzer said, "Right, Jonathan. Job well done." He gave me a calendar. "This is your rehearsal schedule. Since you have no understudy, it will be difficult if you miss a rehearsal. However, that won't be a problem, since you *never will*. I will see you in acting class." The professor clutched his left arm and left the theater.

With Katzer gone, and the other students circling around David like groupies at a rock concert, the boy sitting next to me tapped me on the shoulder. "Hello. Remember me?"

I laughed. "Thank you for saving me. I'm sorry, I forgot your name."

"Et tu?" He offered me a freckled hand. "Barry Goldman."

"Are you related to the department store mogul?"

"Only when I need a new shirt and can find a gullible store clerk."

I laughed again. "Hi, Barry. I'm Johnny Falabella. David named me Jonathan Bello."

He flexed his biceps. "Ah, the powers of David Star."

I laughed louder. "And I'm not rich either."

"Your clothes disagree with you."

"These are David's."

He nodded and his glasses nearly slipped off his nose. "Then we'll have to earn our wealth the real way… by becoming famous."

"Deal." After we shook hands, I said, "Are you serious about doing a scene with me in acting class?"

He looked me up and down. "Well, you aren't much to look at, but after the way you killed it on stage tonight, you're my ticket to an A."

"That was David's coaching."

"It may have been David's coaching, but it was *your* performance. And it was terrific!" Dressed in a red flannel shirt and jeans, he pulled a script out of his denim knapsack. "I read the two *Angels in America* plays a hundred times." He folded over a page. "Let's do *this* scene. We play gay lovers." His sea-green eyes sparkled. "Can you handle me?"

"Didn't you just see me up there with David?"

"Reality check. I'm nothing like David."

"I'm adaptable."

"We'll see. When can we rehearse?"

"How about tomorrow in the lab theater before class?"

"You're on, Johnny." He rose, then stood motionless.

"What's wrong?"

Sitting on the arm of the chair, he said, "Are you and David Star…?"

I smiled. "David's my roommate. He's also my gym workout partner."

He looked at my arms. "That explains your identical bodies… and scarves."

I laughed. "Barry, I'm nowhere near as big as David. And David and I aren't romantically involved."

Swaying back and forth with his hands on his temples like a medium, he said, "But you'd *like* to be."

I blushed. "How could you tell?"

"You aren't *that* good of an actor. Besides, everyone is in love with David… including David."

"Barry, please don't say anything to David about any of this."

He ran a hand through his wavy ginger hair. "No problem. I'm not exactly on David's go-to list." Looking at everyone swarming around David like flies on a carcass, Barry said, "I'm also not good at fitting in with the crowd."

"So you are immune to David's charms?" I asked, rising and getting my scarf.

Barry crossed one sneaker over the other. "David Star isn't the kind of guy I like."

"What kind of guy do you like?"

He moved into the aisle. "*That* is the question. See you tomorrow."

After Barry left, Terrence ended his conversation with David and stood next to me in the aisle. "Congratulations, Jonathan. It's a feather in your cap as a freshman to be cast in a major role." He smiled. "That doesn't happen too often around here." He reached out his enormous hand. "I'm Terrence Falcon."

I shook his hand. "Nice to meet you, Terrence. And thank you. I hope I don't let everyone down."

Terrence's large muscles nearly ripped his skintight navy-blue shirt. "If you do in performance what you did tonight at auditions, we'll have an amazing show." He squeezed my hand. "Don't hesitate coming to me if you need anything." His dark eyes and white teeth glistened in the theater lighting. "Anything at all." He left the theater.

The other students hung on David's every word in the front of the house. Finally, David extricated himself from the adoring mob, put his arm around me, and walked me out.

Standing in the theater lobby, I said, "David, thank you so much for helping me—in our room and tonight."

He pinched my arm. "You were great up there tonight, Jonathan."

"Only because you were with me." I felt like a moonstruck teenager. Rubbing my sore hand, I asked, "Are you and Terrence Falcon... together?"

"What do you mean?"

"I sensed a connection between you two."

David smiled. "Terrence was my roommate freshman year."

"What happened?"

He laughed. "The room wasn't big enough for both of our egos."

When we got outside, instead of walking back to our dorm room, David beckoned me to follow him to the college's front gates. Gray clouds had filled the sky, causing the mountains to resemble an eerie castle. David flashed his thick thumb, and before I knew it, I was sitting in the front seat of a pickup truck. The driver looked about thirty years old, with a crew cut and tattoos on his arms. He had on worn jeans and a faded sweatshirt.

Our host asked, "Where you going, guys?"

I was equally curious.

David said, as if talking to his limousine driver, "We're going to the club at the very end of the boulevard."

The man's weatherworn face sagged. "Have you fellas been inside there before?"

David planted his elbow into my side. "It's the first time for my friend."

Squirming in his seat, the man said, "You know what kind of place that is?"

With feigned naïveté, David answered, "Pretty noisy?"

"I mean, do you know it's not a *regular* bar?"

David was the epitome of innocence. "I don't know what you mean...."

"Clyde."

Fixated on our driver, David said, "Clyde, I'll bet the drink menu is pretty *regular*. The music too."

Scratching the stubble on his chin, Clyde whispered, "It's a place for queers."

"Is that right?" David's eyes doubled in size.

Clyde nodded. "I'd be careful about going in there if I was you."

David turned to me, "Jonathan, did you know we were going to a gay bar?"

Not knowing how David wanted me to play my part, I shrugged my shoulders.

Looking back at Clyde, David said, "How do you know it's a gay bar, Clyde?"

"I was in there once."

"You were!" David clutched at his chest.

Nodding, Clyde replied, "I wanted a beer, and I thought it was a regular bar."

"What happened when you went inside?"

Looking as if he had rotten eggs in his mouth, Clyde replied, "Some guy came on to me."

"He did?"

Clyde nodded like a ragdoll on a trampoline. "He asked if I wanted a beer."

"You just said you *did* want a beer."

"Right. So I had one."

"Good for you, Clyde. Then what happened."

"Then he asked if I wanted to dance."

"With *him*?"

"Ugh-huh. I wanted to puke."

"Did you?"

Clyde shook his head no. "I held it down."

"Good for you, Clyde. Bar owners don't like it when people puke all over their floor."

"That's what I figured."

David looked like a child at story time. "So what happened?"

"I got the hell out of there. That place is against my religion."

"But drinking *isn't* against your religion, Clyde?"

He thought about it. "Dunno."

"You didn't have another beer then?"

"No way. That place gave me the creeps."

David shook his head. "Well, Clyde, thank you for the warning."

Clyde nodded. "That place is right out in the open. Innocent people could stumble in there by mistake. Even kids."

"Were there any kids in there, Clyde?"

"No, but I try to warn regular guys who don't know the truth."

"That's big of you, Clyde. Speaking of truth, did you ever go back into that bar again after that night?"

Clyde spit phlegm out his window. "I went back a couple times."

David acted enthralled. "How come, Clyde?"

"Like I says, to warn guys who might be in there by mistake."

I pulled his arm. "David."

David held still. "And when you found the other *innocent* guys, what did you do, Clyde?"

"Since it's a fag bar, I told them to watch out for their family jewels."

Seeming astonished, David said, "Then what happened?"

"Sometimes a guy left with me."

As if trying to figure out an intricate puzzle, David said, "So you left the gay bar with another guy?"

"Yeah."

"Did you two get into your truck?"

"Yeah, so I could drive the guy home."

"Sure. And what happened when you got to the guy's house?"

Sweat beads appeared on Clyde's knotted forehead. "We talked."

"About what?"

"Guy things."

Again I pulled on David's arm and again David held tight. "What kind of *guy things* did you talk about, Clyde?"

Clyde's tongue rolled around his yellow teeth. "You know, things guys like to talk about."

"Which things are those?"

Clyde scratched his protruding stomach. "Well, I'm a carpenter, so we talked about building things."

"Right. And after you talked about building things, what happened?"

"We had some more drinks. And we ordered a pizza."

"That sounds great. Then what did you do?"

Clyde squirmed in his seat. "I don't know. Whatever guys do."

"Did you stay overnight?"

Clyde's back stiffened. "Hey, it wasn't dirty or nothing like that. Just two guys having fun."

Choking back a smile, David replied, "Of course." David slapped my back. "Just like us. Two guys having fun."

As Clyde pulled up in front of the bar, it started to pour. I got out of the truck. "Thank you, Clyde. Have a good night."

David climbed out after me. "Yes, thank you for the lift, Clyde. Hope to see you again soon."

Clyde leaned out of the truck and called out after us, "Remember what I told you guys. Stay away from that place."

Unable to contain our laughter a moment longer, David and I guffawed as we ran to the club in the rain. Once inside, David put his arm around me and walked me to the bar. "Jonathan, remember Clyde if you ever play a redneck homophobe. Don't forget the tattoos on his arms, his knotted forehead, and limited vocabulary with incorrect grammar. Remember how he spit out the window when he became agitated, and scratched his stomach when he was at a loss for words. Most importantly, keep in mind his fear and frustration at facing who he really is."

After we shook off the rainwater and sat on stools, the bartender, a tall, very muscular, middle-aged, bald Latino wearing a tank top and shorts, winked at David. "Hello, David."

David returned the wink. "Hi, Manuel. This is my roommate, Jonathan."

Without asking for I.D., Manuel placed a beer in front of each of us. "Welcome, Jonathan."

I smiled and reached into my pocket to pay. David placed his hand over mine.

Manuel said, "Any roommate of David's is a friend of mine."

I said, "Thanks, Manuel."

Manuel eyed David. "Is Jonathan going to be a famous actor one day, like you?"

David rubbed his huge shoulder against mine. "We were just cast in lead roles in our college play."

"That calls for a toast." Manuel clinked our beer glasses with his glass of bourbon, and we all drank.

After David and I finished our beers, Manuel served us seconds. "Jonathan, are you interested in working at the club?"

David replied quickly, "Jonathan is interested in dancing with me."

David led me onto the dance floor, where he gyrated to the up-tempo song, and I made an unsuccessful attempt at following him. When the music turned to a slow tune, he took me in his arms and held my chest tightly into his. Then he placed my head on his shoulder, and whispered in my ear, "You really were terrific at the audition tonight."

Looking up into David's sea breeze eyes, I said, "I reacted to what you gave me on stage. Your last name suits you. You're a shining star."

His dimples appeared. "Your last name suits you too since *bello* means beautiful in Italian." He kissed my nose.

We continued slow dancing. It felt safe and incredibly sensual being in David's strong arms. I planted my face into his mountainous pectoral muscles. David pulled up my chin and gave me a deep kiss. I savored his musky scent and warm, wet mouth. He kissed me again. And again. Each time was more intense.

A pretty blond boy rested a shaky hand on our shoulders. "You two look like you're having fun. They say three's a crowd, and who doesn't like a crowd? Can I join you?"

David scowled like a Victorian father. "How old are you?"

The boy's pink cheeks turned crimson. "I look younger than I am. Manuel checked my ID."

"Which is obviously fake."

"No it isn't." The boy ran a twitching finger around David's nipple. "And *I'm* not fake either."

David pointed to a small table in the corner. "Let's all sit down over there."

We followed David's order and sat around the table.

The boy looked about sixteen years old. "I've never had a threesome before."

"And you're not going to have one now," David said. "You won't be in here long enough."

"You can't throw me out of here. It's a free country," the boy said, rising from his chair.

Pushing him back down, David said, "Nothing's free, sonny. Now before I put you over my knee and spank you—"

"That might be fun," said the boy with raised eyebrows.

David said, "Tell me why you're here."

The boy replied, "I told you. I was looking for a hookup. If you two guys aren't interested, I'll go somewhere else."

Noticing a tear brimming in the boy's big blue eyes, I took his hand. "What's your name?"

He looked away. "Mark."

David said, "No it's not. What's your *real* name? And tell me fast or I'm calling the cops."

The tear made its way down the boy's smooth cheek. "I don't have to tell you anything."

David changed his tactics. Smiling at the boy, he said, "I only hook up with guys who tell me their real names."

Feeling David kick me under the table, I added, "I'm Jonathan. This is David. Those are our *real* names. What's yours?"

His eyes were wild and searching. "You aren't going to call the cops on me, are you?"

"Not if you tell us your real name," I said.

He fidgeted with the belt loop of his jeans. "Henry."

"Henry what?" David asked, not taking his eyes off the boy.

"Why should I tell you?"

David leaned forward and his muscles bulged out of his shirt. "Because I don't have sex with a guy unless I know his last name."

Looking at David's handsome face and muscular physique, Henry said, "Henry Wooley," and then he put his hand on David's crotch.

David pushed Henry's hand away. "Now, Henry Wooley, tell us why someone your age is in a bar."

Henry wiped his face with the shoulder of his T-shirt. "I got thirsty and horny. Where else would I go?"

David grabbed him by his thick locks. "Are you going to answer my question, Henry?"

Playing good cop to David's bad cop, I said, "I'd tell him, Henry. He means business."

After looking nervously from me to David, Henry finally said, "I'm older than I look. It's a genetic disorder. Everyone in my family has it."

David pulled his hair.

"Aghhhh!"

"I'd talk fast Henry," I said.

Henry sealed his lips.

David said, "You have five seconds to talk before I pull out every strand of your pretty hair, then use that phone booth to call the cops and ask them to arrest you for soliciting."

"What's *soliciting* mean?" Henry asked.

David replied, "It means start talking or you're going to juvenile hall. And no more stories—except the real one." David released the boy's hair.

"Why are you here, Henry?" I asked with a comforting arm around the boy. "You can tell me."

Henry squirmed in his seat. "How do I know I can trust you?"

I replied, "You must have approached us for some reason, Henry."

He said, "I thought you were both hot."

I smiled. "I think you trusted us. So follow your instincts."

After looking at David and then at me, Henry focused down at the table. "My father threw me out."

"What'd you do?" David asked.

"I didn't do anything!"

David jumped up. "I'll have your ass thrown into a juvenile prison faster than you can wave your fake ID."

"I told him I'm gay."

I asked, "How do you know you're gay, Henry?"

He shrugged. "The same way you do."

David sat again. "This isn't about Jonathan. It's about *you*. What did your dad say when you told him?"

Henry looked at me, and I nodded. As if reliving a nightmare, Henry said, "He said I'm not his son. And God hates me. And I should be ashamed of myself." He was deep in thought. "Two things I don't understand."

"What's that?" I asked with my hand on his.

"God made me. So why would God hate me?"

I replied, "God doesn't hate you, Henry."

Henry said, "And I inherited my father's genes, right? And my mother died when I was young so my father raised me. Either way you look at it, nature or nurture, it's not *my* fault I'm gay."

David stifled a smile. "Parents say crazy things sometimes."

"Did he hit you, Henry?" I asked, afraid to hear the answer.

Henry shook his head and blond hair flew in several directions.

"Don't lie to us." David grabbed Henry by the T-shirt, accidentally exposing a large purple-red bruise on his side. I was never happier to have supportive parents.

Swallowing hard, David asked, "Are you okay?"

Henry nodded.

"Has this happened before, Henry?" I asked.

When Henry didn't respond, David said, "It's not the first time."

Henry didn't argue.

David asked, "Do you have a boyfriend, Henry?"

"No, but I was hoping to get lucky tonight with you two."

Biting my lip to keep from laughing, I asked, "Do you have any family members we can call to come get you?"

"Not in this state… except my dad." It dawned on him. He said almost to himself, "I guess he's not my family anymore."

David asked, "You have any friends?"

Henry shrugged. "The kids in school and on my block call me a faggot. They wouldn't come get me if I was hanging from a bridge."

"Why'd you come in *here*?" David asked.

Henry said, "I heard this was a place gay people go. I'm gay. I had nowhere else to go."

"So you came on to two strangers?" David said like a lawyer in a courtroom with a hostile witness, "Don't you realize how dangerous that is?"

Tears filled Henry's eyes. "I just wanted to be somewhere with people who are… like me. Who understand me."

"This isn't the place." David said.

"Then where *is* the place?" Henry asked.

David took a pen from his pocket and wrote a phone number on a napkin. "Call this number. It's a twenty-four-hour hotline. They'll get you a safe place for the night, and connect you with someone you can talk to." Then he placed some coins inside the napkin and handed it to Henry.

"Can't I just come home with the two of you?" Henry ran his hand down my chest. "I'll do whatever you guys are into."

I removed his hand. "David and I are college students. We live in a dorm."

"I want to go to college someday." Henry searched his pockets, then displayed a card. "I have a college ID card." He smiled. "I'm a senior."

"Then stay in *high* school and stay out of places like this. And get rid of this fake card." David confiscated it and threw it in the trash.

Henry whispered to me, "David's a mean one. You could do better. I'm available."

Obviously concerned about the boy, David said, "Henry, promise me you won't come on to anyone else or have anything to drink?"

Henry said, "You're no fun."

David glared at him.

"Okay."

"And swear you'll call the number on the napkin?" I asked.

"Whatever," Henry said raising his eyes to the stained ceiling.

David said slowly, "Henry, Jonathan and I have to leave now. Go into the phone booth and call that number. They're understaffed, so it might take a while for them to get to you. But don't move from the booth until they talk to you and tell you where to go. Understand?"

Henry looked away and nodded.

Holding the side of Henry's face softly, David said, "Henry, do it."

Henry looked into David's eyes and nodded.

David wrote another phone number on the napkin. "This is how you can reach us at the college. Don't be afraid to call if you need us."

After David and I stood to leave, Henry wrapped his arms around David's shoulders. "Thank you."

David held Henry in his arms and said in the boy's ear, "I know you feel alone, but you're not. Remember that."

I squeezed Henry's arm. "Make us proud, Henry."

Henry nodded.

Back at the bar, David asked Manuel to keep an eye on Henry, noting Henry's fake ID. Manuel agreed to let the boy stay there a while longer.

On our way out, I said, "Poor kid."

David wiped a tear from his eye. "Talk about emotional recall."

"Was your childhood like that, David?" I asked.

David replied, "No. Not at all."

For the first time, I didn't believe David's acting.

Since it was my first time (in a gay bar), I wasn't surprised it was still raining outside. A thick fog surrounded us like a steam bath, making visibility nearly impossible. Unable to see the street in front of us, David stuck out his thumb with no results. With water cascading down our faces, David noticed a bald, heavyset, middle-aged man sitting in his car with tears streaming down his face. David knocked on the window, and the man lowered it.

"Are you okay?" David asked.

The man wiped his face with his handkerchief. "What are you two boys doing out in the rain?"

"We're looking for a ride back to the college," David shouted through the raindrops.

"Get in."

The man didn't have to ask David twice. David reached for the door handle of the large luxury car and we both sat in the wide front seat. I pulled my scarf inside and shut the door.

The man said, "It's not safe for you boys to be outside on a night like this."

Feeling as if we were driving through the clouds, I said, "How do you drive in this weather?"

"Real slow," the man replied, adjusting his leather jacket. After a pause, he said, "You boys go to the college?"

"I'm a senior. He's a freshman," David replied with a flick of his wet, shining mane.

The man smiled. "My son went there too."

"We're theater majors," I explained. "I'm Jonathan and this is David."

"Mike Bodine." He suddenly seemed miles away. "Bobby majored in engineering." He added proudly, "He was the first one in my family to go to college."

David perked up. "Is Bobby your son?"

Mike nodded. A tear formed in his eye.

"Are you an engineer too, Mike?" David asked.

Mike shook his head no. "I'm a contractor... like my father was." He grinned. "And like his father."

As if a dog with a new bone, David asked, "Is Bobby working as an engineer now or as a contractor?"

Mike's face flushed. "Bobby isn't with us no more."

Becoming accustomed to taking on the role of David's sidekick, I asked, "Bobby doesn't live in Colorado?"

A tear dropped onto Mike's sagging cheek. "Bobby passed on." Sadness filled his dark eyes. "A year ago today."

David rested a hand on Mike's flabby shoulder. "Mike, we're so sorry."

"Thank you."

Always ready for a new character study, David said, "Please tell us more about Bobby."

Mike's face lit up like a jack-o'-lantern. "Bobby was a terrific kid. Smart as a whip. Loved his family. Funny as all get-out."

After David's knee jabbed into mine, I asked, "What happened to him, Mike?"

The tear flowed down Mike's cheek. "He was hit by a car... on a night like this."

Peering through the thick raindrops at the cottony road ahead, I said, "That's horrible."

Mike nodded. "It sure was. When the police called, his mother and brother and sisters couldn't stop crying."

"I can see why." David squeezed Mike's shoulder. "How about you, Mike? How have *you* been holding up over the year?"

"Not too good."

"That's understandable," I said.

"No, you don't understand." Mike looked at us. "It was my fault."

"What happened?" David asked with his eyes piercing into Mike's.

Mike took the handkerchief and wiped his cheek. "On the night Bobby... of the accident, Bobby told me something about himself.

"Would you like to tell us about it, Mike?" I asked.

Mike replayed the scene in front of him. "Bobby came home after school and asked me if we could talk. I asked him what was wrong. When we got into the family room, he told me he wasn't like me… or like my father… or like his father." Tears filled Mike's eyes again.

David played along. "You mean because Bobby didn't want to be a contractor?"

"It wasn't about that," Mike said. "Bobby told me he was… gay."

"And what did you say?" David asked, riveted to Mike's story.

Holding back tears, Mike said, "That I would take him to our priest to be cured of what he was. When he refused to go, I said"—His voice cracked—"he couldn't live with us… he couldn't be around his little brother." He wept openly. "I told my wonderful son he wasn't welcome in my home… in his home."

"I'm so sorry, Mike," David said like a mourner at a funeral.

"Me too." Mike wiped his face with his handkerchief. "What was I thinking? So what he was different from me? He was still my son."

Somehow sensing we were getting close to the college, I asked, "What happened then, Mike?"

Mike blew his large nose. "Bobby left. He picked up his friend and they drove to that bar. They had a few drinks. When they came out of the bar, Bobby ran across the street to the car. His friend called out to him, but Bobby didn't hear."

David said, "And since it was foggy and raining, like it is tonight, Bobby was hit by a car?"

Weeping again, Mike said, "He wouldn't have left if I didn't say those things to him that night."

"So you went to the same spot tonight to honor Bobby?" I asked.

Mike nodded, weeping openly.

"What happened to Bobby was an accident. You two would have made up in time." David's biceps bulged as he patted Mike's shoulder. "You've been beating yourself up for a year now, Mike. Don't you think it's time to let yourself off the hook?"

"That's the thing," Mike explained. "Whoever said 'time heals everything' never loved nobody. 'Cause it gets harder instead of easier every day."

"What do you mean?" David asked with empathy in his handsome face.

"You're too young. You don't understand."

"Explain it to us, please, Mike," I said.

"I go to work, spend time with my wife and our other kids, go to church—one that welcomes everybody—watch the game on TV." He let out a bitter laugh. "I even tried yoga. But nothing helps. I can't stop thinking about Bobby. I miss him... more every day." I wasn't sure if he was talking to himself, God, the air, or us. "What do you do? How do you stop hating yourself for the stupidest mistake you ever made? The thing that took away someone you fed, taught to play ball, took care of when he was sick, fell asleep on your shoulder at night watching TV? How do you stop the guilt knowing you killed your own son, and in one night changed your world from sunshine to clouds?"

As we pulled up to the entrance of the college, David said, "Mike, we're getting out here. Thank you for the lift."

Mike nodded, weeping openly.

David said, "Mike, can you do something else for us?"

Mike had a desperate look in his wet eyes.

"Drive back the way you came and park in the same spot where you picked us up. Then go inside the club and ask the bartender, Manuel, to point out a kid named Henry Wooley. If Manuel gives you any trouble, tell him David Star sent you. If Henry isn't there, ask Manuel where you can find him. When you get a hold of Henry, tell him what you just told us, then ask Henry how you can help him. Do you understand?"

Mike nodded as tears fell onto his dark pants.

"Will you promise me you'll do all that, Mike?" David asked.

"I will." Mike said tentatively.

"Good luck, Mike." David gave Mike a hug. "Let yourself off the hook, Mike. Bobby would want that." Then we exited the car.

As Mike drove away, David took my hand and we walked back to our dorm room. The rain had finally subsided.

David said, "Remember everything about tonight, Jonathan. The foggy night, the taste of our beer, how it felt dancing with me, and your emotional reaction to Henry and Mike's stories. Etch in your memory Henry's quivering body, sexual awakening, false bravado, and desperate yearning for protection. Remember Mike's painful loss, paralyzing guilt, and agonizing self-punishment. One day you'll use them as an actor."

When we got back to our dorm room, we put away our scarves and our shoulders touched. David smiled at me and took me in his muscular arms. We shared a kiss.

Thinking back to our time in the bar, I wanted to break out into a chorus of "I Could Have Danced All Night." "Thank you for tonight, David."

"My pleasure." His hands moved down to my buttocks. He squeezed, and I let out a satisfied squeal. We kissed again, and I delighted in David's musky scent and strong embrace.

David looked at his watch. "I have to go."

Feeling as if somebody threw ice cubes at me during a hot shower, I replied, "Where are you going?"

David wrapped a peach and emerald scarf around his neck. "I have an appointment."

"When will you be back?"

"Late. I'll see you in morning."

David left the room.

I felt like someone thrown out of bed during foreplay. Having had enough of David's mystery man performance, I left the room and headed past the lobby outside. Through the fog, I spotted David in the distance and followed him to the college entrance, where he entered a parked car that quickly drove away.

CHAPTER FOUR

IN MY classes over the next few weeks, I enjoyed learning about the Greek, Roman, medieval, Elizabethan, Restoration, Eastern, and Modern stages, plays, actors, costumes, and props. Sitting next to Barry, we laughed about the censorship in television, given the untamed content of the early Greek plays.

In the lab theater for acting class, Barry and I giggled like schoolgirls as Professor Katzer, looking like a cartoon character, demonstrated how various animals move, eat, and communicate.

Catching us, he said, "I'm thrilled you find my performance so entertaining, Jonathan and Barry. Now, since my palpitations have palpitations, it's *your* turn."

Feeling like the characters in the barnyard game for children, Barry and I contorted our bodies and called out, "moo, oink, roooar, neeeigh, whooo, bzzz, and rrrrrr," as Katzer commanded us to become cows, pigs, lions, horses, owls, bees, and flies. Upon his further instruction, we swayed around the stage like trees, crawled like babies, barreled around like construction workers, rolled like aliens, struggled like senior citizens, danced like ballerinas, and floated like fairies.

Next were mime theater exercises called the machine, tug of war, catch the invisible ball, and the magic trunk, where we became the cogs of a machine, played tug of war with an imaginary rope, caught a ball that kept changing size and weight, and used a mimed object from a trunk to enter an imaginary universe.

Then Professor Katzer asked us to pair up with our scene partners for the trust exercise. Barry and I were last.

The professor placed a blindfold over my eyes, then rested my hand on Barry's forearm. "Jonathan, you will play the blind man, and Barry, you will be Jonathan's guide. You have five minutes to make your way through the entire lab theater stage, house, and lobby and end up back here center stage." He rubbed his bald head. "You do that while I take some deep breaths to get my pulse rate down to two hundred."

With total blackness in front of me, I held on to Barry's arm like a life raft in the rapids. "Are we still on stage?" I asked Barry with my voice wobbling as much as my knees.

"Johnny, you've only taken two steps from when we started," Barry said.
"What should I do?"

"Calm down. Hold on to me. And let me guide you."

Barry's forearm became my fortress as he led me all around the lab theater in three minutes flat.

When we returned to center stage, Professor Katzer took off my blindfold, then patted our heads. "Congratulations to Jonathan and Barry. I am pleased to announce you both finished the exercise first. And my heart rate is down to critically rapid. Now everyone keep your current partners for the mirror exercise." When the professor got to us, he said, "You two boys face one another. Barry, you will play Jonathan, and Jonathan, you will pretend to be the mirror—reflecting back in mime everything Barry does as you." Katzer put a hand to his pale cheek. "While you do that, I'll go to my office to check my blood pressure."

Wearing his usual flannel (orange and brown that day) shirt and jeans, Barry took off his glasses and put them in his shirt pocket, unleashing his emerald-green eyes. Since I was his mirror, I mimed the same action (but wearing a green and blue polo shirt and jeans). Then Barry pretended to comb his hair, brush his teeth, and wash and dry his face. I mimed the same actions back to him. Finally, Barry flexed his muscles and kissed the mirror—me.

"Hey, what'd you do *that* for?"

Barry grinned. "I'm you. You're the mirror. You love your own reflection so much, you can't help but kiss it."

I chased him around the stage, and we both laughed hysterically until Professor Katzer returned, stopping us in our tracks. Placing his small hand over his sunken chest, he exclaimed, "Horseplay in my lab theater! Are you two boys trying to give me another heart attack? This is a college acting class, not the track in the Physical Education department. Can we please get back to acting?"

Katzer asked us to sit on the stage of the lab theater facing our scene partner. The professor weaved around the stage on small legs like a spider. "Look into each other's eyes and tell your partner a secret about yourself from your past. This will create a connection between the two of you to build upon for your scene. Acting is about listening, sharing, trusting, and not judging. So open your heart to one another… while my graduate assistant gives me a cardiac massage."

During our scene rehearsals, Barry and I had talked about our pasts. He knew I came from an Italian-American neighborhood in Philadelphia, my father and brother were accountants, and I was a B+ student and a gymnast in high school. I was aware of Barry's upbringing in Highland Park, a suburb of Chicago, by his parents who owned a Jewish delicatessen, where his brother and sister worked. I also remembered Barry was an A student and wanted to be an actor ever since, at four years old, he sang "The Dreidel Song" while doing cartwheels to his "bubbie's" and "zadie's" thunderous applause and shouts of "bravo!" We were both virgins. Neither of us had seriously dated anyone in high school. I grew up Catholic, and Barry grew up Jewish. So we each struggled to try to think of a secret to share with one another about our past.

After a few minutes of pondering, something finally came into my head. "I'll go first."

Barry looked relieved. "Thanks, Johnny."

Staring into Barry's eyes, I said, "I knew I was gay from the time I was a kid, but I never shared it with anyone, not my parents, friends, teachers, or my teammates."

Barry replied, "I know you're gay, Johnny."

"That's not my secret." I cleared my throat. "When I was a gymnast in high school, there was this kid, Gregory, on my team who somehow sensed I was gay. Gregory never said anything overtly, but I always felt him watching me, waiting for me to say or do something different from the other guys."

"Was he good looking?"

"I don't think you're supposed to interrupt me, Barry."

"Who's interrupting?"

I took in a long breath. "He was an average looking guy. During practices and events, Gregory would slap the other players on their butts to support them. But he never did that with me. When we got to regionals, and I won the thirty-yard dash and placed second in the floor routine, Gregory nodded his congratulations like we were businessmen after a corporate meeting."

"Maybe he was jealous of you."

"Barry, can I finish the story?"

He said with an innocent look on his face, "Who's stopping you?"

I sighed. "Gregory would never shower or change next to me in the locker room, and he always covered himself whenever I showered or changed. I had seen the way other gay kids were treated at my high school. So throughout my whole junior and senior year, I waited for Gregory to tell me some homophobic joke, call me a 'faggot,' push me into a locker, or press my head into a toilet bowl."

"Did he?"

"Barry!"

"Are you going to finish your story before we graduate, Johnny?"

I spoke quickly. "But none of those things happened. Gregory just kept watching me and being guarded whenever I was around, as if I was an alien from another planet. So I did the same to him."

"Good for you, Johnny."

I covered Barry's mouth with my hand. "At the end of the school year, everyone on the team signed one another's yearbooks. Some of the guys wrote goofy things like, 'I'm so much hotter than the guy in the picture next to me,' or 'You're so gay.' Some wrote typical things like, 'Thanks for being my teammate and friend.' When Gregory and I exchanged books, I wrote in his, 'Best of luck in your future endeavors.' After Gregory wrote in mine, he closed the book, handed it to me, and walked away. I didn't look at it until I got home that night. Lying on my bed, I opened the book to Gregory's picture and read, 'I never had the guts to tell you, but I really like you. Actually, I more than like you. I know you don't like me. That's okay. For some crazy reason, I just want you to know.' I put the book away and never mentioned it to anyone. Since school was over, I never saw Gregory again."

I removed my hand and Barry's jaw dropped. "And you never called him, Johnny?"

Thinking back, I replied, "No."

Throwing his skinny arms up in the air, Barry said, "That's pretty cold, Johnny. The guy was head over heels for you, and you didn't even talk to him about it. That's more than cold. That's frigid, Falabella."

"I thought this exercise was about trust and no judgment."

Barry's freckles grew. "I'm not judging you, Johnny. I just think you should be nicer to people who are hot for you."

"Who's hot for me besides some kid in high school who probably long ago forgot I ever existed?"

Professor Katzer was at my side like a rash. "Stop arguing like an old married couple, you two. If Jonathan has finished telling his story, it's Barry's turn." Katzer signaled his graduate assistant to fetch more digitalis from Katzer's office; then he moved on to the next couple.

Barry said, "My story isn't about how hot I am, Johnny."

"That's not what my story was about."

"Are you going to argue or listen to my story, Johnny?"

"Do I have a choice?"

Barry sat up straight like a librarian reading a children's story. "My favorite pastime as a kid was watching my bubbie cook. She always gave me a taste of whatever she was making, then made me promise not to tell my parents 'her little secret.'" He was a little boy again. "When I was five years old, Bubbie sat me at the kitchen table while she made potato latkes, my favorite, for dinner. When I asked for a taste, she passed me one and said, 'Remember, Barry, this is our little secret.' I nodded and enjoyed my snack. Back at her frying pan, Bubbie said, 'When you're a grown man, make sure you marry a girl who knows how to make potato latkes.' With my mouth full, I said, 'Bubbie, I'm going to marry a boy, not a girl.' Since I was chewing, Bubbie thought she misunderstood me. So she asked me to repeat myself. I swallowed and said clearly, 'I'm marrying a boy, not a girl, Bubbie.' She dropped her spoon into the bowl of latke batter and clutched at her heart, saying, 'Barry, I'm going to speak to your parents about this!' I replied calmly, 'Bubbie, if you don't tell Mommy and Daddy *my* secret, I won't tell them *yours*.'"

As usual, Barry made me laugh. "Did that really happen?"

"Of course it did."

"Did your grandmother ever tell your parents?"

He shook his head. "She kept my secret to her grave. And I've kept hers… until now."

"Do your parents know you're gay?"

"Of course. I think my fan dance to 'The Dreidel Song' tipped them off."

"And they're okay with it?"

"What choice do they have?"

"They could disown you like some parents?"

"No they can't. We're Jewish. We don't disown. We just nudge and annoy the person to insanity."

Thinking about the story, I asked, "Do you want to get married, Barry?"

He held my hands. "Johnny, I'm touched, but aren't we a little young?"

I hit his shoulder playfully. "I mean someday… when you meet the right person?"

Pushing his glasses up the bridge of his nose, Barry replied, "Yes. If the person is a man… and I love him and he loves me… and he wants to share a home, a family, and a life only with me… and if it's legal."

I leaned back on my elbow. "Do you think it will be legal during our lifetime?"

He shrugged his bony shoulders.

Thinking about David, I said, "What if you love someone and you want to marry him, and it's legal, but he doesn't want to marry *you*?"

"Then you wait until he's ready."

Professor Katzer tapped the top of our heads. "I hate to interrupt your coffee klatch, but can we get back to learning acting?"

And get back we did. The professor taught us a great deal about how to use our bodies, faces, and voices to convey different emotions and experiences. Though Professor Katzer seemed to be on the verge of a nervous breakdown in each class session, we learned how to use various acting techniques (presentational, representational, method, sense memory, emotional recall, imagination, repeating) to get the most out of a scene, and make our characters come to life.

I also looked forward to rehearsal every night when, under Professor Katzer's guidance, we analyzed the script, wrote character biographies, studied the play's time period, blocked the play (determining our stage movements), and rehearsed our roles. David kept a watchful eye on me, never directing me or telling me what to do, but often whispering an idea to me about how to play a scene like, "Don't forget you love her," or "Remember a time when you felt angry." My performance as Valère started out rocky, but thanks to Katzer's directing and David's tips, I grew by leaps and bounds with each practice session.

Whenever they weren't in a scene, I noticed David and Terrence whispering in a corner of the theater. When I asked David what they were talking about, he replied, "We can't believe how far you've come as an actor, Jonathan."

To my elation, David continued to be affectionate with me, often hugging or kissing me in our dorm room after our romantic dinners for two. We also continued our hitchhiking adventures to the bar, where David and I danced together till our feet ached. To my disappointment, however, our physical relationship never went beyond that point, thanks to David's disappearing act. In each case I followed him to the entrance of the college, and every night he drove off as a passenger in the same car.

Barry and I spent a lot of time together doing homework and rehearsing our scene for acting class. When Barry and I kissed in our scene, it felt comfortable with no (pardon the word) drama about it. Nobody could make me laugh like Barry. When I was with him, I was completely myself—for better or worse.

One night after a successful rehearsal in Barry's dorm room, he turned to me sitting next to him on his bed. "We aced that one, Falabella."

"You sure?" I asked, always hesitant to believe my work was good.

"I'm sure." Dressed in his usual flannel shirt (blue and green check), jeans, and sandals, Barry handed me a container of orange juice from inside his mini refrigerator, then sat back down next to me on his bed. "I took these from the cafeteria at breakfast." He raised his plastic container to mine. "Here's a toast to our scene from *Angels in America*. It's heavenly."

"Barry, how'd you get a refrigerator?"

"My mom sent it—with a year's supply of blintzes." He imitated his mother, "So you shouldn't go hungry."

I laughed as I opened my container. "But we aren't allowed to have refrigerators in our rooms."

"My mother sent a year's supply of potato latkes to the dorm manager." We toasted. "How are play rehearsals going?" he asked before taking a swallow.

I leaned my back against the wall. "They're going. Sometimes I feel like I have a real handle on my character. Other times I think I'm just flailing my arms and jumping around the stage like a lunatic."

Barry said, "Lucky you, acting on stage. I'm on the prop crew."

After taking a sip of juice, I asked, "Barry, do you know Terrence Falcon?"

He nearly spit out his juice. "Who doesn't? He's David's second in command."

"Did you know they roomed together their first year here?"

He pushed his glasses up his long nose. "I'm not surprised the elite gravitated toward one another."

"I wonder how Terrence got so big?"

Barry scratched at a freckle on his skinny ankle. "Steroids I guess."

"Do you think David likes him?"

Barry put our orange drinks on his desk, then pulled up a chair next to the bed. As if a psychiatrist at the start of a session, he said in a professional tone, "How long have you had feelings for David?"

I laughed. "I guess since the first time I met him."

He picked up a pad and pen from his desk. "How does David make you feel?"

Continuing Barry's role-play, I said, "When I'm with David, I feel… invincible. When I wake up, go to bed, and in between, what I think about is…. David."

After writing a few notes, he asked, "What do you think about him?"

I closed my eyes. "What he's doing, all the people whose lives have been touched by him, if he likes me, how much I like him, why he's affectionate with me but only to a certain point." As if an afterthought, I added, "And where he goes at night."

Barry's eyebrows rose toward the lightbulb on the ceiling. "Where he *goes* at night?"

Sliding to the edge of the bed, I leaned my elbows on my knees. "Barry, don't tell anyone, but David goes out late every night."

"Where?"

"I don't know. And the strange thing is, David usually hitchhikes everywhere."

"That's not safe."

"It's fun actually."

"You've hitchhiked with David?" Barry hit his forehead with the palm of his hand. "What am I saying? Of course you have. You'll do anything with David."

I squeezed his knee. "Hitchhiking with David is like living a new adventure every day. We meet the most amazing people, and David always knows just what to say to help them." Sounding like David, I added, "It's an incredible experience for an actor's emotional memory."

"But he doesn't hitchhike when he goes out late at night?" Barry rejoined me on the bed.

I twisted my body to face him. "A car picks him up."

"Who's inside it?"

"The windows are shaded, so I can't tell."

"Where do they go?"

"Beats me."

"But you're dying to find out."

I nodded.

He said in a German accent, "Are you ready for my diagnosis?"

I laughed. "Go for it."

Sitting on his feet, Barry said, "I think David is like a matzah ball."

"Come again?"

He gestured like a mime. "Think about a bowl of chicken soup. It's warm, inviting, delicious, and good for you. But smack in the middle is the star, the sensation, the reason you bought it, the thing that makes it famous—the matzah ball. Now there are various techniques to eating matzah ball soup. Some people eat around the matzah ball, saving it for last. Other people break it up and eat a little piece with each spoonful of soup. But the best way to eat matzah ball soup is to eat the entire matzah ball first. Enjoy it. Savor it. Get it out of your system. Then you can go on to eat the real thing, what stays in your stomach, sustains you, supports you, and makes you healthy—the chicken soup."

I laughed again. "Can you translate that for a non-Jew?"

"Johnny, David isn't real." Looking out the dorm room window, Barry said, "He's a shooting star, looking beautiful, demanding everyone's attention, causing havoc in the sky, then disappearing."

"Tell that to my heart."

Barry whispered into my chest, "Get over David."

After I laughed, Barry took my hand. "Maybe we all need a David to help us grow a pair—and help us grow up."

As if seeing him for the first time, I asked, "Have you ever been in love, Barry?"

"I think so."

"Who's the lucky guy?"

Barry squeezed my hand. "*I* am."

We shared a laugh.

I said, "So you're the mysterious type, huh?"

Taking another sip of juice, he answered, "You don't want to hear about this now, Johnny."

"After I sat here spilling out my guts, the least I can do is be an ear for you."

He unleashed a warm smile that enveloped me like a hug. "Hang in there. I'll tell you someday, Falabella."

After my rehearsal with Barry, I headed back to my dorm room, excited about sharing my day with David before his mysterious nightly outing. As I approached the door to our room, I heard voices coming from inside. Upon opening the door, I found Terrence Falcon standing in front of it—zipping the fly of his black chinos. "Here's our Valère," Terrence said with a wide grin.

David hurried a sweatshirt over his head. "Jonathan, how did your rehearsal go with Barry?"

Still standing in the doorway, I replied, "Fine."

"When *we* took Acting I with Katzer, David and I did a scene from *A Few Good Men*." Terrence laughed. "We were not very good."

Pulling down the sweatshirt, then matting his hair back in place, David said, "Thanks for stopping by, Terrence. See you at rehearsal tomorrow night."

Terrence's small features tightened. Not thrilled by the brush-off, he picked up a used condom from David's bed and threw it into the trashcan. "Cleanliness is next to godliness." Then he kissed David on the lips. As he passed by me to leave, he said, "Take care of our boy."

After Terrence was gone, David picked up the towel on top of his bed and threw it into the laundry bin inside his closet. Then he made his bed.

I tried to process what had just happened. "So Terrence *is* your boyfriend."

David laughed. "Hardly."

In an effort to stop my body from shaking, I sat on my bed. "But you two have sex?"

"Occasionally." David stood at his bureau and checked himself in the mirror.

Feeling my heartbeat in my throat, I asked, "For how long?"

David shrugged. "Since freshman year."

"When you two roomed together?"

"Yeah, I guess."

Trying to hold back tears, I said, "And do you *guess* you had sex with your next roommate after Terrence?"

Confusion filled David's handsome face. "Jonathan, what's this about?"

Clenching my fists, I said, "I don't know. Why don't *you* tell *me* what this is about, David?"

David sat next to me on my bed and put his hand on my shoulder. "Is something wrong, Jonathan?"

I laughed bitterly. "Yes, David, obviously something is very wrong… with *me*."

He put his hand on my forehead. "Are you sick?"

Rising on shaky legs, I said, "Let's see, you had… and still have sex with your first roommate, and no doubt had and would still be in the sack with your second roommate had he not moved to LA. But your third roommate, that would be *me*, doesn't hit the jackpot with you. How is that, David?"

"Terrence and I have a past."

"Do *you and I* have a *present*, David? Do we have a *future*?" I tried to hold back the tears, but they flowed freely.

Looking concerned, David sat me back down next to him on the bed. Then he put his muscular arms around me and rested my back onto his warm chest. "You're my little Jonathan. You mean everything to me."

I tried but couldn't stop crying. "Everyone means everything to you, David. You want everybody to love you, and it all works out your way, because they *do*."

He squeezed me closer to him. "I care about you, Jonathan."

Pushing him away, I said, "Then why were you in bed with Terrence… and not with *me*?"

David took my hands in his. "Jonathan, we don't have that kind of relationship."

"Obviously." I pulled away and wiped my eyes with my sleeve. "I'm not as hot as Terrence. I'm just your little pity project."

He pulled me back into his arms, and I wept into his thick neck. "Jonathan, I coached you because I like you."

Moving away from him and sitting at my desk, I said, "In the same way you liked Sarah, Trudy, Jake, Clyde, Henry, and Mike? You advised them too. You cared about *them too*."

He stood behind me and wrapped his arms around me. From my peripheral vision, I could see his bulging biceps pressing against his sweatshirt. "Jonathan, why are you doing this?"

I pushed him away, then stood facing him. "I'm doing this because I don't know who you are."

Laughing, he replied, "We've lived together since the beginning of the term."

"We share a room and some dinners, but not much else."

"What are you talking about?"

There was no turning back. "I'm talking about your wink at Manuel in the bar. Is *he* part of your past too?"

David put his hands in his pants pockets. "I've known Manuel since I was a freshman."

"Have you had sex with him?"

"Jonathan, I don't want to hurt you."

I pushed him so hard David fell back flat onto his bed. "Then tell me where you go every night… and with whom."

Sitting up on the bed, David answered, "It's business."

"What *kind* of business?"

"You wouldn't understand."

"Try me." I knew I sounded like a jealous wife, but I didn't care. "I want to know."

Rubbing his smooth forehead, David said, "Manuel... I work for him."

"Doing what?"

He looked down at the floor. "He hooks me up with guys."

It felt like someone had punched me in the stomach. "You're a *hustler*?"

His eyes begged for affection. "It's not like that, Jonathan."

"Then what's it like?"

He took in a deep breath. "Manuel finds older, wealthy guys who are lonely and want companionship."

"From a hot, young guy?"

"They're nice guys, Jonathan. And very generous. Occasionally it's a new guy, but most of the times it's one of the guys I know. Lately it's been this one guy I've known since my freshman year." Rubbing his sweaty palms against the knees of his pants, David said, "They pick me up, take me out to dinner or to a movie. Then we go back to their place. We talk. They tell me their problems, their hopes, fears. It's great character study actually."

"And then you have sex?"

"Sometimes."

"How can you do that?"

"I look at it like an acting exercise." He shrugged his perfectly sculpted shoulders. "It's good money. And I'm helping those guys out."

"But you don't love them."

"You think every guy loves every person he has sex with?"

"Obviously *you* don't."

Sighing, he said, "This is why I didn't tell you. I knew you'd make a big deal about it."

"Having a prostitute for a roommate *is* a big deal, David."

"It's only a big deal because you're making it one."

"David, it sickens me to think of you in bed with those guys."

"Then don't think about it."

I felt as if I was trapped in an amusement park fun house, seeing David and the world like I'd never seen it before. "You really are Tartuffe—the great pretender, the con man."

He took in a deep breath. "I know you're trying to hurt me, Jonathan."

My mouth was on autopilot. "Hurt *you*! Of course everything is about *you*, David. But how about for once we talk about *me*?"

"What do you want to talk about?"

"For starters, I'd like to know what's wrong with me?"

"Nothing's wrong with you."

"I disagree, David. There must be something very wrong with me. Because you seem to have sex with everybody except me."

"Why are you doing this, Jonathan?"

"Because I want to know. Am I so decrepit you can't face the thought of being intimate with me? Do I need to pay you for services rendered?"

"Stop it, Jonathan."

"How much do you cost, David? Ten dollars? Fifty? A hundred? Two hundred? I could probably swing a hundred, max. Maybe we can barter. I'll do your laundry if you have sex with me with ten percent off your usual fee."

"Stop it!" David took in a deep breath. "Jonathan, please, sit here next to me."

As usual, I did as David requested. Fighting back tears, I looked into his handsome face.

David put his arm around me and rested his square jaw on my cheek. "Jonathan, there are some things you don't know about me."

"Obviously."

"I'm not wired the way you are… the way most people are. Something like sex isn't that important to me. But I want you to know one thing about me."

"What's that?"

"I love you in my way, and I always will."

"But—"

David rose, put on his scarf, and left.

I lay on my bed and cried myself to sleep.

CHAPTER FIVE

As usual I was asleep when David got back to our room, and he was out like a light when I woke in the morning. Looking out the bathroom window at the sun turning the mountains into a field of maize, I tried to process what I had found out the night before about David.

Sitting through my morning classes was an arduous task, as visions of David's secret life permeated my every thought.

When I got to the lab theater for my acting class, Barry met me at the entranceway.

The college's lab theater was in the adjacent building to the main theater. In a room painted black, risers seating a hundred people faced a small stage area.

Standing in the small lobby, Barry asked, "Ready to knock 'em dead, partner?"

I was so wrapped up in my drama with David, I forgot about my drama scene with Barry for acting class. "Barry, are we scheduled to do our scene for the grade *today*?"

"Very funny."

Pretending I had a mind, I said, "Yeah, I was joking."

Reading me like the phone book, Barry said, "You were serious! Johnny, how could you forget?"

I pressed my shoes into the thin carpeting. "I'm sorry, Barry. I've had a lot on my mind."

"Yeah, a lot of David. When are you going to grow a pair, Falabella, and get over Mr. Star?"

Putting thoughts of my roommate aside, I looked at my scene partner. "Barry, there's something… different about you."

"Yeah, *I'm* ready for our scene."

"I mean, the way you look." I checked him out from head to toe. "Barry, you're hot!"

Barry's face matched his hair. "It's for our scene. I gelled my hair, took off my glasses, and borrowed a suit from the costume loft."

I couldn't believe my eyes. "Barry, you're a butterfly!"

"I'm also completely blind. So during our scene, pull me back if I get too close to the edge of the stage." Barry pushed me toward the door to the next building. "Now go to the costume loft and get into your suit. Wash your face and comb your hair. Go over your lines. And remember everything we worked on in rehearsals." He pulled me back. "And forget about David for the next two hours. Katzer scheduled our scene first."

I looked at my watch. "I'll never make it in time. What are we going to do?"

"I'll tell Katzer your mother was in a car accident, and she wants to talk to you before she passes away. He won't think it's a good enough excuse to switch our scene from first to last, but it'll have to do unless I can come up with something better by the time I get inside." He slapped my behind. "Now go!"

I followed Barry's directions, then crept into the studio theater during one of the other scenes. Sitting next to Barry in a rear riser, I whispered, "How do I look?"

He replied sotto voce, "Like an out of breath college student."

"Oh my God!"

"What's wrong?"

"I didn't bring the props for our scene."

Barry pointed to a bag at his feet. "What would you do without me?"

"If Jonathan's mother isn't with the angels, can we see *Angels in America*?" Professor Katzer sat behind a desk in the center of the first riser. With digitalis in one hand and a red pen in the other, he asked his graduate assistant (a good-looking, muscular blond in skin-tight clothing) to bring him a glass of water while Barry and I set up on stage for our scene.

After our furniture and props were set, Barry and I did the scene better than ever. We worked together like a musician and his instrument. It was as if there was an imaginary ball of energy thrown back and forth between us. We found every nuance, emotion, and connection in our performances. When it came time for the kiss, our lips met and nearly exploded. We groped one another's bodies in a fit of passion. When the scene ended, we didn't want to let go of one another.

Wiping the sweat off his large forehead, then checking his pulse, Katzer said, "Jonathan, Barry, excellent work. You have come so far since your first in-class rehearsal. You each embodied your character beautifully. Your actions and objectives were crystal clear. I felt every emotion in the scene because *you* did. I believed every beat. Since you listened and reacted to one another, *I* listened and reacted as an audience member. You will both receive a well-deserved A grade." Katzer turned to his graduate assistant. "Austin, I have a pain shooting down my left arm accompanied by shortness of breath and nausea. Please take me to the nurse."

After Professor Katzer and Austin left, the students congratulated Barry and me, then emptied the lab theater.

As Barry packed up the props, I said, "Barry, you were amazing."

He smiled. "Right back at you, partner."

I gave him a hug. "Thank you for picking me as your scene partner." As we separated, I noticed a tear in his eye. "Are you still caught up in the emotions of the scene?"

"Yeah, that's it."

"You're lying."

"You're right. The truth is I can't see anything."

We shared a laugh.

"Do you need help getting back to your room?"

Barry held out his hand like a southern belle. "I do believe a gentleman caller has asked to walk me to the cotillion. Lead the way, Falabella."

Doing the blind man exercise in reverse, I led Barry back to the dorm. That evening we ate a congratulatory dinner in the cafeteria.

At that night's rehearsal, I kept my distance from David. When I was not needed for a particular scene, I sat on a sofa in the lobby going over my lines. Feeling a large, strong hand on my knee, I looked up to find Terrence Falcon sitting next to me with his enormous muscles bulging out of a cerulean T-shirt and button-fly jeans.

"You're doing a great job in the show, Jonathan."

"Thanks, Terrence."

He smiled. "You're really inventive. I like the physical bits you added to your character to make him lovelorn." His hand worked its way up my leg. "David's coaching has really paid off."

I shifted in my seat and Terrence's hand fell to his side.

"Going over your lines?" he asked.

I replied, "Yeah. We're off book starting tomorrow night."

Leaning back on the sofa and spreading his legs, Terrence said, "I was thinking maybe you and I could go over our lines tonight after rehearsal… in my dorm room." He looked down at the bulge between his legs. "We could help each other out."

"Thanks, but I study better on my own." I went back to my script.

Terrence put his gargantuan arm around me. "The worst thing you can do is stress over learning lines, buddy, believe me. Relax. Let it happen…

naturally." His dark eyes twinkled in the chandelier lighting. "I can show you some *tricks*."

"Thanks, Terrence, but I'll pass."

With a thick thumb, he guided my chin toward him. "We have a lot in common, Jonathan. We could be of… service to one another." His small facial features filled my vision. "I can give you… advice and help you navigate through life here." Terrence's tongue caressed his upper lip. "Guys like you, David, and me need to stick together." He pulled me in toward his huge pectoral muscles. "It's a good thing… sticking together."

Though Terrence was certainly attractive, thinking about him making love with David sickened me. I pushed him away and stood by the window, looking out at the black mountains reaching to the cobalt sky.

Terrence stood behind me and wrapped his powerful arms around my waist. His formidable groin pressed against my buttocks as he whispered in my ear, "Stop fighting it. I know you want this, Jonathan."

I struggled out of his grasp. "I told you, I'm not interested, Terrence."

"Then let's have a three-way hook up—you, me, and David."

"*Definitely* not interested."

Rage overtook his handsome face. "So you're only David's piece of ass. Nobody else can get any?"

"Go away, Terrence."

He threw me back against the wall, then wrenched my hands onto his massive chest. His breath smelled of whiskey. "You know you want me, Jonathan." Wrapping his arms around me, he grasped my buttocks hard. "Take a piece of the action before I lose interest." Before I could respond, he covered my mouth with his.

I tried unsuccessfully to escape his strong hold. When his kiss finally ended, I came up for air. Terrence unbuttoned his fly and pushed me to my knees. With his hand squeezing my throat, he unleashed his long, thick tool from his pants like a snake and forced my face toward it. I called for help until Terrence's hand cut off my ability to breathe.

As he was about to ram his weapon into my mouth, David burst through the lobby door. "What the hell?" David pushed Terrence away from me.

The darkness in front of my eyes brightened. I sucked in air and started to cough.

David kneeled at my side and put his arm around me. "Jonathan, are you all right?"

I nodded, taking more deep breaths.

David rose and approached Terrence.

Buttoning his fly, Terrence said with a laugh, "I had too much to drink during my break. The kid came on to me."

Not buying it, David grabbed Terrence by his T-shirt and came nose to nose with him. David's eyes looked like ignited charcoal. "I'm only going to say this once, Terrence. If you *ever* touch him again, I'll report you to the Dean. And if the Dean doesn't kick your ass out of here, I'll come after you, and I'll kill you. Do you understand me?"

Terrence wiggled free. "Okay, okay. Chill out, man. I was just trying to be friendly." He pulled his shirt back in place. "You can keep your little boy-toy all to yourself."

Helen, the student stage manager, called us back into the theater. During the rest of the rehearsal, David kept a watchful eye on me—and on Terrence.

When we got back to our room, I was still feeling shaky. David sensed it and reached out for me. We lay on his bed with my head on his chest.

I looked up into his perfect face. "I'm sorry for what I said to you last night."

He tweaked my nose. "You didn't say anything that wasn't true."

Tears brimmed in my eyes. "I didn't mean any of it."

David stroked my hair. "Yes you did, and it's okay."

I couldn't hold it back any longer, "David, I love you."

David froze like an icicle. "Don't say that."

I sat up and faced him. "Why not? You said you love *me*."

Backing away from me, he said, "Don't love me, Jonathan."

"Why?"

"Just don't. You… nobody should love me." He looked at his watch. "I have to go."

Flailing my arms like a ragdoll, I said, "Wait, David, please don't go."

"I'm sorry, Jonathan. I have to." David jumped out of bed, put on his scarf, and left.

For the next few weeks, I went to my classes with Barry, hit the gym and ate dinner with David, and stayed clear of Terrence in rehearsals. Alone at night in our room, David was affectionate with me, but only to a point. And like clockwork every night, at ten o'clock he grabbed his scarf and headed out the door.

One day in acting class, Professor Katzer worked with us on improvisations in the theme of relationships. Sitting in his usual spot, front row center, with Austin massaging Katzer's tiny shoulders, Katzer said,

"Jonathan and Barry, it looks like you two are last. Please go up on stage. Bring the sofa, end table, and easy chair downstage."

We did as we were told.

Checking his pulse, Katzer said, "I want you to pretend you are a couple."

This was fine with me since I felt so comfortable with Barry.

After asking Austin to bring a pillow for his back, Katzer continued his instructions. "You have both just gotten home from work. Barry, someone in Jonathan's office called you today to tell you he saw Jonathan out on a date with someone else. Let's see what happens." After putting a digitalis under his tongue, Katzer leaned back to observe our improvisation.

I entered first, flipped off my shoes, and took off my button-down shirt. Comfortable in my white T-shirt and slacks, I lay on the sofa and mimed watching television. Barry came in and tried various tactics to get my attention. When none of them worked, he stood in front of the make believe television set and told me what he had heard at work. At first I denied it, but as he probed, I finally admitted the truth.

Instead of accusing me, ranting and raving at me, or applying a guilt trip, Barry said with adoration in his eyes, "Jonathan, you are the only person I have ever loved. We are the perfect pair. When we're together, I feel alive. When we aren't, I'm… in limbo." Barry sat next to me on the sofa and took my hand. "It may be fun and exciting to be with someone else, but it's not right for you. *I'm* right for you. And you're right for *me*. We fit together perfectly. This… us… here together, this is the real thing. This is love. This is happiness." He wrapped his arms around me, took my face in his hands, and kissed me like his life depended on it. His sugary scent filled my nose. His goofy face and warm breath felt like home.

As Barry's glasses slid down his nose onto mine, Professor Katzer said, "Excellent work, you two. Your tactics were crystal clear. Great work with your bodies and voices as well. I liked how each moment propelled into the next." Motioning for Austin to dab water on his wrists, Katzer said, "Barry, I totally believed you were in love with Jonathan. And Jonathan, good work, but it didn't seem as personal for you. Think about the cognitive dissonance and duplicity of someone who is a fool for love, unable to stop himself from making a huge mistake and possibly losing his soul mate. How would you feel if that were *you*? Are you two boys working together for the next class scene?"

I must have been daydreaming about David in class, because doing a second scene was news to me. Since everyone else in the class was already paired up, I prayed Barry was on it.

I thanked the heavens when Barry said, "Jonathan and I are working together on a scene from *Love! Valour! Compassion*! We're playing a gay couple."

"Great play," Katzer said, motioning for a compress to be placed on his forehead.

One of the other students in the class asked, "Professor, aren't there any great plays about straight people?"

"Yes, but our library is out of them." Katzer winked at Barry. "See everyone next class. And don't stomp out of here like a herd of buffalo. It makes my angina flare up."

As the students left, Barry squeezed my shoulder. "Good job, partner."

"Thanks for saving me again, Barry."

"No problem." As we walked back to our seats, Barry looked more excited than a televangelist waving his tax-exempt corporation certificate. "I picked a great scene, full of humor, drama, and romance."

"Will you look hot again?"

Picking up his book bag, Barry said before leaving, "You'll have to wait and see, Falabella."

With everyone else gone from the lab theater, I noticed Professor Katzer writing notes at his makeshift desk. I stood in front of him. "Thank you for the nice words today, professor."

He looked up at me. "Thank you for the fine improv performance, Jonathan."

"The emotions hit home for me. I think they did for Barry too."

"So I noticed." Katzer motioned for me to sit next to him on the riser. Rubbing his small chest, he said, "Jonathan, believe it or not, I can still remember being your age and in college."

I imagined it. "You must have been a phenomenal actor, professor."

He waved me away like smoke. "Stop."

"Sorry."

Sliding to the edge of his seat, he said, "*But* since you brought it up, I played all the classics—Puck, Ariel, the clowns, and quite a few contemporary roles as well." He laughed. "Well, contemporary a million years ago, when I was young."

"You're still pretty spry, professor. It was amazing watching you demonstrate how to be an owl."

"That's what I am now, a wise old owl, sharing what I know with my students. So may I give you a bit of advice?"

"Of course, professor."

"Jonathan, you're going through college like an astronomer looking into a telescope… focusing on one star. Sure, the star's amazing, but there's a whole galaxy out there of wonderful stars for you to gaze at. And there's one special star shining into your own window."

I blushed. "I think I understand what you mean, professor."

"Good. At least one of my students learned something today."

"Professor, did you look at a lot of stars when you were in college?"

He laughed. "You have no idea." Winking at me, he added, "But I'm glad I wished on only one—for the last forty-five years."

I smiled. "I'm going to miss you when this class… and our show… end."

"Didn't you take Acting II with me next semester?"

I smacked my forehead. "Is registration going on so soon?"

Sighing, he replied, "It was last week. You received a letter from Registration, and I announced it in class. I also overheard Barry remind you about it…." He added with a smirk, "…during my lecture on the importance of actors *listening* to one another on stage."

"Thank you, professor. I'll hurry over to Registration now."

"Don't run, Jonathan! It makes my heart murmur."

"Sorry, professor. See you next class."

I left the lab theater and headed to the Registration building. As I walked across campus, I gazed at the mountaintops disappearing into the white fluffy clouds, forming vanilla ice cream cones.

When I got to the Registration Office, I found the staff members walking from cubicle to cubicle like mice in a maze. After standing in line for twenty minutes, I stood in front of a large African American woman wearing a leopard sari and matching turban with enormous gold earrings dangling from her ears. "May I help you?"

I shuffled from foot to foot. "I missed freshman registration last week, and I need to register for next semester."

The woman's dark eyes met mine. "I would have made registering a priority."

"I know. I'm sorry."

"You realize many of the classes you need will be full?"

Feeling like a criminal being read my rights, I said, "Can you please check them for me?"

"What classes do you need?"

I opened a college catalog sitting on the counter and read from the second semester listing on the Theater Major page. "Theater History II, Acting II, Voice Production II, English Literature II, Modern Dance, and General Science."

She laughed. "And you think there are still open seats in all those classes?"

I swallowed hard. "I can hope."

Shaking her head, she ran her long blood-red nails across her computer keyboard. "What's your name?"

"My stage name or my real name?"

She raised her eyes to the fluorescent light above her head. "Since we've barred the autograph hounds from entering the building today, let's start with your real name."

"Jonathan Falabella."

She froze like her computer screen. "What's your stage name?"

"Jonathan Bello."

The woman's hard expression melted like ice in spring. "I'm Selma. Jake's girlfriend."

I smiled. "Pleased to meet you, Selma."

She extended her hand. "And I am pleased to meet *you*, Jonathan." After we shook hands, she said, "Jake told me about the advice he received from you and your friend David when he gave you a ride back to the college." She giggled. "You two boys are wise beyond your years."

"I hope we didn't meddle too much in Jake's personal life."

Selma let out a hearty laugh. "Jake may be a fine worker in the maintenance department, but he needed some meddling in the romance department." She raised her hand to reveal a diamond ring. "Thanks to your advice, Jake and I are engaged."

"Congratulations, Selma! Jake is a terrific guy."

"He sure is. And *you* are pretty terrific too. You should write for a newspaper advice column."

"My roommate David Star gave Jake the romance tips."

"How did David learn so much about relationships?"

I felt the blood rushing to my head. Not wanting to shock her, I kept quiet about David's nightlife. "David likes helping people."

"Let's see if I can help *you*." Moving her nails across her computer keyboard like lightning, Selma said, "Well, Jonathan, it looks like all of your classes are full."

"I was afraid of that."

Selma continued typing, then hit the print button.

As she handed me the printed paper, I asked, "What's this?"

"Your schedule for next semester."

"But you just said my classes were all full."

She winked. "I squeezed you in."

"Selma, thank you!"

She leaned over and whispered in my ear, "One good turn deserves another."

CHAPTER SIX

THAT EVENING over dinner in our room, I told David my good news about Jake and Selma, and my spring semester schedule. After taking the last bite of his fillet of sole almandine, scalloped potatoes, and creamed spinach with shiitake mushrooms, David put on his leather jacket and gold and maroon scarf. "Let's go."

"Where?"

David was out the door. I grabbed my jacket and scarf and followed him to the entrance of the college. The sun had begun its descent, painting swirls of lavender, vermillion, and amber onto the blue canvas sky.

I caught up to David and asked, "Are we hitchhiking somewhere?"

Raising his palms to the heavens, he answered, "Is there a better way to travel?"

When we arrived at the gates to the college, David stuck out his thick thumb and unleashed his winning smile. A car slowed down in front of us but David waved it forward.

"David, why'd you do *that*?"

"Your story about Selma inspired me. I want to check in on our *other* drivers."

Zipping up my jacket, I replied, "So we're going to wait here all night hoping someone we know drives by?"

"Not all night," David said. "Just a few more minutes."

A car stopped in front of us.

David opened the door to the station wagon, hopped into the front, and beckoned me to join him inside. After I shut the door behind me, I said hello to Sarah Hampton, sitting behind the wheel. Had it not been for Sarah's car and housedress, I would not have recognized her. Sarah's short, straight blonde hair was combed into waves. The bags under her eyes and haggard look on her face were replaced by a radiant glow.

"Are you two boys movie stars yet?" Sarah asked with a smile.

David replied, "Not yet, but we are starring in the college play the next two weekends."

"If I can get a sitter, I'll come see it."

Pressing his firm shoulder against hers, David said, "We'll look for you after each performance."

Sarah looked happier than a right-wing politician voting on tax cuts for corporations. "I feel honored."

"You're special to us, Sarah." David squeezed my knee.

Picking up my cue, I replied, "I'll wave to you at the curtain call, Sarah."

She laughed joyously. "I'd love that!"

David said, "We were waiting for you, Sarah."

Sarah did a double take. "How did you know I'd be driving by the college and passing the movie theater?"

"At our last excursion together, you said you were picking up your kids from scouts. I guessed you'd be doing the same thing at the same day and time each week."

She laughed. "That's me, all right. Always on the mom schedule."

"How are the paper dolls coming, Sarah?" David nudged my side.

Taking the hint, I said, "We'd love to see your work."

"My *work*? They're only paper dolls."

David batted his long eyelashes. "But they're *your* paper dolls, Sarah. And I have the feeling you're a terrific artist."

Sarah looked like a princess at a ball. "You two are so sweet!"

"So how's it going, Sarah?" David asked on the edge of his seat.

Sarah replied, "I started by creating a paper doll of my daughter with separate cut-outs for her clothes. She loved them. Then I did the same for my son. He loved them too. So I moved on to other family members and neighbors. It's just a hobby, but everyone seems to like them. My neighbor, Morty, is a security guard at an art gallery in the next town, and he said they're really good."

David replied, "See? Someone in the business recognized your talent. I knew you had something special, Sarah."

Using the improvisation skills I learned from Professor Katzer, I said, "Sarah, you should do paper dolls of celebrities. Draw their faces and figures with different tabbed wardrobe pieces for swimwear, casual outings, dress up, and formal wear."

"That sounds like fun," Sarah said.

David said with twinkling eyes, "I bet each celebrity you draw will want one. You'll become so big, they'll have you on the TV talk shows."

Sarah pulled in front of the movie theater. "You two boys inspire me!"

David said, "Get to work on those drawings, Sarah. Bring them to the theater."

"We can't wait to see them," I added.

"I will."

"Good luck, Sarah," David and I said in unison as we got out of the car and shut the door behind us.

When we got to the ticket window, I couldn't believe my eyes. Trudy Ingham sat behind the ticket counter like a movie starlet waiting for her close-up. Trudy's dirty blonde ponytail was replaced by a platinum bun sprouting ringlets like waterfalls down the sides of her powdered face. Her beady eyes were transformed into wide radiance, peeking out under flowing eyelashes, blue mascara, and brown eyeliner. Rosy cheeks, red lipstick, and silver nails completed the picture. A skintight pink angora replaced Trudy's frumpy brown sweater.

"Trudy!" David's giant pectoral muscles pressed against his designer polo shirt. "You look amazing."

She cocked her head as if toward the camera. "Hi, David."

After David kicked my shin, I said, "Trudy, you look like a movie star."

Trudy replied, "I registered for classes at the college next semester. I'll be a Theater major like you guys." She blew a gum bubble.

"Good for you," David said.

I chimed in. "Welcome to the department, Trudy."

David pointed above his dark mane. "The name Trudy Ingham will be up in lights before you know it."

"That's the plan," Trudy said, popping her bubble.

David said with a winning smile, "Until we can see a Trudy Ingham film, Jonathan and I will have to settle for what's playing tonight. Two tickets please."

Trudy blew another bubble as she took the money, then passed David the tickets. "See you guys soon."

"You got it, Trudy."

Sitting in the last row during the coming attractions, I said, "You really helped Selma, Sarah, and Trudy, David."

"As actors, it's important for us to cultivate our audience base, Jonathan."

As the movie began, I rested my head on David's warm shoulder, and he kissed my forehead. Though I relished my time with David, as always, I was surprised to find myself wondering what Barry would think about what David and I were doing, and the people we encountered. I made a mental note to contact Barry about starting our new scene rehearsals for acting class.

The film was a terrible war movie. David studied every frame, whispering in my ear his critique of each actor's performance. One of the supporting actors reminded me of Barry, which made me think about Barry's heartfelt performance in our acting class scene and improvisation.

When the movie was finally over, David kissed me on the lips and filled my nostrils with his musky scent. "You're my favorite date, Jonathan."

I kissed him back, enjoying his warm, moist lips, glad to be rated higher than Terrence and David's elderly clients. As we exited the theater, after waving good-bye to Trudy, David took my hand. "Let's go to the club."

I froze like a car windshield in February. "David, I don't want to go in there again."

"Trust me, Jonathan."

Thinking about David's pimp and clients, I said, "It's hard for me to think about you doing… what you do."

"I won't be *doing* anything except looking around. Come on."

Following David like a lapdog, I heard Barry's voice in my head say, "Grow a pair, Falabella."

As we entered the bar, David nodded to Manuel and the two of them spoke sotto voce.

With his bald head shining in the overhead lighting, Manuel's biceps bulged as he filled two glasses with tap beer. Handing me one of them, he said, "Jonathan, have you decided to work at the club?"

Before I could reply, David took his beer and said, "Jonathan doesn't need to work for you, Manuel. He's going to be a big star."

"Like you, David?" Manuel asked with a sneer.

"You'll see." David looked around the room, then led me to a table where young Henry Wooley and Mike Bodine sat talking.

I cleared my throat. "Hello, Mike. Hi, Henry. Do you remember us?"

Their faces beamed like car headlights.

"Jonathan and David!" Henry called out.

"Please, join us." Mike pulled out two chairs and we sat.

David smiled. "You two guys playing nice together?"

"We're doing more than that. I'm living with Mike and his wife," Henry said. "I taught them how to make tacos."

"Henry's staying with us until he figures things out," Mike explained.

"I'm sleeping in Bobby's room." Henry winked. "I like Bobby's old magazines."

Grateful to see Henry was drinking a soda, I asked, "What are you two doing in here?"

Mike took a sip of his beer. "Henry wanted to come. I gave him my permission, but only if I could tag along, and only if we could leave at a decent hour."

Henry smiled. "We'll see about the leaving early part."

Squeezing the boy's shoulder, David said, "Stick with Mike. He's *good* people, and that's all that matters."

"I know." Henry ran a hand through his shining blond hair. "Thanks to Mike's tutoring, I'm doing really good in school."

I said, "I think you are doing *well* in school."

Henry nodded. "I'm doing that too."

After David and I invited them to our upcoming play on campus, to Henry's dismay we called it a night, and Mike drove David and me back to the college. As we got out of Mike's car, he whispered to David, "Henry is what I needed."

David whispered back, "Looks to me like you're what *Henry* needed."

As David and I walked back to the dormitory, the sky and mountains surrounded us like a gray blanket. I put my arm through his and enjoyed the feeling of David's strong forearm resting against mine. "You're amazing, David."

He looked surprised.

"You transformed those people's lives."

"No, I didn't. *They* did." David said, "Do you think Mike and Henry will come to our show?"

"I hope so."

"Too bad we didn't run into Clyde outside the bar. I hoped he would beg a guy not to go inside, fall in love with him, then take the guy to Sweden to register as domestic partners."

We shared a laugh.

"David, do you want to get married someday if it's legal?"

"No."

I did a double take. "That was fast."

"Jonathan, I watched my parents destroy one another. I don't want any part of that."

"But what if you fall in love?"

"Love and marriage have nothing to do with one another."

"There are plenty of married people in love."

"Maybe, but not with each other."

After we got back to our room, I thought about what Barry said during our improvisation in acting class. "David, wouldn't it be amazing to share a home, family, and life with the person you love? I want that."

"Then I hope you get it." David kissed me. "I have to go."

As I lay in bed remembering our amazing night, and trying to put the pieces of David together like a mystery puzzle, I heard Barry's voice in my head, "You'll find out, Falabella."

The next week was Tech Week, meaning we rehearsed the play each night in the theater with props, costumes, sets, lighting, sound, and makeup. Given the propensity for technical things to go wrong during Tech Week, and the high emotional level of everyone involved, Professor Katzer was popping digitalis like popcorn.

We all missed our classes, gym workouts, and even some meals, and slept during the day like vampires, saving every ounce of energy for the evenings.

David told me to keep hydrated, stay focused during my scenes, and go over my lines or take naps when the lighting crew called breaks so they could fix the lighting—sometimes well into the night. It was good advice that helped get me through the challenging week.

David was like a warrior going to battle, practicing his stage movements, working out his emotional arc in each scene, timing his costume changes, and checking his placement in the light onstage. Nothing seemed to matter to him except the show and his performance.

During our breaks between scenes, Terrence looked at me like a priest scouting a new altar boy. I kept my distance and concentrated on the show.

Barry and the rest of the prop crew worked hard to finish, repair, set, and reset the period furniture and props. On the rare occasions when he and I had a break at the same time, we met in the green room and rehearsed our new scene for acting class. Barry and I played longtime lovers having a lovers' spat and making up. Since I had grown so close to Barry, it was easy for us to play the scene. We were quite comfortable with one another and enjoyed an easygoing rapport. It was also fine for us to critique one another's performances and to offer each other suggestions on how to play the scene more realistically. When we kissed in the scene, it seemed natural and comfortable.

After we rehearsed the scene a number of times, Barry, clad in his usual flannel shirt (yellow and brown) and jeans, pushed his glasses up the bridge of his nose. "I'm bushed, Falabella."

"Me too." Sitting on the greenroom floor, I rested my back against his. "Katzer will love the scene."

"Then he'll call for an ambulance."

We shared a tired laugh.

"My aches and pains have aches and pains," Barry said rubbing his hands.

Peering into the backstage area, I said yawning, "It looks like we'll be here all night. Professor Gero and Professor Katzer are battling it out over the lighting for the scene changes. Poor Jacob has to keep changing the light cues." Leaning further against Barry, I added, "Professor Gero has quite a temper."

Barry said, "We get Gero as sophomores for Tech Theater. Assuming you remember to register for fall semester."

I poked his side. Then looking down at my frilly blue satin jacket and pants, I said, "I hear Professor Canniby is nice for Costuming."

"That's Junior year. We may not live that long." Barry closed his eyes. Then hearing my stomach growl, Barry said, "You want me to go to my room and get you a blintz?"

"I'm too tired to eat." Thinking about my latest excursion into town with David, I asked, "Barry, have you ever been to the gay bar in town?"

As he faced me, Barry's eyes opened like rockets. "Johnny, I have a confession to make." He bit his knuckles and shrieked, "I'm a heterosexual."

I pushed him away.

"Why would I go to a gay bar, Johnny? I'm a theater major, surrounded by dozens of gay guys... and the girls who love them."

"I went with David."

Barry groaned. "Did everyone at the bar fall at David's feet?"

"It wasn't like that."

He rested his leg over mine. "What was it like?"

Happy to get the chance to talk about it, I said, "David and I talked and danced, and he brought together this homeless gay kid with a guy who lost his gay son."

Barry sneered. "Give David Star the Purple Heart."

"Barry, why don't you like David?"

"Everybody likes David."

"But *you* don't."

"Johnny, David's like a fancy box with a pretty pink bow. What's outside is nice to look at, but when you open the box a plastic snake pops out."

"That's not fair."

Barry took my head in his hands. "David's breaking your heart, Johnny. And it's *not fair* to the person who will have to help you repair it."

"You don't understand, Barry."

"I understand more than you think." Barry rose and rejoined the prop crew.

Somehow we all survived tech week. Thanks to theater magic, and our naps during the day, our energy level was boundless on opening night, and the show was a smash. Even the torrential rain outside (as always on firsts for me) couldn't put a damper on the energy and power onstage. The characters were all strong and believable, and the comic timing was slick. The audience was with us at each beat, laughing in all the right places and remaining quiet at the appropriate times. Our hell week for tech paid off since every set, lighting, prop, sound, and costume cue went off without a hitch, as our professors wept in each other's arms.

At the curtain call, we were elated with the audience's generous cheers and applause. I was shocked when the level of applause rose at my bow, and not surprised at all when the audience gave the star of our show a standing ovation.

I was disappointed my parents weren't able to make the trip due to my dad's work schedule. However, after the show David and I were happy to be greeted at the stage door by our *fans*. Jake patted our backs proudly. Selma gave us a beautiful bouquet of flowers. Henry asked for our autographs on his program, happily announcing he was "letting Mike look into adopting" him. Trudy shared her excitement about joining the department next semester. Finally, Sarah gifted us with an original Sarah Hampton paper doll book of famous stage actors—including David and me!

After they left, I said, "That was amazing!"

David replied, "It sure was. Great show tonight." He kissed my cheek. "See you in the morning, Jonathan."

My jaw dropped to my makeup case. "You're going to work *tonight*?"

"That's the plan. Don't stay up too late."

Though the rain had stopped, I stared after David's back, like someone caught in a hurricane.

Barry came out of the stage door. "Going to the cast party at the student center, Falabella?"

With tears brimming my eyes, I replied, "I think I'll head to my room."

"Want some company?"

"Thanks, Barry, but I'm wiped out."

Looking at David in the distance, Barry said, "So I see." He took my hand in his. "You were terrific tonight, Johnny. I'm so proud of you." He squeezed my hand and was gone.

The rest of the performances the first weekend went just as well. After the Sunday matinee, I made it back to our room before David. Standing in our bathroom, I washed the makeup off my face and heard David enter our room with someone else. With the bathroom door slightly ajar, I could see and hear what was going on in our room.

The other man looked like an older version of David, however, his face had deep lines and his eyes were bloodshot and void of emotion. Wearing a Native American ribbon shirt, jeans, and a brown leather jacket with his hair pulled back in a long ponytail, the man seemed out of place.

David took off his scarf and leather jacket, then tossed them onto his bed. "Can I take your coat, Dad?"

The man shook his head no.

"Here, have a seat." David offered his father his desk chair.

"I can't stay long," the man said in a hoarse voice. "Your mother will worry."

David asked, "Did you like the show, Dad?"

The man nodded. "You had a lot of lines to learn."

David smiled tensely. "Yeah."

"I noticed that right off."

"Thanks for coming, Dad."

"I've seen every one of your shows, David. Your mother would be here too if she could stand the long drive. I don't know if you appreciate that."

"I do." David moved to his bureau. "Would you like something to drink, Dad?" He opened a drawer. "I have wine and juice."

"No." His father looked around the room. "This is a nice room."

"Is this the first time you've seen it?"

"Over three years and you never invited me. So today I invited myself."

"Well, here it is."

"You live pretty well here, David."

Wearing a designer purple polo shirt, David shrugged his large shoulders. "I guess so."

Looking out the window at the mountains, his father said, "You have a nice view. I saw the cafeteria when I walked up here." He pressed down on the bed. "Firm bed."

"I'm happy here, Dad."

As if asking for the first time, his father said, "Do you ever think about your mother and me?"

"Of course I do. All the time."

Gesturing around the room, his father said, "While you live here, do you ever think about your mother and me in our little house?"

David's chest caved in like an avalanche. "Is Mom okay?"

"How can she be okay? She never hears from her son. It makes her cry at night."

"I'll come visit after the show closes, I promise."

"The show comes first, then your mother." His father let out a sad laugh.

"I've been really busy."

"I know."

"Dad, did you get the money I sent you?"

The man nodded. "It all went for your mother's operation. And you didn't even visit her in the hospital."

Sounding like a little boy, David said, "I'm sorry, Dad. Is Mom going to be okay?"

"For now. The doctor said the cancer could come back."

"Does she feel okay?"

"She sleeps a lot."

David opened another bureau drawer and handed his father a wad of cash. "Take this, Dad. It's all I've got right now."

His father pocketed the money. "You're here on a scholarship. You work at the bar. This isn't all you have, David."

David replied, "It is, Dad, I swear. I'll get you more as soon as I have it."

He stood over David. "After giving birth to you, your mother couldn't have any more children. Did she ever tell you that?"

David slowly nodded as if in a time warp.

"When you came out of her it messed something up inside her. I wonder if it messed something up inside you too?"

"What do you mean, Dad?"

"There's something wrong with you, David. You don't feel things like other people. You're cold. And arrogant too. The whole world revolves around David Citlali." He threw his play program on the bed. "Since you turned your back on your heritage and your family name, I guess it is David Star now." His face was inches away from David's. "You believe all that applause, but I know what those people clapping don't know. You're a fraud… and a phony. Your mother would die if she knew what you do with those men in that bar. My father would turn over in his grave."

David sat on his bed, staring straight ahead as if hypnotized by a magician.

"I'm dishonored and disgusted to call you my son. You spit on the Citlali name."

Tears streamed down David's face. As if a walking zombie, David went back to his bureau and handed his father a smaller wad of cash. He said in a shaky voice, "This is everything I have."

After pocketing the money, his father said, "You bring shame to our family, David. The wrong person in our family got sick. Why was it your mother? It should have been you." David's father shook his head and walked out of the room.

As if hit by lightning, David's whole body writhed. I ran out of the bathroom, sat next to him on the bed, and rested his head on my chest. As David wept, I ran my hands through his thick dark hair. I said what my heart felt, "I love you, David."

David pushed me away, and I toppled onto the floor. "Don't love me, Jonathan. Didn't you hear my father? I'm unlovable. I'm toxic!"

Looking up at him, I said, "That's your father's reality, not yours."

David's eyes were wild. "He's right, Jonathan. I'm inhuman."

Rising to my feet, I said, "Nobody's inhuman."

"I am." He grabbed my arms. "I can't feel anything, Jonathan. I'm a stone."

I wrapped my arms around him. "That's not true. You're a good person, David. Everyone knows that."

He laughed bitterly. "Not everyone."

"*I* know it, David. You said everyone's special. *You're* special, and I love you."

He pushed me away harder and screamed, "Don't love me, Jonathan. You'll end up hurt… like my mother."

I held on to his hands. "You deserve to be loved, David. You deserve more than Manuel's sex for pay or buddy sex with Terrence." I begged him. "Please, David. Please let me love you. Let me *show* you how much I love you."

He wept again. "No, Jonathan. I can't."

I wrapped his arms around my waist and clasped mine around his shoulders. "Love me, David. Please, love me." Leaning him back onto his bed, I lay on top of David and kissed his tears.

"I can't do this, Jonathan."

"Yes, you can, David. Let yourself love me." I kissed his lips. "Make love with me, David."

His eyes met mine. "Is this really what you want?"

"I want *you*, David." I slowly took off David's clothes; then he took off mine. Lying in bed naked next to one another, I said, "David, I'm so glad my first time is going to be with you."

David said, "I can't do what you want me to do, Jonathan."

"I just want you to love me."

"Love and sex are two different things for me."

"It doesn't have to be that way, David."

I wrapped my arms and legs around David as if we were glued together. Then I ran my hands along his incredibly muscular shoulders, back, biceps, pectorals, and abdominals.

David kissed my forehead, nose, mouth, chin, and neck. He breathed into my ears. His tongue encircled my nipples, abdominals, and navel. After he kissed me on the lips, he said pensively, "Jonathan, are you sure this is what you want?"

I kissed him and nodded.

David took me inside his mouth and in seconds I cried out in ecstasy. Then he rose from the bed, reached into his bureau drawer, and put on a condom covered with lubricant. After he lay on top of me, I screamed as he entered me. The pain soon turned to pleasure as he kissed me again and again in perfect timing with each thrust. I held on to his powerful thighs and buttocks, caressing them with each pounding. Then David took me in his hand. As we both climaxed, we held on to one another like shipwrecked men in a storm.

Lying in one another's arms, I said, "Let's stay like this forever, David."

He kissed my lips and laughed. "My little Jonathan." Then he rose from the bed and started to get dressed.

"David, please don't go out tonight."

With a look of regret on his handsome face, he said, "I have to go, Jonathan."

I reached out for him. "Please stay with me. Just for an hour."

"I can't. I warned you, Jonathan." And David left.

Lying back in bed, I heard Barry's voice say, "David's breaking your heart, Johnny. And it's not fair to the person who will have to help you repair it."

CHAPTER SEVEN

I was busy the next week with classes, scene rehearsals with Barry, and our final weekend of play performances. With each performance the show became even tighter and more professional. We were all proud of what we had created, including Professor Katzer, who miraculously survived the play's run without a cardiac episode.

The closing night party was held at Ayisha (Mariane) and Ling Chow's (her understudy) house. Both coming from money, the two best friends lived in a huge apartment in town with cathedral ceilings, a large sitting room with a veranda, an eat-in kitchen, and two bedrooms—each with its own fireplace.

After the show ended, I went back to my room to change into my (rather David's) button down pumpkin-colored shirt, black slacks, and a white ribbed sweater. By the time I arrived, the party was in full swing with rock music blasting from large speakers in the sitting room. The kitchen table was stocked with hero sandwiches, beer, wine, and chips. The bedrooms sported "Do Not Disturb" signs dangling from their closed doors. I looked around for David, but couldn't find him through the haze of bodies and smoke.

"Johnny, you finally got here." I turned to find Barry on the floor of the sitting room, resting his back against the white wall trimmed with fancy gold molding.

Sitting next to him, I said, "Wild party, huh?"

"I've seen wilder."

"Where?"

"My bar mitzvah. My mother made me dance with my Aunt Sophie. The woman nearly suffocated me with her bosoms."

We shared a laugh.

He asked, "Are you sorry the show is over?"

I thought about it. "It was an amazing experience I'll never forget. But I'm ready to move on to something else."

Barry grinned. "Are you talking about David or the play?"

Taking his hand, I said, "Barry, I've been dying to tell you something, but we've been so busy I haven't had the chance."

"You're in love with me?"

I hit his knee. "Stop kidding. This is serious."

He leaned forward. "What is it?"

Feeling like a teenage girl on her princess phone, I said, "Last week after the matinee, David and I made love!"

Barry looked away. "Congratulations, Johnny. I know that's what you wanted."

I leaned my shoulder against his. "Barry, it was amazing. I told David I love him."

Staring down at the Oriental rug, Barry said, "Did David say he loves you too?"

Thinking back, I replied, "No, but he called me his 'little Jonathan.'"

"Sweet." Barry looked at the bedroom door nearest us.

"Why aren't you looking at me?"

Pushing his glasses up the bridge of his nose, Barry answered, "Johnny, it's too loud and smoky in here. Let's go back to my room for some blintzes."

"I want to find David. Have you seen him?"

Barry picked at a button on his blue flannel shirt. "No, I haven't."

Looking into his eyes, I said, "You're lying. Where's David?"

He rose and lifted me to my feet. "Let's get out of here before our lungs and ears go on strike."

I pulled away. "I'm not leaving until I find David."

"Johnny, wait."

I searched the sitting room, veranda, and kitchen with Barry following me like an antigay politician in a public bathroom. Next, I peeked into the bathroom. Finally, I knocked on the first bedroom door.

"Johnny, you might disturb Ayisha's parents."

"Ayisha's parents live in Hawaii."

Ling Chow answered the door with a sheet wrapped around her. I looked inside the room and saw Ayisha and Jacob (our show's lighting crew head) in bed waiting for her.

"Sorry," I said, then moved on to the next bedroom.

After I knocked on that door, Barry took me by the shoulders. "David obviously didn't come to the party. Let's go back to your room and rehearse our scene for acting class."

The door opened and David, wearing only red briefs, scratched his washboard abs. "Jonathan, is everything okay?"

I looked past him and saw Terrence lying naked on the bed with the sheet up to his waist.

The room spun around like a top.

Barry put his arm around me. "Let's go, Johnny."

I stood like a statue. "David, how could you do this?"

Terrence leaned back on his elbows, causing his pectoral muscles to expand like melons. "Come back to bed, David."

As if a mourner paying his respects at a funeral, David said, "I told you not to love me, Jonathan."

"You were right. I wish I never loved you, David. I wish I never met you." I started hyperventilating.

"Jonathan—"

Barry led me out of the party.

When Barry and I got back to my room, I fell onto my bed, still in shock. "How can I be so stupid? I think about him every minute of every day. I worry about him. Care about him. Love him. I let David take my virginity!" Looking up at Barry sitting next to me on the bed, I said, "What's wrong with me, Barry?"

He took my hand. "Johnny, you're not the first person in the world to fall in love with someone."

Tears streamed down my face like waterfalls. "But how stupid was I to fall in love with someone who doesn't love me back?"

Barry smirked. "It happens all the time. I should know."

I looked into Barry's loving eyes and suddenly everything clicked in my head. It felt like watching my life as a movie in front of me. "Barry, oh my God, I've been so stupid."

"Johnny, I—"

Throwing my arms around Barry's neck, I pressed him close to me and covered his mouth with mine.

Coming up for air, Barry said, "Johnny, let's talk about this."

Covering his face with kisses, I said, "We've talked so much, Barry. I don't want to talk anymore." I unbuttoned his shirt and caressed his lean, hard chest. "Do you love me, Barry?"

"Johnny, we—"

"Do you want to be with me? Only with me? Show me, Barry. Show me how much you love me." I pulled at his belt.

Barry held my wrists. "Johnny, stop!" After he finally got my attention, Barry said, "Johnny, I fell in love with you when I first saw you at the auditions."

Nuzzling my head into his chest, I said, "Prove it, Barry."

He grasped my arms tighter. "But I don't want to be David's sloppy seconds."

"You aren't. I want to be with you. Now."

"We'll make love one day, Johnny."

"When?"

He pushed his glasses up the bridge of his nose. "When instead of thinking about David, you're thinking about *me*." Barry gently pushed me back onto the bed and covered me with the blanket. "Think about that as you fall asleep, Johnny." He kissed my forehead. "Pleasant dreams." Barry shut off the light and left the room.

During the next week, I felt like a patient on anesthesia. Barry and I pretended my night of desperation for him never happened. I woke, ate, worked out, went to my classes, rehearsed my scene with Barry, ate, and went to bed as if caught in an invisible bubble. I touched no one, and no one touched me. Like David, I was an island unto myself.

As usual David was out during the nights and asleep early mornings. Since I went to the gym on my own and ate dinner with Barry in the cafeteria, I didn't speak with David the entire week.

Auditions for our next production, *Death of a Salesman*, were scheduled in the theater the following evening. The director, Professor of Directing Bruce Beamer, had arranged for two professional actors, married in real life, to play the leading roles of Willy and Linda Loman as guest artists. His plan was for students to play all the other roles. It was automatically assumed by all of the students that David and Terrence would be cast in the pivotal roles of Willy and Linda's adult sons, Biff and Happy. However, Barry convinced me to audition.

So the afternoon of auditions, Barry and I met in his dorm room to practice the Biff and Happy scenes from the play. After hours of character analysis, script dissection, improvisations, and reading from the play, Barry threw down his script and fell back onto his bed. "We're ready, Falabella."

Standing over him, I said, "Are you sure?"

Sitting up, he said, "I'm sure."

"It doesn't matter anyway. Beamer has probably precast David and Terrence in the roles." I flailed my arms like a penguin. "Still, this is a classic play, Barry, and I want to do it justice. *Everybody* will be auditioning. If we are going to have any chance at all of getting—"

"Jonathan!" Barry motioned for me to sit next to him, which I did. "You have to stop this."

"Stop what?"

"Behaving like someone in drug rehab."

"I'm not doing that."

Putting his arm around me, he said, "Yes, you are, Johnny. In an effort to not think about David, you're throwing yourself into your acting."

"What's wrong with that?"

"Nothing, except in not thinking about David, you're cutting yourself off from your emotions. And that's never a good thing for an actor to do."

"So you're telling me I sucked in my readings?"

"No, Johnny, your work has paid off. Your readings are intellectually perfect. What you need now is to *feel* what you're saying. Let yourself connect with your own emotions, so you can use them to connect with Biff's."

I rose and paced the room. "But Biff is nothing like me."

"I disagree."

"What do you mean?"

Pushing his glasses up, getting ready to make a point, Barry said, "Biff has found out something he doesn't like about someone he loves. He's hurt and angry. He wants to get away from the people he loves… and from himself."

My shoulders dropped. "How come you're always right, Barry?"

"Probably because I'm so cute."

We shared a laugh.

Barry stood next to me. "Now, are you ready to knock their socks off at the audition, Falabella?"

I squeezed his hand. "Ready, partner."

When Barry and I got to the theater, we took our same seats in the second row.

Immediately upon entering, David made his way up to Professor Beamer on stage. Wearing a skintight cherry-red sweater and black chinos, David held up a stack of papers. "Professor, I took the liberty of making copies of each scene for the auditions."

The tall, thin, bespectacled professor smiled below his large mustache. "Thank you, David, but that won't be necessary." He patted a briefcase at his side. "I have everything under control."

David said, "Terrence and I are ready to read first, professor."

Looking at David through narrow eyes, Professor Beamer said, "We missed you in directing class last week, David."

David unleashed his winning smile. "I was resting after the show, professor. Were you able to see one of the performances?"

"Of course. You did a fine job, David. But you already know that." Beamer rubbed his bony hands together. "Now, please take a seat in the house, and we'll get started."

David walked in confusion to a seat next to Terrence in the front row.

Professor Beamer tugged at his vest and cleared his throat. "I trust you have all read this great, classic play and are ready to audition. I have sides for each of you." He looked down at the sign-in sheet. "I would like to start with Jonathan Bello reading for Biff."

I wasn't sure if I heard right until Barry nudged my shoulder and motioned for me to go up to the stage.

Handing me the pages, Beamer said, "You did a fine job in the Molière play, Jonathan."

I croaked out, "Thank you, professor."

"Who would you like to read with as your Happy?"

David started to rise from his chair.

I said, "I'd like to read opposite Barry Goldman, professor."

Beamer shielded his eyes from the stage lights and searched the audience. "Mr. Goldman, are you here?"

"Here!" Barry ran on stage like a game show contestant.

David shrugged his broad shoulders and sat down.

"Whenever you two boys are ready." Professor Beamer took a seat in the front of the house.

It came as no surprise to me that Barry and I had a great rapport on stage. We kidded, teased, cajoled, and confronted one another as the Loman brothers. Our emotions were raw and volatile yet natural and spontaneous. Knowing each other so well, we weren't afraid to be affectionate with one another or to engage in battle when appropriate. We hit every level and beat in the scene like a baseball player hitting a home run. When we finished, Professor Beamer said, "That was quite nice, boys. Next, I would like to see David Star and Terrence Falcon."

Barry and I watched from our seats as David and Terrence took the stage. Besides their physical beauty and large size, their confidence and experience came through clearly. Commanding the stage as if they owned it, David and Terrence forced the audience to keep their eyes on them. When they finished, the students in the audience applauded loudly, and Beamer said with a huge smile under his mustache, "Good work, men. Very good work."

None of the other boys auditioning came close to David and Terrence's performance. After everyone had read, Beamer mixed and matched us all, calling us up to read with a different partner each time. I was relieved he never matched David and me.

When the auditions were concluded, Professor Beamer reentered the stage. "Thank you all for auditioning. I don't believe I will need to schedule a callback. It was a difficult decision, but I have cast the play."

It was so quiet in the theater, you could have heard an ant falling off a ticket stub on the floor. Barry held my hand as everyone waited for Beamer to announce David and Terrence would be playing Biff and Happy.

After taking a long breath and staring down at his notes, Beamer said, "The roles of Biff and Happy will be played by...." The drum roll I heard was the pounding of my heart. "...Jonathan Bello and Terrence Falcon. Their understudies will be David Star and Stuart Singleton."

After Beamer finished reading the cast list, he thanked us all again for coming, distributed a rehearsal schedule to the cast members, then met with the tech crew in the rear of the house. I sat stupefied, not believing I was cast as Biff, and in total shock at having David as my understudy.

Barry squeezed my shoulder. "Congrats, partner. You'll be terrific as Biff."

Coming to, I said, "Barry, thanks. Sorry you didn't get a role."

He smiled. "I'll sign up for set construction and make friends with the butch students."

We shared a laugh.

As we all filed out of the theater house, Terrence said, "I'm looking forward to working with you, Jonathan."

Not looking at him, I replied, "Thanks, Terrence," and continued walking toward the door.

Once Barry and I were in the lobby, I said, "Thanks for reading with me, Barry. If it hadn't been for you, I'd have never gotten the role."

He pinched my cheek. "Don't sell yourself short, Johnny. You're a terrific actor. You deserve this."

I hugged Barry, enjoying his sugary smell and the safety of being in his arms.

Barry whispered in my ear, "I'm proud of you, Falabella."

Then we headed back to our rooms.

Still in my sweatshirt and jeans from the audition, I sat cross-legged on my bed reading the play rehearsal schedule. To my surprise, David came into the room and sat next to me. "Put on your coat and scarf. Jake's picking us up at the college entrance in five minutes."

Not looking up from my reading, I replied, "I have some studying to do."

"It can wait. You got cast as Biff. We should celebrate."

"You can go to the bar with Terrence. I'm busy." I opened a book and pretended to read (upside down).

His handsome face hardened. "Stop acting like a jealous wife."

"Stop acting like you're happy for me and not devastated to be understudying your little mentee."

David looked like someone had punched him in the stomach. "You think I'm jealous of you? I've never been more proud of anyone in my life. You aced that audition, Jonathan. And you deserve that part."

I stared into his piercing eyes. "David, tell me something. What am I to you?"

"Someone who is keeping me waiting."

Closing the book and sitting closer to him, I asked, "Honestly. How do you feel about me?"

"I like you."

"Do you think we'll be friends after you graduate in May?"

"I hope so."

"Will we be lovers?"

He rose. "Jonathan, let's not get into that again."

I stood next to him. "David, I want to know."

He exhaled loudly. "I don't know."

"Why don't you know?"

"Because I don't think the way you do."

"What do you mean?"

"I think with my head, not my heart." He raised his arms. "You heard what my father said. I don't love anyone and nobody loves me."

"You think you're unworthy of love because your father doesn't love you."

Walking away, he said, "Don't psychoanalyze me, Jonathan."

I clutched at his leather jacket. "Everyone deserves love, David."

He laughed bitterly. "Not according to my father. I'm not even worthy of the Citlali name."

"Is that your real last name?"

He nodded. "It's his Native American tribe's word for *star*."

I looked out the window at the array of stars matted into mosaic clusters by the dark sky. "David, your father is wrong. Unlike everyone else, including me, *you* are a star."

"That's why Beamer cast me as your understudy."

I held him by his muscular shoulders. "David, you are a gorgeous, charismatic, caring, incredibly gifted individual. Stop selling yourself short by wallowing in your father's anger… and punishing yourself by spending your time with creeps like Terrence."

His radiant smile appeared. "Who should I spend my time with?"

Trying to stay angry with him but quickly losing the battle with myself, I replied, "Your roommate."

"I'm trying to spend time with my roommate by celebrating his good news, but for some reason he's still keeping me waiting."

I heard Barry's voice in my head say, "You're gonna get hurt, Falabella."

David held out my jacket and scarf. "Are you coming?"

Forcing Barry's thoughts out of my mind, I grabbed my things and followed David out the door.

As David and I rode in the back of Jake's compact car, David leaned over the front seat. "My roommate's playing Biff in *Death of a Salesman* at the college, Jake. We're going out to celebrate."

Jake beamed with pride. "You two boys will be rich and famous one day."

"That's the plan." David squeezed my knee, then asked Jake, "How are things going with you and Selma?"

Jake unleashed his infectious smile. "Terrific, thanks to you."

"We didn't do anything," David said.

"You helped me sort things out, David, and I appreciate it. So does Selma. She likes you two boys."

I said, "Selma's pretty terrific herself."

"Ain't that the truth." Jake scratched his curly gray hair. "Now we just got to get through the wedding."

Like a police dog picking up a scent in the woods, David asked, "Is there a problem with the wedding?"

Jake replied, "Not really."

"But?" David asked.

"Selma wants a big blow-out affair, and I want to keep it simple."

David said, like a mind reader, "And you two have been arguing about it."

Jake answered, "Not really arguing." After looking back at David's questioning eyes, Jake added, "Well, maybe we've had a few... discussions." He grinned. "Which got pretty heated."

David held court. "Jake, how many more times are you going to get married?"

"This better be the last," Jake replied.

"Do you love Selma?"

"More than I love my own life."

"Then give Selma the wedding she wants. It'll be something you two will look back on with pride for the rest of your lives. Instead of saying, 'We could have done this' or 'We should have done that,' you'll be saying, 'Remember when we had the wedding of a lifetime?'"

A line appeared across Jake's forehead. "A big wedding can cost."

David had an answer for everything. "You and Selma both work. I bet if you look at your finances, you'll figure out how to swing it." He laughed. "Plus, think of all the gifts!"

As Jake pulled up in front of the bar, he smiled. "Will you two boys come?"

"Of course," I said.

David added, "Jonathan and I will do a dramatic reading of your choice."

Jake laughed. "Won't that go over big with my family from Newark." We all shared a laugh.

"Thanks for the lift, Jake," I said as we got out of the car.

"Any time, boys."

"Now go and plan that fancy wedding with your bride," David added.

As we walked into the bar, I said, "You should be a counselor."

David replied, "I just listen and react... just like in acting."

When we got to the bar, David checked in with Manuel, handed me a beer, then led us to a table. As we clinked glasses, David said, "To the best Biff Loman who ever was and ever will be."

After taking a sip of salty foam, I said, "Will you rehearse with me?"

"You don't need my help. You've got this one, Jonathan."

Thinking back to our discussion in our room, I asked, "What did you mean when you said you think with your head and not with your heart?"

"Jonathan, ever since I can remember I wanted to be an actor. No, more than an actor. A *star*. There's nothing more important to me than making it in show business. It's the only thing that keeps me sane. It's my ticket out of my family, this state… and out of my own head. So everything I do, every thought in my head is geared toward that one goal."

"A lover could help you achieve your goal."

"Or take my focus away from it."

"David, plenty of successful actors are happily married with families."

"Relationships take time. I need to devote every ounce of my energy to acting."

"And what if stardom eludes you?"

His eyes clouded over. "I can't think about that."

I ran my fingers through his luxurious hair. "I hope you make it one day, David. And I hope I'm a part of your life when you do."

David kissed me and I melted like grilled cheese. Though I was still nursing mine, David had finished his beer. So he went to the bar and got himself a second, and a third. Then David took my hand and led me to the dance area, where I danced in his strong arms.

"David, I need to make a confession."

"I'm not a priest, Jonathan."

"Obviously." I took in a deep breath. "I was glad when Beamer cast you as my understudy."

"I know."

My eyes doubled in size. "How did you know?"

"It's human nature." He pulled me closer to his massive chest. "So you're human."

"I thought you'd want to hurt me."

"This isn't *A Separate Peace*, Jonathan."

I laughed. "I'm so glad I met you, David. I don't want to lose you."

"You're my little Jonathan, and you always will be."

We danced and kissed through several love songs. David smelled like musk and barley.

"David, tell me about your parents."

"I don't want to talk about them."

"Please? Tell me why your father is so angry."

He exhaled loudly. "My father married outside the tribe to a white woman. His parents had a fit. My mom's parents looked down at Dad as a 'red man,' and made my mother feel like she abandoned them."

"That's awful."

David nodded. "Unfortunately they took it out on each other."

"And on you?"

David didn't respond.

Choosing my words carefully, I said, "David, do you think your father is continuing his father's cycle of guilt with you?"

"No."

"How come?"

"Because I don't think about it." He kissed me. "And neither should you."

I looked at my watch. "Don't you have to work tonight?"

"Tonight's *your* night, Jonathan."

I caressed his huge back muscles, and we kissed and danced some more.

When it was near closing time, David was a bit tipsy from having a few more beers. "You're my little Jon-Jon. And you're going to play Biff."

"I know." I helped David outside, then raised my thumb to the passing traffic. It was such a clear night, the mountains looked like fingertips reaching for the shining stars.

A familiar-looking pickup truck stopped in front of us, and David staggered into the front seat. I followed, shut the door behind me, and the truck took off.

A voice I'd heard before said, "I told you two guys not to go into that bar."

Feeling no pain from all the beer, David said, "Clyde! It's great to see you again. You remember us? David and Jon-Jon."

"I remember you," Clyde said.

I said, "Clyde, we're headed back to the college."

"No problem," Clyde said before spitting some phlegm out his window. "The problem is, why didn't you two guys listen to me?"

David giggled. "We didn't listen to you, Clyde, because unlike you, we aren't bigots." David laughed at his own joke.

I explained. "David had too much to drink tonight."

"Which wouldn't have happened if you two boys didn't go into that bar. I told you it's not safe," Clyde said shaking his head. "And I'm not no bigot. I'm just following what it says in the bible. Guys who go into that bar are an abomination to God."

David pressed his shoulder against Clyde's. "Let me ask you something, Clyde. Do you eat shellfish?"

"What's that mean?" Clyde asked.

"David, stop," I said.

Sobering up a bit, he replied, "I'm just asking our friend Clyde here a simple question. Clyde, do you like shrimp, lobster, scallops, clams?"

"You don't have to answer that, Clyde," I said.

"I don't mind." Clyde rubbed his stomach. "Sure, I eat them kinds of fish. Who don't?"

David continued. "And that sweatshirt you have on. Is it one hundred percent cotton, or is it a cotton blend?"

Shrugging his sagging shoulders, Clyde said, "How should *I* know?"

David said, "Does your neighbor have the same religious beliefs as you, Clyde?"

"Hell no!" Clyde said, "She's an atheist piece of crap."

I pulled David away, but he relented. "Did you stone her to death, Clyde?"

"No." Clyde added, "She'd probably kick my butt in a fight."

David announced, "Then you, Clyde, have broken three rules in the Bible. *You* are an *abomination*."

Scratching his chin stubble, Clyde said, "I don't know what you're talking about, sonny. But I do know one thing, that bar is a place for faggots. And being a faggot is wrong."

I tried to change the subject. "It's a clear night out."

David was like a cat with a rubber mouse. "But, Clyde, last time you told us *you* go into that bar."

"To warn guys like you who'll go anywhere for a drink, but don't know it's a fag bar."

David pushed my arm away. "Now let's get this straight, Clyde. Straight." David giggled. I whispered into his ear a plea to stop, but David ignored me. "Now, Clyde, you said you go into that bar to warn guys it's a gay bar, but then you go home with them."

"So?" Clyde said scratching a tattoo on his neck.

David continued. "So it seems to me, Clyde, you and those guys are gay."

"Are you calling me a homosexual?" Clyde asked, his eyes ablaze.

"Clyde, David was only kidding you."

Looking at David, Clyde said, "Was you kidding me, David?"

"We're almost at the college, "I said. "We can walk from here."

Clyde glared at David. "Was you kidding with me, David?"

David looked Clyde square in the face. "I was dead serious, Clyde. You are as gay as Jonathan and me."

I said, "He's drunk, Clyde. Don't listen to him."

Clyde yelled at me, "Shut up, faggot."

"Leave him alone!" David pushed Clyde, sending Clyde reeling into his car door.

In a flash, Clyde rebounded, scrambled for the latch of his glove compartment, and before either of us could stop him, Clyde pointed a gun at David. "I'll talk to your boyfriend any way I want, faggot!"

"Calm down, Clyde." I said, "We were just playing with you. That's all."

Clyde pulled up to the entrance of the college. I grabbed David's arm and reached for my truck door.

Pointing the gun at me, Clyde said, "You open that door, faggot, and I'll blow you to fairy land."

David shouted, "I told you to leave him alone!"

It all happened so fast, it felt like a dream. I bent over to open the door and Clyde pulled the trigger. David leaned in front of me. As my ears exploded from the deafening noise, the gun went off into David's chest. I turned back to see Clyde's shocked expression as David's body fell into my arms. Panicking, Clyde opened his door and ran. I heard screams from outside the car, and the sound of footsteps chasing after Clyde.

David leaned against me, and blood flowed from his chest onto mine like a river. With my arms around him, I covered his wound with my hands and kissed his neck. "Stay with me, David. People outside are calling for help."

He looked up at me. "I'm sorry I couldn't give you what you wanted."

"You gave me so much. I love you. Don't leave me."

"You're the only person I ever loved." Struggling to take in a shallow breath, he said, "Do it… for both us."

I looked down at my red hands. "No, David! I need you. Don't leave me."

He gasped for air. "I'll be with you." Blood gurgled out of his mouth. "Always." David breathed his last breath.

EPILOGUE

NOW, TWENTY years later, which details of my story are facts, and which are products of my illusive memory, no longer matter. Whether David Star was a sorcerer, a people puppeteer, an angel, a shaman, or just a college student with high aspirations who perished too quickly, he will always be a part of me.

I feel comforting arms wrap around me, and my nostrils become filled with his familiar sugary scent. Standing behind me, my husband whispers in my ear, "And the Academy Award for Best Actor goes to Jonathan Bello. I'm proud of you, Falabella."

Turning to face Barry, I reply, "You're just saying that because you're my agent."

The face I've loved so deeply for so many years is full of adoration and devotion. "I'd love you even if you didn't win, Johnny." We kiss. "But I'm glad you did."

We kiss again. "I didn't do it alone, Barry."

"I know."

Barry and I look out our double-story great room window at a star shooting through the sky. Its white arc speeds through the blue velvet sky and disappears into the gray pounding waves over onyx rocks.

David Star kept his promise.

JOE COSENTINO began as an actor appearing in principal acting roles in film, television, and theater, opposite stars such as Bruce Willis, Rosie O'Donnell, Nathan Lane, Holland Taylor, and Jason Robards. Watching him on YouTube, his students said, "You were cute when you were young." He moved on to playwriting and directing, where his plays were published and produced in NYC, regionally, and on tour. Upon writing fiction, his mother said, "Don't you have anything better to do than write books?" He replied, "I wonder if Shakespeare's mother said that to him?" All's well that ends well, as his mother, other family members, and friends love his published books. He hopes this book is made into a movie and he can play Mr. Ringwood, bringing his career full circle. It's all in the family since his spouse is an audio book performer.

Joe received his MFA from Goddard College in Vermont, and MA from SUNY New Paltz. He is currently Head of the Department/Professor of Theater at a college in upstate New York, where he and his spouse designed and had built an environmentally friendly home. Joe is a member of an open and affirming church, and does fundraising for GLSEN.

He hopes people young and old will be infatuated with this book, and he loves to hear from readers at joecosentino.weebly.com/ and www.goodreads.com/author/show/4071647.Joe_Cosentino.

Bobby McGrath's Christmas trip to the beautiful Italian island of Capri to meet his eccentric extended family offers stunning views—none more stunning than his third cousin, Paolo Mascobello, a real stocking stuffer. As the two young men embark on a relationship, Bobby, a driven law student, learns to relax and bask under the old Italian moon, and Paolo realizes there's more to life than a frolic on the beach. For the two to find everlasting *amore*, Paulo must overcome his fear of commitment and learn to follow his dreams, and Bobby must get his wish for happily ever after.